SUNCATCHER

SUNCATCHER

Romesh Gunesekera

BLOOMSBURY PUBLISHING
LONDON · OXFORD · NEW YORK · NEW DELHI · SYDNEY

BLOOMSBURY PUBLISHING
Bloomsbury Publishing Plc
50 Bedford Square, London, WC1B 3DP, UK

BLOOMSBURY, BLOOMSBURY PUBLISHING and the Diana logo are
trademarks of Bloomsbury Publishing Plc

First published in Great Britain 2019

A catalogue record for this book is available from the British Library

ISBN: HB: 978-1-5266-1041-6; TPB: 978-1-5266-1037-9;
EBOOK: 978-1-5266-1039-3

2 4 6 8 10 9 7 5 3 1

Typeset by Newgen KnowledgeWorks Pvt. Ltd., Chennai, India
Printed and bound in Great Britain by CPI Group (UK) Ltd, Croydon CR0 4YY

To find out more about our authors and books visit www.bloomsbury.com
and sign up for our newsletters

Helen

in memory of departed friends

A & N

The sky is round, and I have heard that the earth is round like a ball, and so are all the stars ... Birds make their nests in circles ... The sun comes forth and goes down again in a circle.

Black Elk, Oglala Sioux

CONTENTS

I

CROW

I

I first met Jay in a church car park off the high road, mid-way as the crow flies between the mosque and the temple, one June afternoon in 1964; two boys on the brink of a bond that would alter the course of our lives, neither knowing which one would blink first, or fall furthest – nor the cost of finding out. He rode in, hands on hips, freewheeling on the dusty tarmac using only his weight to steer his bike as he leant from side to side. Blue stripy feathers and rawhide tied to the upside-down handlebars twirled in the hot, sticky air; the sun-baked streaks on his proud boyish cheeks shone like warpaint.

'Wanna race?' He lobbed the challenge, veering close.

I wheeled around the hooded statue of Saint Thérèse. 'Where?'

'The scarp: Torrington.' Jay stretched his long, slender neck – more like a swan than an eagle – strands of damp hair playing across his open face. 'If you dare.'

'Been down that.' From the beginning I lied. Although it might have been the steepest slope in my part of town, I didn't see why that should be a problem if it didn't bother him. My only misgiving was the rivalry I felt rising in my chest, seeding trouble.

Jay spun his pedals backwards. A big bowie knife – a real one with an antler handle – leered from his belt. 'Scary, huh? The graveyard over that wall? Dead men's bones?' His lips opened wider, revealing a crescent of awkward adolescent teeth.

'Nah.' The word came out wrong, stretched and warbled instead of strong and defiant.

Even if I had ventured into the cemetery and been scared, I was not going to admit it to some maverick floating by – whatever he had strapped to his belt. Jay was taller, probably older by a couple of years – neither of us could tell exactly by how much for sure – but that did not discourage us from circling closer and finding a nervous delight in the novelty of each other. For days, I had been worried by the idea that the more you savour something, the sooner it might disappear, but I said nothing more. I'd learnt young the uses of silence: others would always fill it with the words they wanted to hear, and you'd be let off.

He dismounted and pinned a tightly folded piece of flutter-paper to the rear strut of his bike. He strummed the spokes, then got back on and set off, the wheel whirring as if it had wings attached.

I needed a guide, a hero, illumination; Jay, I now know, needed an acolyte.

At the turn-off, where the big tamarind trees brooded, he stopped and waited for me to catch up. 'Pedal hard – even if you think you are hurtling. Streamline everything. You have to build up a heck of a lot of speed, like a bullet, to climb up the other side.' He blew at his loose hair with an upward puff.

Hurtling? Like scarp, another word no other schoolboy I knew would use. I tightened my hands on the rubber grips. He must have guessed I hadn't zoomed down the hill before but didn't seem to care that I had pretended.

'Actually, I haven't done this before. Not really.'

'So, you ready?' he grinned, planting dimples in both cheeks. 'When you get to the bottom, ring your bell and start pedalling like mad.'

'Okay.' I fingered the trigger of my bell, absolved.

'Right. One, two, three. Go.'

A fraction of a second behind Jay, whose silver bike did hurtle, I bent low, gripping hard, and flew. The grey cemetery wall, stray bougainvillea and mimosa melted into a thin blur. We whizzed past two sun-dipped women collecting water from a standpipe, tyres spraying spar-klets, thumbs jabbing tinkle-tankle, flooding the valley with peals of laughter. Then the road reared up; every-thing slowed.

'Come on,' Jay called out from the summit. 'Pedal harder.'

Even standing on the pedals would not make them go around fast enough. I ground to a stop and had to push my bike the rest of the way, ashamed that my muscles proved to be the dead loss I'd always suspected them to be.

'Too much, huh?' Jay called out, his long body slouched in the saddle.

'Couldn't do it. The last bit.'

'You need another gear.' Jay clicked the lever on the decorated handlebar with his thumb and ran through the changes. He did not mock me. 'Let's go for a Chocolac.'

'I've only got ten cents.' My parents didn't believe in pocket money and I had to operate on the black market, trading books, selling off Christmas presents, scavenging small change from jam jars. But that unforgettable day, eager and chaste, my finances were in a trough – as were the country's, according to my maddening father.

'We'll take a shortcut.'

He whipped down a small, stony lane that dog-legged to join Bullers Road and picked his way, carefully avoiding the sharper stones. I followed, sticking to the smoother edge. The house on the corner had a garden of pink and purple bordered by bushes with tiny glittery leaves, a hideout for rustlers and outlaws from the ordinary world in which I, too, did not belong. I yearned for adventure, far from my ma and pa, even though I loved them – if love was what I believed it was and had nothing to do with girls and boys.

When we reached the main road, Jay accelerated to top speed again, riding the wave in the flabby ribbon of tar that had softened and swollen in the lazy afternoon sun.

Halfway along, on the other side of the avenue, a red and white striped awning marked the new milk bar – the first of its kind in Colombo – where, I had read in a Sunday ad, you could get a flavour of the future: Chocolac, Vanilac or even Tangolac.

Jay, sidling up to the smart zinc counter, asked the man behind it for a chocolate milk and then turned to me. 'And you? What d'you want?'

Confused by the heady mix of fresh paint and scented syrup, I plumped for the same. 'Yeah, me too.'

Something moved inside me, something mysteriously *more*, that I longed for but could not yet put into words.

Jay squeezed the soft ear of his bronco: the brake handle squeaked. 'I always come here at five thirty. Mahela's last customer.'

'Why so late?'

'To catch the sun when it falls,' he sang with a goofy grin. 'Stick around. I'll show you.'

No one had ever spoken to me so easily, with such an open heart; the invitation kept ringing in my head. Sure, I'll stick around.

We stood straddling our bikes: two mustang riders waiting for the sun to go down and the shooting to begin. Jay tall enough to have both feet on the ground; me, a few inches shorter, having to angle my bike and keep one foot on a notched-up stirrup. Both with the same blue Bata rubber slippers to slap dirt and spur our innocent hopes towards a safe corral.

Behind the milk bar a screen of pink oleander marked the boundary of the censored racecourse. Farther in, beyond the clumps of pampas grass, sprouted the metal rods and concrete pods of a new industrial exhibition complex that would soon replace the redundant gymkhana rings, pens and paddocks.

'You see my little sunbird today?' Jay winked at Mahela, the milkshake man.

'That *chuti* sootikka?'

'Like a sunbeam. I've got to catch him.'

A flash of yellow and glistening purple darted out of a chenille bush and flew over the pampas.

'There he goes,' Mahela flicked his dishcloth in the air after it. 'Off to his girlfriend. Waiting, no?'

I could wait too; most of my time was spent waiting: waiting to grow up, waiting for childhood's demons to die, waiting for my life to start. Waiting for someone like Jay to turn up and switch on the lights.

☀

When he had finished the last of the milk, Jay pushed his empty bottle to one side and wiped his lips, manfully, with the back of his hand. I sucked the final drops of mine through my straw and did the same.

'Come on,' Jay wheeled his bike around. 'Show you something phenomenal.'

'Be careful,' Mahela called out.

Jay led his two-wheeled horse in through a gap in the shrubbery and onto the outer verge of the racecourse; I followed, stepping gingerly between the razor leaves and cat's tails. Ahead, the unkempt turf curved in an arc around the building works; the flaky white wooden poles of the main track leaning to take the turn.

Jay checked over his shoulder. 'Another race?'

'You can't on this grass.'

'It's a racecourse, no?'

'Made for horses: Arabians, thoroughbreds.' They were all in my father's racing almanac.

'So, you know the genus *Equus*.' Jay recoiled widening his eyes in exaggerated surprise. 'But now, use your imagination.' Then he mounted his bike and was away before I could show off some more.

Only power and technique, not imagination, could get wheels moving in such thick grass. Jay had the knack. He drew ahead. One of the white poles marking the circuit had come off and he charged through and across the sand track into a bank of green and purple sage. On the other side of the bushes, pieces of colossal concrete macaroni and fattened cement cubes lay scattered; the main paddock had been gouged out.

'Come up here,' Jay called out scrambling up to the top of the biggest of the piles of building blocks.

Joining him at the top, I found we were higher than anything else around: the milk bar, the old flame trees, even the grandstand on the far side looked puny in the velveteen light.

Jay oblivious, shielded his eyes and pointed to the horizon. 'Look, can you see them?'

A seam of perforations appeared in the sky, dot by dot, stitched by the rhythmic flap of black wings, growing larger by the second, blotching the amber sky in dark puffs with every beat.

'What are they?'

'Bats. Amazing, no? Every evening they come this way. Two by two, in one beautiful straight line.'

'It's a formation. Like bombers going on a raid.' I'd never noticed them before.

'There are always two at the head. I wonder how long a pair lasts.'

I stole a glance at him, wondering what he meant. Was any join also a potential fault line? At home, between my parents, small differences quickly grew large, needles turned to spikes.

'Is the feeding ground nearby?' I was keen to show we had a common interest.

'Dunno.'

'If we follow them, we'll find out.'

'It'll be too dark soon.'

'We could start over in Havelock Town tomorrow,' I suggested, surprising myself. 'The grounds there.'

'Yeah?' The peaks of his cheekbones softened in the light of the sinking red sun.

'Sure.' I tried to absorb the glow. 'I live that side, on Grebe Road.' Halfway to nowhere, until now.

'Corner of Dickman's Road, same time tomorrow then?'

'Okay.' I kept my voice steady, avoiding any thought of what might happen if he were not to appear.

☀

Inside our house on Grebe Road, on the edge of Colombo's newest residential block, the morning sun never reached the breakfast table. Our beige curtains were permanently drawn. The next morning the gloom hung heavier than normal.

'It is utter chaos.' My mother dropped the telephone handset back in its cradle and sharpened the dark look she gave my father. Although slight in size, she had a high forehead and a tense mouth. 'Dilini says no classes again. School closed.'

'Those madcaps probably think idleness might be the best hope for the youth of today.' My father dismissed her worries and opened the back issue of *Tribune* he often returned to in times of uncertainty. He relied on a comfortable compromise between idealism and action which now, with socialism back in the fray, was beginning to show some strain.

My mother, a modern convent girl, preserved a strong orthodox work ethic; her aversion to disorder and need for sanctuary bordered on missionary fervour. She provided both frame and engine for our family's fortunes. 'So, what are we going to do about Kairo's education then?'

My father studied the photograph of Che Guevara meeting our Governor General in his journal: one bearded, the other bald. The Cuban Missile Crisis was over. 'The boy can read, no?'

And so, they left me to another day of aimless browsing and drove off to work. My father to the Labour Department where he held the position of an amiable senior executive officer and had the dispensation to come home for lunch, and a nap, before going back to the office to analyse columns of fictitious numbers, as he said, while waiting for a peon to appear with the high point of his afternoon: a cup of sweet, milky tea from a tin pot. My mother to Radio

Ceylon from where, revelling in the buzz of national broadcasting, she hardly ever returned home to eat.

I finished my Zane Grey and spent the rest of the morning using stolen chalk to connect the random parallel lines and sunray motifs on the back wall of our mishmash of a house.

At lunchtime, emboldened by friendship, I decided to extract some information from my father to impress Jay and cement our alliance; one thing I'd picked up from my father's ramblings was the importance of firm alliances.

'You know where bats come from, Thaththa?' I asked as my father steadily chomped, eyes half closed, in the final stages of the meal.

'England.' He splintered a curried drumstick with his teeth, revealing a dark vein of marrow which he then proceeded to suck with severe concentration and a whistling sound. 'English willow trees.' He shifted an eye and studied me. 'You want to play cricket?'

Unaware that we were talking at cross-purposes, I recalled a *National Geographic* article that recorded the journeys of the tiniest birds – swallows, wagtails – flying thousands of miles, crossing oceans and continents in seasonal migrations.

'Actually, bats don't have to be English,' he added. 'There wouldn't be enough trees for all of us from the West Indies to Australia if that was the case. India alone has enough cricketers to denude all the shires of England.'

'No, Thaththa. Not cricket bats. I mean bats like flying foxes.'

'Oh.' He bent his leathery head sideways to catch the sound the chicken bones made as he crunched them.

I gave up and curled up with a second-hand *Rawhide Kid*.

My father, marrow-drunk and drowsy, tried to discharge his duties paternal and political. 'Enough comics, son. Read Gorky or, if you must go American, Steinbeck. Improve your vocabulary and learn to understand the choice you have. This country is at a crossroads. No one knows which path will lead us out of the quagmire.'

Having made his point, he dug into his teeth with a toothpick. Once his teeth were clean, he called Siripala – who did the housework, the cooking and the driving, when he was not too busy smoking cheap cigarettes – with a single-word command: 'Take.' Succinctly meaning that the plates should be cleared. He always spoke in an abbreviated Sinhala to Siripala, as if he had to use a code to speak to a servant in a modern democracy. He stood up and rolled back his shoulders one at a time. 'Time for a quick kip.'

I drifted in and out of my comic book until Siripala had also surrendered to the afternoon's stupor. Then I took up my position on the balcony upstairs from where I could survey the road and plot the Wells Fargo route to Sacramento, dream of a life more exciting than one punctuated by my father's snores.

Across from the house, a large tract of wasteland – a jungle – fenced off with barbed wire, steamed in the afternoon sun, primed for my daydreams of cowboys and cougars.

In the buckskin map of my mind, a serene meadow of tepees and smoke signals began to form in the warm layered air when, across the road, the weekly paper collector, one of the many itinerant hawkers in our neighbourhood, turned the corner and made a beeline for our house. My father hoarded newspapers and my mother constantly tried to flush them away. Siripala would push piles of newspapers out or pull them back in according to who happened to be presiding in the house on the day. Today, the man was early.

Because of the yard-round basket he carried on his head, he could not see me but I crouched low anyway, making the intruder into a gunman with a sombrero and turning his reddish sarong into chaparajos. An unwitting desperado, he lifted the iron hasp of the gate and clanged it, clearly not understanding the risk.

Siripala hurried out, barefoot, shushing to silence him. He pointed to his wrist. The paper collector checked his wrist too. Neither had watches but both pretended their lives blossomed richer than they did. The man patted his headgear and drifted downstream; Siripala retreated.

The realm of make-believe, I could see even then, was not mine alone.

⁕

Every evening, the eastern corner of Dickman's Road and Havelock Road by the sports ground melted into a patch of yellow grass and scruffy shadows of upended rickshaws. Skinny bullocks would sniff the pissed-on ground and drift drunkenly on. Rugby veterans, cutting a fast corner to get to their own watering hole in time for a sundowner, sometimes foundered. I arrived at exactly five thirty, after the dog-catcher had been, nervous: would Jay turn up?

The sky had a half-hour or so to fully ripen but the slope up Dickman's Road was already restless; the jacaranda trees swayed, gathering up their wind-tipped leaves, brushing against nests and cocoons, stirring their dozy residents into action. Crows bristled, beaks open; other birds jostled in the branches, ready to join in the frenzy and herald the dance of the sun rolling out his rug of darkness and shaking out the stars, as he did above the canyons of the West.

'Hey, man, watch your back.' Jay yanked the *Beano* I had clipped to the rear mudguard carrier for emergencies. 'Anyone could just flick that, *machang*.'

'No-o.' The syllable went off-key. 'I was looking out for those bats.'

'If you wanna be a hunter, you must become invisible.'

Jay was hardly invisible; he was wild and gangly – his limbs shooting out in all directions, big enough to be everywhere – even though he appeared so suddenly, like a gun in the hand of a gunslinger.

'There are more trees on the other side of the grounds.'

'Bats would launch off from a much *wilder* place.'

'There's a jungle on our road,' I declared, bewildered by my audacity.

'So, let's check it out. You lead.'

The thrill he unleashed in me surpassed anything I had ever known: trusted so quickly to lead. Trusted by the one who was the natural leader. I wheeled my bike around and sped down the road before Jay had a chance to change his mind.

The sweeper by the toddy shack raised his broom in a salute as I flew past. At the shortcut, I waited for Jay to catch up. Hardly any cars came along that road – a blind corner where I had once almost ridden straight into Mr Selvarajah's shiny Studebaker. His driver had given me such an evil look that if I ever found that car parked out on the road, I vowed to let the air out of all the tyres.

'Down there?' Jay jerked his head, pointing with his chin.

I did a snake with my hand and led the way, ringing my bell along the narrow lane lined with the high wall of a Bavarian fortress on one side and crumpled black-jacket trees on the other until we reached my green dream-swell.

Jay let out a low whistle. 'This is a real *kalava*. How big?'

'Massive. It goes on and on.'

'Ad infinitum?'

'I keep watch from the balcony.'

'Is there a path in?'

'Dunno.' I said the word the way I had heard Jay say it. 'You can go in anywhere.'

Jay lowered himself to search the perimeter, then began to move forwards holding his bike lightly by the centre of the downturned handlebars, uncoiling a muscle at a time. Only on a page had I come across anyone move so quietly and so alert – all there, body and soul clenched tight.

'What have you spotted in there?' Jay asked.

'There's a bear, maybe.' Bears and bison would be an improvement on the usual stray cats and bullfrogs.

'You've seen tracks?'

'Weird sounds.'

We came to a break in the fence where the barbed wire had snapped and lay in loose coils. Two red-eyed butterflies floated lazily into the lantanas.

'Hear that? Yellow-eared bulbul.'

'Let's put the bikes in my garden first,' I suggested. Jay followed me home and we hid them snug next to each other in the front yard.

He crouched, already in hunting mode, as we slipped back out of the gate and across the road. His slippers made no noise while mine flip-flopped with every step I took. How did he do it? Suck the rubber up through the soles of his feet? I suppressed the urge to own up, tell Jay that there really was nothing in there to see except grass snakes and caterpillars. The *kalava* was a jungle of illusions, a dream-hole framed by a gate of whispery ivory and thorns. Nothing more.

Jay lifted an umbrella of white flowers out of the way and cleared a safe passage. Working carefully, dipping his head here and there and noting every broken twig and over-turned blade, he took the lead. Within minutes the fence, the road, the house, all signs of human life disappeared. The colours became brighter and denser, the air stiller and fuller, trapped in a dome of green. He whispered the names of plants: castor, veralu, nelli, nika. As we reached a clearing near the centre, the whoop-whoop-whoop call of a coucal echoed over the crackles of leaves and insects. Jay twisted back and put a finger to his lips.

A coucal – an ati-kukula – a large black bird buttoned up in haughty, toffee-brown wings, was hardly wildlife. One could be found in every other garden in Colombo, admonishing smaller animals like a stern, sozzle-eyed squire, but this one's sombre warning had set off several other creatures. A small scarlet bird, close by, puffed up its chest and sounded its own shrill alarm.

Jay paused, drawing the birdsong into himself before whistling back. 'Fantastic. Minivet. Male. This could be the place. If there are bigger trees farther in, they might be there hanging like bobos – those bats.'

All I could spot hanging were dried scimitar pods and swollen breadfruit. An orange-throated lizard scrambled up a tree and froze, sensing danger. Jay picked up a small stone from the ground; a second later it flew and hit the tiny animal, knocking it into the bushes.

'I don't like it.' I swallowed hard. 'We should go back.'

Jay raised his hand, palm up, scout style. 'Not yet. We go as far as the jak tree.'

I was beginning to feel hemmed in by all the thick, fuddling chlorophyll. My father had once warned me: 'Don't go off track, son. Put your head above the parapet and it is bound to get blown off. Understand?'

Jay reached the target and circled it stealthily, studying the patchwork branches, the big, prickly fruit, his eyes sliding from side to side, measuring, sorting, solving.

'What is it?'

'Look, there it is. Not an ordinary ati-kukula. See the beak? It's green. I've not seen a green-billed one before, have you?'

Not in the dark, I wanted to say. The sun's wake was fast coagulating; soon you would see only a mass of tangled shadows and fangs snarling at the moon. 'There is a bigger jungle farther on, you know.'

'Where?'

'After our house, there is only one bungalow and then it is like swampland.' Siripala was adamant that illicit *kasippu* distillers did moonshine executions of any nosy parker down by the creek and fed their bodies to the crocs you could hear snuffling through midnight.

The green-billed coucal took off, heavily, crashing through the bushes of carambola and sparking a chorus of frantic birdsong. I watched Jay's pleasure glow as he followed its bumbling flight. Then, through a gap in the trees, I spotted the convoy of bats pricking a line in the distance. We were in the wrong place to follow them – wide off the mark. Mortified, I tried to distract Jay.

'I saw a snake.'

The ground could have been crawling with reptiles, but Jay searched the treetops instead and noticed the distant formation.

'They've changed the flight path.' He didn't dwell on it, quickly shifting his interest to what other birds might be hiding in the foliage. 'Is that an orange babbler?'

The shame of failure that always hung around my shoulders seeped in deeper. I knew I should apologise for leading him astray, but couldn't bring myself to do it. To admit inadequacy as a navigator would double the agony of the blunder and I could not handle that; no, better hurry nightfall and bring on the howl of coyotes and mooncalves.

Outside our house, Jay was cheerfully upbeat. 'That green-billed coucal was phenomenal. So rare. Miles better than following any dumb bat.' He collected his bike and waited for a few seconds at the gate before climbing onto the saddle. His long lashes caught the last rays of the sun and brightened the corners of his eyes.

A car horn beeped farther up the road.

'So, see you around, pardner.' Jay rang his bell. I waved him off.

A small and difficult truth dawned on me as he disappeared: I wanted Jay close, but I did not want him inside the house. I did not want him to see the clutter of cheap furniture and useless newspapers that filled the sitting room; the ordinariness of my parents. The promise of blameless companionship I had found in him had nothing to do with anyone except the two of us, and I was determined to keep it that way.

☼

The black-framed spectacles my father wore for reading were narrow at the bridge and thick at the sides; balanced precariously on his flat nose, the plastic arms often acted as blinkers helping him to focus on the serious business of form.

Twice a week he would have the opportunity, before my mother came home, to fold his 'race paper' into a small rectangle and carefully mark it with crosses and circles, calculating form to potential. His pencil would hover between the 'place' and 'win' decisions until the last minute, juggling the bookie's odds against the five-and-a-half-hour time difference, as it was then, between Colombo and Goodwood or Kempton Park; then, tucking his pencil behind one ear, he'd call Siripala and hand him a clutch of green rupee notes and the scrap of paper on which he had written the time of the race and the names of the horses. 'This one for place, this one for win. Understand? So, go.' He'd set Siripala on his own race up to the bucket shop by the main junction on Havelock Road and warn him to be back within half an hour. It didn't bother him that he rarely won, or that even when his horse did win, against the odds, Siripala claimed he'd got the bets confused and had put the money on the wrong one.

The day after the jungle expedition with Jay, my mother came home early – soon after Siripala had been dispatched on his mission. My father had settled down to the rest of his newspaper unaware of her frustrations at the studios or the transformation in my life. He smoothed the damp paper to try to stiffen the headlines in the climate of permanent humidity that swathed his marriage.

Undiverted, she noticed the yellow pencil stub lodged behind his ear. 'You are not betting again, are you?'

'Now? No, not now.'

'Where's Siripala?'

He peered over his thick spectacles. 'Fellow was here a minute ago.'

I couldn't help but admire my father's ability to wriggle out of a corner.

But she zeroed in: 'You haven't sent him to the bucket shop again, have you? Aren't they all shut down? New law, no? Isn't that what enforcement is meant to do?'

'A foolish legal aspiration of the morally demented. They can ban racing here in Colombo, my dear, and stop a local punt. But, you know, even this government can't stop horses running in England.'

'You are betting on what – English races?'

'We have the radio, Monica? Your medium. So, time to turn the tables. They are the jockeys and we wear the top hats now. The age of imperialism is over.' He chortled and clicked his big toe with his second in a kind of raspy salute, the way normal people snapped their fingers. 'If you form a club, you see, dearie, you can do whatever the heck you like.'

Converting an immediate retort into a reproachful sigh, my mother went over to the sideboard where several unopened pinkish envelopes stood pressed between two small, carved ebony elephants. She picked up one of the envelopes, her hand shaking with the charge.

'You haven't even paid the electricity bill. Another red-letter warning. Ignore, ignore, but what next? They'll cut us off – then what?'

'I told you, they'll never cut us off.' He scraped the edge of one thumbnail against the other, prising out an argument hidden under the white, uneven tip. 'Electricity they need us to use. Otherwise what's the point? Bet those jackasses don't even know where the off switch is. Don't worry. Why give money sooner than necessary? "Just-in-time" is all the fashion now.'

'We can't live like this, Clarence. It's madness. On a tightrope all the time. Any minute, we'll fall.'

I slipped out of the house before the quarrel escalated and took off on my bike.

At the bottom of Greenlands, a familiar figure ducked into the teashop where bare-bodied idlers huddled smoking and drinking endless cups of syrupy *kadé* tea. Siripala, an expert at his own calculations, could always shave time for himself on his errands.

As I took the turn, Wolfman, the neighbourhood thug, stepped out onto the road swinging a thick, black stick in his hand. I braked. The bike skidded, sending me sprawling. The man advanced, uglily. Siripala didn't even peek out, but a woman in the teashop jeered at Wolfman's bloated belly flopping over his sarong; it gave me just enough time to pull up the bike and escape.

At the milk bar, safe again, I asked for a Chocolac. 'Did my friend come by?'

'That boy? Come and gone.' Mahela, his face round and irrepressible, jiggled the milk drink to the Jim Reeves tune playing on his radio before passing it over.

'But he always comes at this time, no? To catch the sunset, he said.'

'Caught bloody enough today. The bird in the pocket. Clever as a monkey, that boy. He could catch the sun in a thunderstorm, if he wanted to.'

'The yellow bird?'

'Shah,' he wagged his head in admiration. 'Set a trap with the cage up there.' He indicated the laburnum. 'Don't know what he put inside but that sootikka flew straight in and pop – he had the fellow.'

I imagined Jay's big face breaking into a smile. 'Lucky for him.'

'He went with the cage hanging off a pole. He'll be at home teaching it to sing hymns now.'

'Where's his house?'

'Don't you know it? The Alavis residence: Casa Lihiniya?' He noticed the tiny spots of blood on my elbow. 'What happened? You fall, *putha*?'

'Just a stupid kerfuffle.' Casa Lihiniya: a charmed House of Swallows for a boy who could catch even the light in the sky.

⁕

My own sanctuary was a ten-minute ride away, at the top of St Kilda's Lane: a second-hand bookshop where a quick dip into an adventure annual, or an illicit paperback, never failed to give me a boost.

Most of the time, Mr Ismail, the proprietor – hair oiled and neatly parted to the left – would be marooned on a brown cane chair behind a school desk on the front veranda surrounded by piles of salt-speckled books. His papery hands would sort them carefully by category, binding, size. Crusty old hardbacks would then be lodged close to him; the stacks of comics, organised by superhero, farthest away at the back of the shop. In six months I had gone through all the *Green Lantern* and *Batman* series, then the column of smaller pocket-sized *Commando* war comics. Recently I had discovered motor magazines, paperback detective stories and mystifyingly adult thrillers. The credo at Mr Ismail's shop stated that you buy, sell and exchange all in one go at a fixed price. 'No credit,' was Mr Ismail's favourite line. No credit meant you sometimes had to make do with two paperbacks, instead of three. Or a *Beano*, instead of the latest *Boy's Own*, or the new Saint escapade. The transaction became a ritual, almost sacramental. Although the books – except for the Soviet ones – were second-hand and had been pored over by many pairs of greedy eyes, for me only one other person floated in that world: Mr Ismail – a man with millions of words at his fingertips and a capacity for remaining silent at will.

On this late afternoon, the glare had been nearly all sucked out of the sun and the thin orange lozenge foundered in its final dissolve while Mr Ismail, wedged between two cardboard boxes overflowing with blue-backed Pelicans, contemplated the inch of inky sea on the horizon with more suspicion than usual. His neat shirt with the dog-eared collar tucked deep into the waistband of his faded trousers, he rocked back in his chair, a bare, skinny foot crossed on his knee, toenails bared.

'After more war stories?'

'No more, Mr Ismail. Read all those.'

'Ah, new shipment coming this week. American adventures. The education attaché at the U.S. embassy has a big family and they get through a lot, he says. Americans know how to turn even an argument into an adventure, the stuff of dreams.'

'Any argument?' Could the feud at home one day become profitable?

'Can't make out his new friend though. Tourist, apparently, but more like a lapsed beatnik to my eye.' He snuffled back the unwelcome note of incomprehension. 'So then, what are you looking for today, young man?'

'Information, Mr Ismail.'

'An encyclopaedia, is it? Cost a lot, you know. And the exchange value of pure knowledge these days is abysmal.'

'Jus' curious.'

Mr Ismail wiped the desk with the back of his hand, sending a small storm of paper flakes and silverfish shells into the air. He fixed me with a ropey eye. 'You have acquired a new curiosity?'

'Only birds.'

'Really?'

'Actually, birds and bats. Wanna know how they fly.'

His face eased, relieved. 'They applaud, young man. They clap with their wings and applaud the sky. That's how.'

I moved my hands together cautiously. 'How? This does nothing.'

'Smart fellow to go for the bat. An unusual wing, the bat wing. A cloak, not a feather. It changes the shape completely, and can hide everything or reveal it all, like a heart with wings. You should learn from that.'

Mr Ismail bent down and pulled out a thick, squat book, making a sharp creak which might have been his chair, or his spine or the book's spine cracking. He placed the book on the table and patted it. *'Pears' Cyclopaedia*. Good place to start for basic facts. Prominent people. Events of world importance. Maybe not our Sufi poets, but it covers some science and philosophy. Maybe even puzzles of nature. Take a look.' He pushed it forward: a rook on a chessboard.

I opened it and leafed through, conscious of Mr Ismail's eyes on me. The thin paper made a whispery sound as I flicked each page over, a rolling surf of words.

'Can't see nothing about bats.'

'Another lacuna? Check the index. Might be under general information.'

Sure enough, an entry on bats: L15. Listed under a letter and a number. Could the whole world, and everything known about it, be ordered in this way? They didn't teach things like that in my school. L15: the right-hand column boasted a two-inch paragraph on bats and their extraordinary ability to navigate in the dark using ultrasonics.

How did a word so wonderful come into being? Ultrasonics. As mysterious as a boy being born. How is it possible that I am here, alive, with a word like that in my head?

'Mr Ismail, you always come up trumps.'

'If you look, you will see.'

'It doesn't explain actual flying, but they find their way using ears not eyes. It's all to do with soundwaves. According to this, fishing bats in Central America can even find fish by detecting the echoes from the ripples that the fish make in the water.' That, for sure, would surprise Jay.

I could see those brown eyes freshen and Jay's face brighten into an ultrasonic sparkle. 'Wow.'

'We can all feel ripples, son,' Mr Ismail mumbled. He rose from his chair and shuffled to the edge of his small veranda, breathing noisily. He squinted as the last tints of the sun darkened his freckles. 'When a storm is coming, we can all feel the signs.' All I could see were golden feathery ridges over the rooftops trickling down the lane. I now wonder if Mr Ismail, bigger and older, could see things in the reddening clouds that I could not then: his hopes blistering, sinking, his long-held memories slowly winnowed by the gusts of a failing day.

☼

The following afternoon, school done, I waited until five before heading to the milk bar again. Turning into Bullers Road, I tore past a succession of old colonial mansions crumbling in their large sad gardens and a half-naked soothsayer bewailing the future on a tree stump, tuning my ears to a higher frequency, hoping to pick up a sound-silhouette of my friend slurping chocolate milk; instead I heard only Mahela's frothy laugh spilling out. Jay was at the counter teasing him.

Mahela mopped the zinc counter and leant over it. 'Good timing, cycle *kolla*. The ace is back: our maestro catcher.'

'You caught the bird?'

'Yup.' Jay popped his lips in delight. 'Sunbeam.'

Time to be ultra-cool. The information on the sensitivities of bats seemed the best bet. 'You know, bats hear ultrasonics. They can even catch fish from the sounds of swimming.'

'Not from my fish tank.' Jay gulped down his milk.

'You have a tank?'

'*Aquaria infinita.*'

'I'd love one, but my father says it's a waste of time. A bourgeois hobby, he calls it. He doesn't approve of anything that's fun, unless it's something *he* likes.' Even the radio was condemned as a mouthpiece for government propaganda, although he listened to it constantly and advocated state control of everything under the sun.

'You wanna see my fish? Come on, I'll show you.' Jay raced ahead.

Casa Lihiniya, Mahela had called it; a house with a name had to be more special than one with a number. I followed Jay down a zigzag lane until we reached a paved private road – and there it stood: a massive, modern, white house with a parapet protecting a winged roof. Next to the tall iron gates, firmly shut, a small metal door gleamed, tucked into the concrete wall. Jay had rigged it up with a secret wire that he could pull to release the inside bolt and make it chuckle open.

'Nobody knows when I come and go.'

We pushed our bikes through and stepped into a kingdom guarded by two agave plants with their yellow-bordered swords frozen mid-wave. A small tongue of tarmac split, leading to a tiled porch on one side and a line of whispery bamboo that shadowed the building on the other. An open concrete stairway hugged the outside wall of the house. Jay lodged his bike under the staircase and then leapt up the steps, two at a time. I did the same. At the top, we entered a vast covered balcony, bigger than my room, halfway between a zoo and a shipyard: a jumble of fish tanks big and small, workbenches piled with timber and boards, trays of hammers and saws and screwdrivers and pliers. A broken pane of glass and several sheets of Formica, propped up by a broom, shielded the back section.

'You have tons of tanks.'

'I keep eleven different species. Each aquarium has to be special.'

I stepped carefully across a wooden frame which had nails pointing up. 'What's this? A man-trap?'

'The fish are okay in the tanks. I can keep the Siamese fighters separate and watch them fence. But the birds are the problem. I'm making something better for them.' The budgies clustered in a blackened square cage in a corner of the balcony. 'They need protection, but they also need something more. You know, something *capacious*.'

He shook some seeds out onto a tray and pushed it in. The small grey, blue and green bundles exploded into a flurry of chirping. Jay crooned soothingly. Next to the budgies hung a separate small bell-shaped birdcage, a yellow orb framed in glistening purple brightened in it: the sunbird from the milk bar puffing up to add its sharp two-pronged whistles.

In our house we had no pets. I had never been surrounded by so many creatures swimming and fluttering, breathing out their given measure of life. I don't know why but despite the abundance, I felt we were all in some sense endangered. Jay poured some water from a jug into a saucer in the budgie cage, then he stepped over to the fish tanks.

'You'd think these fish were made especially for glass aquariums, no? Look at them. All the markings are on the side. Who would see those if they were just in a stream? Even that silly bloody tetra has a neon stripe on the side.'

Sparks swerved in the water.

'Are they your favourites?'

'Tetras you can catch easy-peasy. The ones I really like are my angel fish: this pair from Lumbini's. I'd like them to breed. That would be really something. They say it's a doddle but even keeping them alive is hard. See how they move? Sudden acceleration and then everything slows down. That's the way to live. Sudden motion. Then to be very still.' He tightened his jaw, moving closer to the water. 'If reincarnation is true that must be how it works. When you are born, you move. When you die, everything is still... Then, you are born again. Like a heart pumping.' He opened and closed his fist, repeatedly. 'The pulse of the universe, you see?'

Sudden acceleration sounded good, but I did not want time to ever stop. At that age, I did not like the idea of breeding either – whatever that might involve.

'But right now, the birds come first. So, I'm making an aviary in the garden.'

That was a new one too. I had heard my mother mention ovaries but had not bothered to listen more. 'Uh-huh. Right.'

'Big *ca-pacious* space, you know. So they can really fly around and not see bars all the time.'

The garden was enormous: eagles could fly in it and they'd think they were free. Casa Lihiniya even had coconut trees in the garden. Whatever an aviary was, it could certainly be put in there and no one would notice.

'Wanna help?'

Something in me accelerated; everything else slowed down. I breathed in, and then out. Angels flew. Swam.

'Sure. Aviary. I can do that.'

Jay handed over a bundle of wood strips. All precisely cut to size: six pieces, each as tall as him. 'Bring these. I'll show you.'

He collected a roll of chicken wire and a toolbox and led the way back down.

Skirting around the house, we ducked under an archway of blue flowers onto a patio. The lawn stretched out ahead: a carpet of creeping broadleaf grass.

Two men seated on butterfly chairs paused their conversation. While the trimmer one in a tightly buttoned shirt perched uncomfortably, his languid companion clicked his fingers jokingly. 'How's tricks, Batman?'

'No tricks today, Uncle Elvin. No bats, only budgies today.'

'But isn't that Robin with you?' A dry laugh escaped as if from a puncture in his throat.

'Kairo,' Jay said.

I half repeated it, swallowing a syllable, unsure of what to do.

32

'Very opportune. Add an 's' at the end, and you will always be our providential one. Kairos – good timing, no?' He gently pinched the skin under his Adam's apple and pulled it. 'Your father studies Greek?'

I stared at the long, lengthening throat. 'He wanted to call me Nasser, but my mother wouldn't have it.'

The other man plucked at his moustaches and burst out, 'Not a bloody socialist, is he?'

Jay hoisted his roll of wire mesh higher. 'Come on, let's go.'

'Those budgies are too damn loud, son.' Unrestrained, impatient, the buttoned-up man barked, 'A chap can't think with that racket. Put them somewhere out of earshot, will you?'

'Will you, will you?' Jay mocked, already half across the lawn.

'The thing is, Marty,' Elvin coaxed his agitated companion back to an earlier, less emotive, argument, 'a drought is a serious matter, but we need meteorologists not astrologers. The buggers in the ministry just don't know what to do. Never mind the university, there are not enough teachers at any level. No wonder the damn school keeps closing every other day.'

I made a mental note: no teachers. The tantalising possibility of not having to go to school – any 'damn' school at all – edged closer.

Catching up, I asked Jay, 'Was that your dad? The one who doesn't like your birds?'

'Yup.'

'Looks really upset. Is he a teacher?'

'He does business. Makes him a misery guts half the time.'

'Must be tough.' My father often worked himself up into a froth over private companies. 'Only one letter away from pirate,' he'd fume.

'Packaging and paper. Boring as hell. Uncle Elvin is forever trying to get him to do other stuff.'

'Your uncle looks cool. Like a secret agent.'

'He's a coconut planter.' Jay laughed. 'Also likes planting wild ideas in my father's cerebrum and cerebellum. They're cousins – Uncle Elvin and Dad, I mean. The only two. No brothers or sisters. Like me.'

'Me too.' Until then, I had assumed I was the only one.

At the end of the garden, in a cleared out area big enough to park a car, several posts marked out a rectangle. One side had chicken wire stretched across it; at the far end a row of bird houses stood on individual poles: a toy town on stilts. Jay put his roll of wire mesh down on the ground. A jeery flight of parakeets swooped past; shrikes and koels and fuzzy barbets cheered.

'Today we'll finish pinning the mesh. Then we have to figure out how to put in a full-size door so we can walk in. Cool, huh?'

'Your budgies are going to be in heaven.'

'I want to have lots of different sorts of birds in here, like my Sunbeam, that pretty yellow bird I caught, and bee-eaters and Java sparrows.' Jay took the wood strips and laid them out in a pattern of squares, constructing the outline of a new world. 'Trouble is those budgies can be vicious. So, have to see. Buggers need to learn how to live together.'

Jay knew so much: how to make cages, how to trap birds, how to breed. Stuff you couldn't learn from books – even an encyclopaedia. Despite the big words Jay sometimes used, he didn't look like a reader; his hands moved too much: long fingers drumming the air. Not fingers for turning pages, or holding a pen. And now, measuring his sticks against the blueprint in his head, Jay was biting the tip of his tongue.

'How?'

'Okay,' Jay said. 'Here's what to do.'

He made me stand at one corner with two strips of wood held aloft while he nailed them to the posts, then unroll the chicken wire to pin to the frame. Within an hour, most of the basics were done. Back at the house, Jay's father and Elvin carried on wreathed in smoke. I wondered if they too, like us, were engaged in drawing up a future for a better world.

2

'Madness.' My father tossed the party newspaper onto his cane chair, the first dip on the road to the archival pile. 'Just when we need to be united, what does our party leadership do? Split, split, split into bloody factions. What next? Another Three Stooges?'

Mooning over a new-style cashew-studded chocolate bar, I couldn't care less until he mentioned the Three Stooges.

'Those MP fellows are fascinated by a female in power, no?' To my mother the errant behaviour of politically driven men hardly amounted to a mystery with the world's first woman prime minister running the country. 'Anyone can see they can't wait to jump into her pocket.'

'Flummoxed, not fascinated. They say now is the beginning of socialism in this country, but I fear it is the end.'

'Isn't Madam Prime Minister a bona fide socialist?' A faint tone of incredulity crept into my mother's voice. 'And now with your far left joining her too.'

My father twirled a finger, stirring the air.

'The alliance of our LSSP leaders with her is seen by the purists as collaboration.' His voice slithered as he tried to control his frustration with orthodoxy. 'So, now all three – N. M., Cholmondeley and whatshisname – have been expelled from the Fourth International...' He acted as if he was talking about his Hotel De Buhari buriyani buddies, instead of the oldest left-wing political movement in Ceylon, predating independence, and powerful trade union champions.

'Never mind party politics, what about the language proficiency tests the government has started? Everyone has to pass or resign, no? So, hadn't you better start doing something to improve your Sinhala, Clarence?'

'How to be learning grammar at my age?'

I felt for my father. He had been brought up speaking English more than Sinhala; his mother tongue was not his strong point.

'If those posh fellows in parliament can come back from Oxford and speechify in Sinhala, why can't you learn enough to pass a simple test?'

'Okay, Monica, okay.' My father used the small blue rag that was kept by the telephone to clean his spectacles. 'You better learn too. Your English Service broadcast is not exactly the national priority, you know.'

Ma laughed, light and briefly carefree. 'We *have* to be international. Our listeners hear us in Nairobi, in Kabul, in Singapore. Not like your lot who can't even hear each other in the same room.' She collected her straw harlequin carry-all. 'I've got bridge now. Will you make sure Kairo does his homework?'

She walked out without waiting for an answer. The hot air slowly settled in the room. Flies prayed drowsily.

I retrieved the newspaper which had prompted the initial outburst and smoothed out the columns choked with acronyms and ungainly words: hegemony, Stolypin, GCSU, CMU, proletariat.

'Thaththa, why does it say "a proletarian revolution is impossible now; we must build a consensus"? What does *that* mean?'

'Glad you asked that, son. Always question – how else to learn? You see, our erstwhile party leader says there is no chance of revolutionary action in Ceylon and that the only road to change is through parliamentary reform. So, now he'll join the government and build consensus.' He struggled to express his discomfort in suitable terms. 'But I'm not so sure, son. The reason revolutionary action is not possible might be because our leading communists prefer to preserve things as they are – for themselves. Have you read *Animal Farm*?'

'Farming?'

'You should. Orwell describes this same process. The excuse the pigs use is that they are employing "tactics". But who benefits?'

'Is he a pig farmer?'

'I tell you, if Trotsky could see what is going on in what is surely the biggest Trotskyite party in the world, he'd be livid. It is a betrayal, he said, when leaders seek to preserve themselves. They become nothing but *dried preserves*.' Fingers locked together, leaning forwards, head lowered bullishly, he seemed both enthralled and horrified by the prospect of raisins in the sun. 'You must understand, son, language is the issue. If you don't understand the meaning of a word, you are at its mercy. "The fight against unclear language is part of the struggle for purity and beauty," quote, unquote. Comrade Trotsky again.'

'Are you a communist, Thaththa?'

'Ah, this depends on one's definition, does it not? The Communist Party is distinct from our LSSP.'

'So?'

'I have never been a member of the Communist Party. I do not support the Stalinist route. My creed has always been the abolition of inequality, as in our first manifesto. And for this I believe we must nationalise the means of production, distribution and exchange...'

'Okay then.' I turned the pages of the newspaper over to muffle the drone: bring it on, the revolution of Neapolitan ice cream.

'What's wrong? You want to go somewhere?'

'Don't they do even a single cartoon in your paper?'

This was not the kind of questioning he had in mind; it made him suspect I was being led astray by forces outside his control. 'Where do you go on that bike of yours?'

'Just cycling with a friend.'

'You be careful of fair-weather friends, son. *Amba yaha-luwo*. It's a fickle air we have to breathe these days.'

He chuckled, briefly pleased to have used the Sinhala phrase 'amba yahaluwo' — mango friends — drawing a distinction between a summer pal and a fellow traveller.

The milk bar became our fixed rendezvous. The hub from which we would cycle out in ever-widening circles. Jay never showed any curiosity about my parents, but one afternoon as we rode past the radio station I mentioned that my mother worked there.

'She has a job?'

'On radio shows.' It gave her a sense of freedom from family and that puzzled most of her friends.

'Amazing.' But Jay didn't ask me anything more.

Over the next few weeks, I became a regular visitor to Casa Lihiniya, sometimes cutting badminton club, or a swimming lesson, and going straight up to Jay's balcony with him to help clean the tanks, scooping tetras and guppies, tiger moths and mollies, from one to the other. Jay showed me how to siphon the water out, a half-tank at a time, using a short hose. He held one end underwater and handed me the other. 'Now suck the air but whip it out of your mouth before the water comes.' I didn't always get it out in time and preferred scraping the algae off the glass with a razor blade. Jay taped one edge of the blade with electrical tape, so I could use it safely. To polish the outside, I used cotton rags Jay soaked in a solution of vinegar and baking soda.

The gourami and angel fish, Jay dealt with himself. The cleaning and the feeding needed a special touch, he said, suggesting there might be a nourishment in his fingers that only he could offer. Triumphantly he would produce a tin of fish food and a jam jar filled with roast bread and clink them against each other.

'You crumble it over the water, but you must get it just right.'

He'd circle his thumb around his fingertips and weave a pattern of fine wheat dust on the surface, drawing the fish up, his hand a fleshly magnet and they shiny metal filings saved temporarily from sinking.

In each tank, Jay had favourites: fish that stood out, looked different, or listed to one side impeded. He had names for each and called them out, pretending his voice could carry under the water. They came to his finger when he tapped the glass and then he would dip his hand in and separate them from the others and reward them with an extra pinch of breadcrumbs.

I only saw Jay's father again on about the fifth visit.

We slipped in under the archway to the patio and found Marty, this time sunk in his butterfly chair, puffing a cigarette and blowing bluish blooms into the climbers, his face taut as if recovering from another argument he had lost. He had a soft, beige knitted tie on, but somehow it looked tight.

'So, back for more?' He, too, sounded wary of his son making dubious new pals.

'We'll be finished on the aviary by the weekend.' Jay moved across to shield me. 'Sunday.'

'No more Sunday weekends, son. It'll be religious holidays to appease the Buddhist vote instead – Poya holidays and pre-Poya days to match the phases of the moon. Those will be our weekends.' He began to shred a piece of paper meticulously into the large, shallow glass ashtray on the mosaic table next to him. He studied the debris, his face narrowing. 'I don't understand it. Those ruddy Marxists in parliament are meant to be anti-religion. What happened to the business of ridding us of the opium of the masses? Can't they even do that right?'

Jay hurried me out onto the lawn. 'Come on.'

'Cool to make every Sunday a moon day.'

'Works the other way.' Jay strode ahead. 'Poya day will be our Sunday. Except the fit is not easy. Moon months are not the same as regular months, so it'll not be the same as the Sunday week. Every month it'll shift a day apart. That's the problem.'

'So, we get more holidays?'

'More chaos. We'll be on a different planet from the rest of the world.'

As far as I could tell, we already were. The world I saw around me bore no resemblance to the wider world I read about. Everywhere else in the world things worked differently – from star charts to song charts.

'My dad says the trouble is the government's teeny cabin is too full.'

'Mine says the whole Cabinet is up the creek.' Jay tested the tension of the wire mesh. 'This kind of thing needs careful calibration.'

Soon he had us both focused on right angles and mitre joints, making the final additions to the aviary. The door he had designed — framed chicken wire — was ingenious, sliding sideways instead of being hinged, so that it could be opened unobtrusively.

'Not just lift and push. It should slide like a Japanese paper screen,' he explained.

He got me to lay a track for it: two straight pieces of wood — one first, then the other — with a flat waxed strip in the middle.

'Good work, pardner.'

Is this what growing up was all about? Hard work and feeling good. Two lines forming one track: a road leading from emptiness to fulfilment.

'Those birds need to feel they are out in the wild,' Jay said.

'Aren't they your pets?'

'Even we can feel wild.'

'Here?'

'In the countryside. Have you never been outstation?'

'I have too. On the school rice-planting trip. And a rubber plantation. My father said our rubber is the thing that China and Cuba are most crazy about, but the Americans are trying to sabotage the business.'

'Rubber is a colonial hang-up.' Jay tested the movement of the door, too absorbed to notice the severity of the implied judgement. 'Coconut is the real lifeblood of this country.'

'My dad is not colonial. He's always complaining that people don't take control of things.'

'He's right. You've got to take control. You won't get where you want to go unless you are captain of the ship.'

44

After we had measured out the roof sections, Jay said we should stop for the day.

Back in the house, I met Jay's mother, Sonya, for the first time.

'Is this your new friend?' As she spoke, her curved face brimming with expectation, she swayed gently to a music no one but she could hear.

'He has a name. I told you, no? His name is Kairo.'

She lightly fluffed up her bouffant curls with her fingers. 'Of course you did, darling.' A bubbly laugh escaped her pink painted lips.

I stared and tried to say 'Hello', but the syllables were too knotted to be audible as my mind raced from the word 'friend' to her potent term of endearment – one I associated only with the flickering romances of screen goddesses.

'What happened to that other boy?' Her large lids fluttered as she returned to a more domestic orbit, shuffling faces and names. 'Ravi, no?'

'He's an idiot.'

'Like your father.' She smiled at me. 'But this one looks very sweet.'

I saw that in this special house the rest of the world had only the most precarious of footholds. Any minute one could slip and fall devastatingly out of favour.

Her caftan – oyster-blue – could have adorned Cleopatra in some Technicolor oasis. She flicked it up at her shoulders, letting air swirl in. 'I'm so happy you are here, Kairo. Otherwise this darling boy of mine will be just talking to himself like you-know-who.'

My head spun, not knowing what she meant.

Then she picked up an elegant, saucer-shaped glass of pale rosé by its stem and started up the stairs. The whole room below darkened in her wake.

'What else to do?' Jay called after her. 'You never listen, no, to what anyone says.'

She stopped at the top and turned. 'When a man can speak without punching a hole in his hat, then I might listen. But you, my darling, I listen to all the time. So, now you listen to me.' She took a sip from her glass. Then looked, I thought, directly at me. 'You must learn to live, and to love, without regret. That is paramount.'

'What'd she mean?' I asked when she had gone.

'She's the crazy one. She says, if not for us, she'd be a film star. But if not for Pater, she'd be in some loony bin. Come on, let's go for a loaf.'

'Pater?'

'You know, Dad.'

As we wheeled out the bikes, I wondered if I should call my parents pater and mater too. We could both be like college boys then. I looked back and soaked in every ray radiating from Jay's Casa Lihiniya. A gilded castle complete with secret passages, captured animals and a mesmerising queen. A whole cosmos far, far more thrilling than the one I had been born into.

☼

I had not mentioned Jay, or Casa Lihiniya, to my parents, afraid my father would disapprove given the apparent wealth of the Alavises. So, when my mother asked where I had been, I dodged the question: 'Someone is building a really big thing in the middle of the racecourse.'

My father, pleased at this new interest in construction, let a rare puff of parental pride inflate him around the gills. 'Building is a sign of progress. The engine of growth.' He made a podgy block with his short yellow fingers and started to erect an imaginary tower, placing one fist on top of the other. 'Brezhnev and Johnson both agree on that.'

My father had never been a practical man. He lived in the hope that good things would happen naturally and was dumbfounded when they didn't. Dialectical materialism, in his opinion, governed everything – even luck. A win at the bookies, he believed, was inevitable – much to my mother's dismay.

Sadly, both thrashed around in the same hole making do – nothing more. A hole I knew I had to escape from. If only I could have spent my whole life in Jay's house; a place full of mystery where the adults, like his fish, floated in a diaphanous ether, where you made the world in the shape that you wanted it to be, where a screen goddess could walk in a regal gown and pronounce your name making you believe she'd known it from the day you were born; a house so large that no single place offered a view of the full extent of it, no single room gave even a hint of the number of doors that could open and close, and who might be hidden behind them, or any idea of the magnitude of the garden that sang out beyond the patio.

When I returned to Casa Lihiniya at the end of the week, it had not diminished. I rang my bicycle bell three times – our special signal – but instead of Jay a tiny woman, aged and shrunken by a lifetime of service, creaked open the side door.

'*Jay baba na,*' she whined. '*Eliyata giya.*' Her brittle, sugary eyes crinkled up. 'Didn't say, no? Just went on that cycle.'

A car honked angrily from the porch behind her. She retreated and opened the main gate. A white Daimler growled out with a tight-lipped Marty hunched over the wheel. At the end of the lane, it turned sharply onto the main road and disappeared.

I took off for the milk bar. No sign of Jay. Not slurping milk. Not racing on the turf. Not monitoring the building site inside the racecourse. A man, working on the concrete tubes, raised his sarong and pointed his thing at me and shook it.

Ignoring the taunt, I headed towards the upper school that I would be moving to when the day of reckoning came. Tall, imposing, red-faced, it too was undergoing renovations. Thick bamboo poles formed a scaffold at the front and stacks of bricks clogged the darkened colonial cloisters. The bicycle sheds I'd been looking forward to had been demolished to make way for compact new hatcheries.

☀

Before Jay turned up, the boys I knew all had an uglier side to them that revelled in elbow jabs and a rough craving to cause harm. He, too, could unleash cruelty: pouring boiling water on a termite nest, knocking the knotted spike off a chameleon with his catapult and leaving it bleeding in the hot sun. Those small acts of delinquency troubled me, but they did not poison our friendship. If I wanted to, I reckoned I could stop him. I began to believe that the world could be as you wanted it and nothing bad need ever happen in it.

We were on the last roll of mesh when Jay stopped: his face sharpened, his hackles rose.

'Thalagoya,' he whispered.

He pointed at the jambu tree in the small strip of the Amazon at the end of the garden and got me to fix my eye on the cluster of pink fruit, then slowly brought his finger down the trunk to the ground and, like a pencil drawing the world, led my eye to the clump of brown roots right at the edge of the wall. And there, camouflaged as a root itself, was a large monitor lizard motionless except for the thin black flickering tongue.

'Watch it,' Jay said and slipped away.

Hardly daring to breathe, I kept my eyes on the three-foot long lizard. The animal seemed to draw silence into the space between us.

When Jay returned, he had an air rifle in his hand. Sinking down, he slowly pulled the pump to prime the gun. He cocked the trigger and took aim, but before he could fire a door at the back of the house creaked open and a couple of scoured coconut shells flew out. Instantly the thalagoya was off, scuttling through a hole in the wall.

Jay lowered the rifle. 'He'll be back for the budgies. They won't have a chance trapped inside the cage.'

'He won't get in.'

'When he sees them, he'll find a way.'

'He can't work that out.'

'Sure. Why not? He can think. Thinking is going on everywhere, all the time.' He scratched at the ground with his bare toe. 'We have to stop him.'

'Could you have killed him with that?' I had seen adverts for his high-powered BSA Meteor, but never one in real life.

'Sure I could. That rubbery skin may be impenetrable, but if you hit the eye the bullet goes straight into the brain. He's a goner then. Ever shot a rifle?'

'A BB gun. Nothing like that.'

'We'll do some target practice soon, but first we need to sort out this problem.' He carefully un-cocked the rifle and placed it upright against a corner of the cage.

'Do we have to kill it?'

'Find a better solution, then. You'll have to think like a thalagoya.'

'If I was him, I'd dig a tunnel and get in from underneath.'

'Good point. If there is even one weak spot, he'll find it.'

The cage, originally designed to stop multicoloured birds from escaping, now had to protect them instead from a flat-footed predator that came from the age of dinosaurs.

'We could put cement on the floor. Make it unbreakable.'

Jay squeezed his upper lip with his fingers, pulling it and letting it plop. 'Can't have concrete. It's not a prison we are building here.' He picked up the rifle and started back towards the house.

'If not cement, we could try broken glass bottles like they put on top edges of walls to stop burglars.'

'I have another idea.' Jay carefully did not say 'better' again.

Upstairs, he pulled out a key he kept on a cord around his neck and opened the cupboard by his bed. A holster hung on a hook on the back of the door; also the bowie knife he had the first time we met, and two shotguns and two handguns on a rack inside. He put away the air rifle and locked the cupboard.

'That's an armoury.'

'Yeah.'

'Where'd you get so many guns? And the knife?'

'Here and there. I'll give you a demo next time. Right now, we have to fix the visitor problem.' A long high bird-call pierced the air. 'That's the kingfisher from the pond next door eyeing the fish tanks. Better cover them before we go.'

At the top of the lane, we crossed over the main road and scurried up an alleyway half hidden by a margosa tree. It brought us to a footpath that ran along a drainage cut. We kept single file for a hundred yards before coming to a low broken-down wall marking the boundary of a large untended back garden. Jay jumped across the ditch and clambered over the wall.

Beyond the mess of thorn bushes, papaw trees and banana lances, three decrepit barns leant on each other. 'Are we allowed?'

'Come on.'

'Is it someone's estate?'

'Don't be daft.' Jay marched ahead. Plum-headed parakeets rose squealing from the fruit trees.

'What's in those buildings?'

'Cars. Uncle Elvin's cars. He collects cars.'

'A collector?' My collection of miniature Dinky cars started on my seventh birthday and was kept in my treasure chest along with plastic figurines of Cowboys and Indians with their hats and headdresses and removable tomahawks and carbines. I couldn't let any of them go even though I had grown out of that kind of thing.

'He has six real stunners in there and a couple of jalopies on the other side of the house.'

'Eight cars! That's crazy.'

At the back of the barn, we climbed over broken Dutch tiles, burnt bricks, the rusting remains of a tractor, and bits of machinery embossed with names of a bygone era: Birmingham, Coventry, Nuneaton.

Jay pulled away some discarded planks. 'I saw a pile of *takarang* somewhere here. Corrugated sheets six or seven feet long.'

'Must be inside,' I said, wanting a peek.

'Let's have a look at the back of the stables.'

'Horses also?'

'Only two: Pegasus and Hermes.'

I'd seen horses trot along the shadier roads near the racecourse with smart Colombo riders – men and women in beige jodhpurs and beaked hats – but I had never imagined they were stabled in back gardens.

We circled a bed of cannas spouting red petals.

Jay squatted on his heels and studied the stained bluish earth. 'If you look carefully you'll see two sets of hoof marks. You can tell the animals apart from the depth of the prints.'

'How come he has horses? Does he collect everything?'

'Pretty much.' Jay raised his large eyes and grinned. 'Cars, horses, guns, girls. He calls himself a collector of good taste.'

Dr. No was on at the Savoy cinema and Jay's uncle billowed from a secret agent to a Bond villain installed in a Colombo lair.

'I'd like to see: horses, girls.'

'Stay focused. One thing at a time. You can do a ride maybe later, but not now. First, we need to find those metal sheets. Wait here, I'll check the back.' Jay disappeared down the side of the stables.

He could have been making it all up. Even in those early days I could tell, Jay had a chronic hunger for dreams. Maybe there were no horses, or cars, or girls; just empty sheds. Then I heard an unmistakeable animal sound: a whinny.

The stable door opened: a man knee-deep in polished brown riding boots stepped out. I recognised him and caught a whiff of horse. An animal stamped noisily behind him.

Jay reappeared at the same time. 'Uncle, you are here.'

'Hello. What are you up to? Is it Batman or Tarzan today?'

'Uncle, I am me today. Me am I.'

'And who is this young fellow? I have seen him before, have I not?' Elvin lifted a pair of wire-rimmed spectacles that hung on a black cord around his neck and examined me.

'My pal, Uncle.'

'Oh, yes. Little Robin. That's good. You need a proper friend, not just another squirrel or chimpanzee.' He curled his upper lip. 'You are not a chimp, are you my boy?'

'No, sir.'

'That's good. Our Tarzan here could do with some human company, otherwise he's going to turn into a jungle animal himself one of these days.'

'We are all animals, Uncle. No life without wildlife.'

'Ah, but *we* do not have to be wild. That makes all the difference. Some of us can behave in a civilised manner.' He glanced at me again. 'What do you think, dear boy?'

'Yes, sir.'

'Quite. "Yes" is probably not what you think, but at least you are civil – which is halfway to civilised – and might have a beneficial influence on our Tarzan here. You have a name?'

'Kairo.'

'Good. You were Kairo when I saw you at Marty's house, were you not? Unusual enough, but remind me next time. I shouldn't be calling you "boy", should I?'

Jay climbed down from a broken heap of furniture. 'What happened to all that *takarang*, Uncle? You had sheets

54

of *takarang* here, like thrown away.' He pulled a piece of cane from a broken rattan chair and twisted it. 'I could use them to protect my birds.'

'Did you forget about a roof? Better off with asbestos, you know. The miracle mineral, advocated by Charlemagne no less.' He checked the weeds by his boots.

'Obviously, we have the roof.' Jay quickly sketched out his plan to fortify the base of the cage against underground predators. Using the palms of his hands, he showed how the sheets of metal would be laid three inches under the ground with the edges bent up to meet the wood frame of the cage. Fresh earth over it and it would look normal, but it would have a metal shell to it that would make it as safe as Fort Knox. 'Good, no, Uncle?'

'I like it,' Elvin said. 'You can be quite cunning when you put your mind to it. I like that too. Not that deviousness should be encouraged, but the way things are going in this country it might be very handy.'

'So, you know where the *takarang* is?'

'That damn stable boy probably sold it to the tinkers. He'll sell anything given half a chance.' Elvin's expression softened, loosening the ruffles gathered at the edges of his eyes. 'Tell you what. Let's go get you some new sheets. Those old things wouldn't have done the job anyway, if they were already rusting. We might even find some galvanised sheets which would be a lot better for your purposes.'

Jay brightened. 'We'll go in the…?'

'What else? You couldn't get all your *takarang* in our sporty little Austin, could you?'

'Austin 1800?' I let out the name under my breath. Surely no one in Ceylon had one yet. Even London was waiting.

He chuckled. 'Think sportier, dear boy. The tops.'

'Austin Healey?'

'You know the little beauty? The 3000 Mark II?'

'I've never seen one. Except, I mean, in *Autocar*.'

'Ah, motoring magazines. What a dream world.'

☀

Elvin pulled open the door of the smallest barn: it had just one vehicle inside, shrouded in a grey cloth. 'Take the covers off, chaps.'

Jay unclipped one side, showing me how to do the other. We peeled back the cloth, rolling it into a bundle and revealing a creamy-white open-top sports car with a vibrant red racing stripe down the side.

Elvin patted the curved haunch. 'Get in, dear boy. Feel the leather. Calfskin.'

'Kairo.'

'What?'

'Kairo,' I repeated, haltingly. 'My name is Kairo. You said I should remind you.'

'Quite right. So, you should. Get in, young Master Kairos.' He added the 's', unable to simply obey a boy's wish.

Carefully opening the door, I slipped into the red cocoon of the front passenger seat. Twin round dials stared back from under the surprised brow of the dashboard. I half expected it to eject me and send me flying out.

'You like it? We'll go for a spin another day. Beauty needs appreciation, and the adoration of the young is a wonderful thing. But today we have a rather serious job to do with the old warhorse next door.'

The warhorse turned out to be a big, muscly jeep; its massive wheels belonged on a battlefield. Elvin climbed into the driver's seat and banged things about.

'It's been modified by the army.' Jay pointed out the alterations. 'Wheelbase extended, metal braces and an extra roof rod also.'

The top was off and the spare tyre – a black rosette – was fixed to the back. Elvin started it up.

A red setter appeared, barking furiously.

'Hey, Garibaldi.' Jay pulled the dog close and nuzzled him.

'Open that other door some more,' Elvin shouted above the clatter of the engine.

Jay pushed the warped wooden door and the jeep juddered out.

Elvin gestured vigorously with his right hand. 'Let's go.'

I climbed in the back and Jay jumped in next to his uncle. The jeep jerked forwards and Elvin beeped the horn. Garibaldi started racing around the jeep, bouncing from yelp to yelp.

Elvin charged down the drive and into the lane without even looking to see if the way was clear. On Jawatte Road, the breeze rose: I let my hand float in the flow, more carefree than I had ever imagined possible.

I assumed we were going to Imperial Stores, but we pulled up at a Maradana junkyard barricaded by piles of tyres and oil cans. Elvin beeped the horn and a weedy, white-haired man emerged from a shack, blinking at the sunlight.

'Cornelius, how? I need some metal sheets,' Elvin said in brusque broken Sinhala, not unlike my father's. 'Galvanised,' he added in English.

Cornelius ran a hand over his head. 'Rust-proof? Those sheets so hard to find today, sir.'

'You tell him,' Elvin said to Jay. 'Tell him your devious plan.'

Jay began to explain and Elvin burst out laughing: 'Ever heard of stopping a bugger trying to get into a cage instead of escaping from it?'

Cornelius continued trying to dig into his brain.

'Sir, sheet is not the answer,' he said eventually, resort-ing to English. 'Not only cost but when it rains sheets make all the ground muddy – galvanised or not. You end up with a big puddle problem that is not good. Your birds are not waterfowl, no? Better you put chicken wire. Two layers of wire mesh can stop even a Bolshevik. Water goes through and no thalagoya can get in without the will of God.'

'I should have thought of that.' Jay looked at me. 'Obvious, no? We'd have had to put perforations in the sheets. Mesh will be a helluva lot easier.'

I had failed him; was it not up to me – the cool-headed pardner – to anticipate those things Jay missed?

'You have enough mesh?' Elvin asked.

'Could do with more.' Jay did a calculation with his fingers. 'Maybe five more yards.'

Cornelius's eyebrows shot up in a triumphant arc. 'We have high-grade mesh. Nothing can bite or break it. But where the sides meet the ground, young sir, what'll you put?'

'Batons.'

'Two-by-two? Not enough. There you must put *takarang*, or galvanised plate. Wood they can break like matchsticks. Pin the mesh on the ground to the batons but also line the batons with metal strips. Cover the mesh with sand. Then you'll have a number-one safe place.'

'Then we'll need some metal strips also.'

'How long, Jay-baba, sir?'

'Let's see what you have.' Jay followed Cornelius. The stronger gravitational pull around Elvin held me back.

Elvin opened a packet of filter cigarettes and shook one out. He put it in his mouth and flicked open a chrome lighter; he scraped the emery wheel shielding the flame with a cupped hand even though the air was still. The tip of the lit cigarette brightened into an orange star.

'So, my boy,' Elvin let the smoke drift out with his words. 'Are you also mad about birds like our friend?'

'Budgies?'

'You have a couple more years to go, my boy, but he should have moved on from the feathered kind by now.'

'Kairo.'

'Right you are, Kairo. Yes. Good, you remembered. You must persevere, otherwise you get nothing in this world.' He blew a smoke ring.

I reached out to make something more of it than a coiled puff waddling to nowhere. A glimmer of recognition flared in Elvin's eyes briefly before he sucked more smoke from his cigarette and obscured it.

Jay came back carrying two rolls of wire mesh under his arm. Beaming. 'I got two different gauges. No way the bugger can get through.'

'And the long strips for the sides?' Elvin asked.

'Chap is bringing them.' He leant the rolls against the spare tyre.

Cornelius appeared with a bundle of long metal strips balanced on his shoulder, bouncing at the ends as he walked.

'Can't fit those in the jeep.' Grey smoke trailed out of Elvin's mouth.

'Easy.' Jay undid the buckles and locks of the windshield and swung it down flat on the bonnet. He then laid the metal strips along the length of the jeep and chucked the rolls of mesh in the back. 'See? No problem. They'll hardly stick out at all. We'll fit in some *takarang* also for extra cover, if that's okay, Uncle?'

Elvin flicked his cigarette to smoulder on the oily ground, threatening to send the whole yard up in flames. 'Good.'

After the metal sheets were loaded, he climbed in and told Cornelius to bill his account. We two boys perched at an angle and held the cargo in place. Elvin reversed straight over his cigarette butt the way another man might have used his shoe to grind it out.

And then we were flying down the main road.

※

That evening my parents had formed a coalition and when I came down for a bite, they pounced.

'Son,' my father started, 'it has come to our notice...'

'Oh, for God's sake, Clarence, speak normally,' my mother interrupted.

'So, you tell then, mother superior.'

'You were seen today Kairo, not on the badminton court where you were meant to be but in a jeep shooting down Bullers Road. In fact, the coach says he has not seen you at badminton since God knows when.'

'I was there last week.'

'Well, you didn't make much of an impression on him then. But you certainly made an impression on all and sundry today in that ridiculous jeep.'

'What is this jeep?' My father craned his neck, aloof but puzzled.

In my father's view, the best defensive action is to launch an immediate attack, so I went for it. 'Who saw? Is it Siripala? How can you believe him? Do you know what he's up to?' A salvo at both. The next question directly at him, the weaker point: 'Have you ever wondered why you never get any winnings?'

He squirmed. 'Don't change the subject.'

'Funny how he says he got the bets confused every time your horse wins. He's no fool.'

'Not every time.'

'You are the fool – to believe him.'

My mother intervened. 'Don't call your father a fool.'

'I only meant…' It was not the right word; not to fling at a father whose need was a lifebuoy more than a son to keep him afloat.

'Whose jeep is it? And what were you up to charging around in it?' My mother remained implacable.

'I wasn't driving it.'

'I should hope not.'

'It belongs to Jay's uncle.'

'And who the heck is Jay?' My father tried to wrest back control.

'My friend.'

'I've warned you: be careful with fair-weather friends.'

'He's a good friend, not like your friends.'

'I told you – don't be cheeky, Kairo.' My mother's voice rose a notch.

I knew I was not going to get the better of her. It might be best to come clean. The Alavises were lucky. Their good fortune surely could not be a fault. I sketched out for my unhappy parents the dreamy grandeur of Casa Lihiniya and Elvin's mansion.

'Well, well, well,' my father's attempt at admonishment betrayed more than a hint of grudging admiration. 'You certainly move in nefarious circles. No wonder you've kept it a secret.' He sucked in a dose of parental seriousness and converted it into a manifesto point. 'You should not be consorting with the class enemy, son, however dazzling they may be. Fool's gold – that is all they accumulate.'

'It has nothing to do with school.'

'They are the *haute bourgeoisie* par excellence, your Alavises. Stay away or you'll end up on toast.'

'What your father means is that these people are not like us. You don't belong with them.'

'Why? What are we?'

'It's not so much a matter of what you are, but what you believe.'

'Is this not a free country?'

That was a dangerous challenge at the best of times, with or without a sulk, risking a parental lecture in response that could last for hours. But, oddly subdued, my father barely managed a few short sentences: 'Freedom is not easy in a state like ours, son. Greed motivates these people, not need. Mark my words.' He paused, trying to decide between a warning and a prohibition. 'Better you stay away,' he added, without resolving the deeper issues that troubled him.

'I'd prefer to be over there any day than in this dump.' I could not stop the words, cruel as they were.

☀

Over the next week, I managed to avoid the subject of Jay coming up again until my mother took me to the KVG bookshop in Fort to buy a science primer.

'You have to start preparing for tests in all your subjects. It's a big reorganisation next year and you'll be reassigned to new classes. If you do badly in January, you'll be consigned to a dustbin.'

'The schools may not even open next term – Jay's father said.'

'You can be sure families like your Alavises will be fully prepared.'

'That shop makes my skin itch.'

'How can that be? You like books, Kairo.'

'Not schoolbooks.'

At the bookshop, she marched straight to the textbook department where she dispatched an assistant, caught idly cleaning his fingernails, to seek out the recommended primer. The whole dismal section made me feel ill with its exhortations of required learning so far removed from the pleasures offered at Mr Ismail's treasure island. Worse, my mother added a Sinhala grammar to the science primer before starting the complicated procedure of settling up through multiple dockets and fistfuls of carbon copies.

'Can I check out the comics section, Ma?' The single ray of sunlight, a hint of hope squeezed between the stacks of stultifying sermons.

'No, Kairo. You have enough comics. You need to start concentrating on these.' She handed over the parcel of books and gave me a push towards the door.

'But these are for dopes, Ma.'

On the way back home, niggled by maternal remorse, she tried to mollify me. 'How about a sundae at Fountain Café?'

'Knickerbocker Glory?'

'If that's what you want, my dear, but you must be a good boy and really start studying now. Also, enough of that rudeness to your father. Don't pick up bad habits from those posh people.'

Three scoops with nuts on top and a glacé cherry, as well as chocolate sauce, was possibly fair recompense for putting up with more schoolbooks.

The famous fountain in the front garden of the fashionable café was in full flow. My mother drove steadily down the drive, past the see-saws and the red swing, to the parking lot at the back where the old boundary walls crumbled between the clumps of orchids and weather-beaten notices for children's parties and tea dances. She parked in her usual place and quickly dabbed the sweat from under her eyes with a hanky before opening the door. As I got out of the car, someone cried out. A cry of helplessness more than a plea for help. A muffled sob. I patted the gun I always carried in my mind – a Colt .45 – and flexed my fingers.

My mother held the car door open, puzzled, uncertain.

'Over there.' The sound had come from behind the green delivery van by the bicycle shed on the far side.

Another cry. This time fear in it, not disappointment. A boy's fear. My mother pulled at the stirrup-handles of the round canister handbag she'd lodged under my seat. 'Only a dog, no?'

She looked for the convenient, easy explanation, whereas I immediately imagined the worst: death, destruction, disaster.

'It's not a dog. I'll go see.'

She tried to catch my hand but clutched air — way too slow for a boy who lived with imaginary gunslingers and metaphors of greased lightning.

On the other side of the van, three older boys had ganged up around a small, chubby younger one pushed against the wall with his white shorts in a puddle at his ankles, his hands spread out in front of his crotch.

'Let's see, fatso. Come on.' The leader of the gang reached for the boy's speckled mesh Y-fronts.

The cornered boy searched for help, his eyes uncertain. I did not know what to do.

Then something whizzed past and exploded against the wall. The bigger bully spun around, going off-balance.

'Wha——?'

'You touch him and I swear I'll bust your balls with the next shot.' Jay had come up from behind and had a huge catapult in his hand, fully drawn.

'Why the fuck are you protecting his arse?' The gang leader pulled back, perplexed, searching with his foot for his rubber slipper.

'Get lost.' Jay raised the catapult and took aim.

'Okay, okay.' The big boy lifted his arms. 'Have the roly-poly. Who cares?'

The gang edged away.

Jay told the boy still huddled by the wall: 'Get dressed, *men.*'

The boy pulled up his shorts and fastened the long tongue on the waistband, struggling with the buttonhole.

'You have a bike?' Jay asked.

'In the shed.'

'I'll ride with you up to the roundabout, so they don't jump you.'

'I'll be all right.' The boy rocked back on his feet.

I'd seen him looking lost in the playground during interval but never made any move to speak to him, thinking he must be one of those bussed in from the outer districts who did not speak English, and that we would have nothing in common. Until that day I had never spoken to any boy from the Tamil class. I still don't know whether that was an unintended consequence, or part of a deliberate policy of separation that would one day create a tragic gulf in our lives.

'It's okay,' I tried to reassure him. 'Jay saved you.'

I felt a hand on my shoulder.

'What's going on, Kairo?' my mother asked. 'What happened?'

'Some boys bullying the kid,' Jay told her. 'It's all right now.'

'Jay sent them packing. This is Jay, my friend. I told you about him, Ma.'

She studied the catapult in his hand. 'Well, you boys look like you could do with an ice cream?'

A Knickerbocker Glory sounded all wrong after what had happened, so I asked for a float instead. Strawberry. The other two asked for the same. We waited at the table in silence, unsure; the fountain in the garden showered sporadic silver arcs into the blue water of the paddling pool. My mother rummaged in her round handbag and pulled out a long, thin, black address book with a tiny gold-coloured pencil attached to the side. She turned to an empty page at the back and asked the boy his name.

'Channa.' He hesitated. 'I didn't do anything.'

'Who were those boys?'

'Don't know.'

'Have they bullied you before? Are they from your school?'

Channa's face tightened. 'They just came. I was only putting my bike there.'

'I've seen them in the upper school, Auntie,' Jay said. 'But they won't bother him again.'

'If they are from the school, they should be reported.'

'No. Please don't.'

'Why not? Shouldn't they be punished?'

The ice creams came, and a lime soda for my mother. Jay leant forwards. 'What he means is that if you report them, then he's marked as trouble. Even if it wasn't his fault.'

'That's not right.'

'Especially boys like him,' he added.

She considered Jay, and wavered. 'So, what do you think we should do?' she asked.

'I'll watch out for him. Don't worry, Auntie.'

My mother tapped the table with her pencil, assessing the options. 'You should tell your parents,' she said to Channa. 'Who are they?'

'My father is Ronny Kanagaratnam, Auntie.'

'Oh, our master dancer? Mr Cha-cha-cha?' She inclined her head to mask a smile, charmed by the connection and an echo of *Oye Como Va*.

'He's a journalist.'

'I know.' She tore out a page from her book and scribbled on it. 'This is my phone number. Tell him he can talk to me about it. Kairo, you finish your ice cream, I need to go now.'

'I'll get a ride back with Jay.'

'Yes, Auntie. Can go double on my bike.'

'Before it gets dark then. And don't go anywhere near those scallywags.'

After she left, Jay let his breath out. 'No nonsense, no, your mater?'

'She doesn't like to waste time.'

Outside, the trees began to fill with birds; the banyan on the other side of the road seemed to grow larger to catch the stragglers lost in the sky.

Channa drained the last of his float. 'I'll go now.'

'Where d'you live?' I asked.

'Other side of Beira Lake.'

'Stick to the main road,' Jay said. 'Those fellows are scaredy-cats but if they see you alone they might try something funny again.'

'They won't catch me.'

After Channa had gone, I continued to chew the paper straw of the float, flattening it, rendering it useless. Sweetness all sucked out, the flavour had turned papery.

'Some people are screwed up,' Jay said. 'They like to crush anyone who isn't as strong as them.'

'But why?'

'They get a kick out of it. Gives them power.'

When Jay said it, I saw how those boys pulling Channa's shorts down, the teachers who caned children any chance they got, Wolfman at the junction, Siripala on a bad day, all shared an anger that gnawed the deepest bones of their being.

'What can you do?' The last time I had punched Siripala back, it had only spurred another round and he had thumped me even harder than the first time.

'You've got to be smarter than them, that's all.'

※

In the days that followed, my father grumbled at everything from the ants in the biscuit tin to the cartoons in the daily paper. I was worried he had gone into a tailspin because my mother had confessed she'd met Jay, but then his friend Abey dropped in and my father was able to give full vent.

'A bloody abomination. Have you seen the newspaper, Abey? It's not a parliament, it's a bloody madhouse. Parity of language for Sinhala and Tamil was one of the foundation stones of our party. It goes back to the beginning. That brought everyone, whatever their tune – Sinhalese, Tamils, Muslims – together under a socialist banner. Equal status, officially, for both languages.'

'They'll do that in the North and East at the local level.' Abey stuck a finger in his ear to mitigate the next blast.

'Why the hell in two regions *only*? Is the plan to segregate them now?' My father flung an arm out, emulating an orator on the steps of Caesar's Forum, but the main repercussion was that he knocked the shade off the standard lamp. Luckily, I was there to catch it. He was chuffed. 'Nice catch, son.'

Abey acknowledged my promise as a cricketer too. 'Good at gully, you'll be, no?'

'We must rise above communalism, not wallow in it like bloody buffaloes. Look at America: despite everything, at least now they have a Civil Rights Act. But while LBJ and Dr King shake hands, what do we do? Pell-mell in the opposite direction. I tell you, at this rate we are heading for a complete societal breakdown.' My father took the lampshade from me and carefully placed it back on the metal holder. 'Sinhala socialism, limited socialism, is a nonsense. There should be no "national", except in "international", Abey. Not in today's world.'

I took note, but found a greater allure in Jay's much simpler axiom: no life without wildlife.

※

To reinforce the floor of the aviary, we dug out a shallow tray the length and width of the cage and laid the wire mesh Cornelius had provided, covering it with three inches of earth. Floor and sides secure, we added the roof: pitched corrugated metal at the back and mesh for the front slope.

'Truly capacious, huh?' Jay laughed. 'Now they need things to do: amusements, playthings, or they'll go off their heads.'

'Birds don't go crazy.'

'Oh, yes they do. Any creature can go crazy if it feels trapped. It happens when you have a brain, dodo.'

'Rubber rings are not going to stop anyone from going crazy.'

'Why not? A few rings, some swinging bars, a couple of whalebones.'

'You don't have whales. The biggest fish you have is that blue gourami.'

'Whalebone is stuff you pick up on the beach. Like clam shells. Birds like to sharpen their beaks on it. You are the book owl, no?'

'Driftwood?'

'For the finishing touch we need a flowering something and a bush with lots of twigs.' He found a dwarf mulberry plant and a forgotten peachy hibiscus on the other side of the garden and moved them in.

By Sunday afternoon, when I returned, the job was complete. He had even made a pond inside, using a broken butler's sink which he had half buried in a corner. The sliding door had a hasp fitted.

'Who's going to be first in?'

'Sunbeam.'

'Lucky.'

'Then the budgies, then bee-eaters and then parakeets.'

'All of them?'

'And more. I want to get some walkers also. And maybe a couple of Java sparrows.'

'Won't they fight? All those different types of birds. They can't all live in the same place, can they?'

'They'll learn. They live in the same world, don't they? Lovebirds might teach them something.'

'You said when trapped they go crazy.'

Jay picked up a stick and drew a square on the ground. 'If they feel trapped and crowded and there's not enough food, then there'll be trouble. But if there is enough space, and they have their basics needs met, then they can co-exist.' He was beginning to sound like my father. 'It doesn't matter if they are different species. You just have to make them feel safe.'

'But some birds hurt others. Peck them. Smash their eggs. Animals can be mean. Just like some people are nasty, no?'

Jay's face lengthened. The beads of moisture along his upper lip touched each other and broke into rivulets. 'If some do go like that, then we have to get rid of them: help natural selection make the right choice.'

Sunbeam was easy to carry in his cage but the budgies had to be gathered, one by one, and put in a large cardboard box to be transported. Jay had cut tiny breathing holes in the lid and a bigger hole in the centre of the box with a sock – toe-end cut off – fixed to it to make a floppy tunnel. He slowly collected each bird and gently transferred it through the sock into the box, making a low whistling sound. They waited for him hypnotised – all twenty-two of them. The last one he gathered was a dark bird with blue-black feathers. He kept that one out in his fist and stroked its head, holding it in such a way that it couldn't get its beak on him. 'We'll let this one see where he is going. He'll be chief of the tribe.'

He picked up the sunbird cage with his free hand and asked me to bring the box.

At the new enclosure he said, 'Leave the box closed, by the door, and take the cage in. Let Sunbeam out first.'

'Me?' A sharp needle picked holes in my back and around my knees.

'Go on.'

Jay murmured softly to the budgie in his hand while I lowered the box and took the birdcage in.

'Hang it on the pole and open the wire door. Then stand back. He'll come out when he's ready.'

'The ones in the box must be so scared.'

'Let Sunbeam get settled. He's got to feel this is his place.'

'But it isn't just his, is it?' I could not understand the exhilaration I felt. Was it power over liberty? Or the fact that Jay had offered me this inauguration?

'For the next few minutes he can believe it is his and that's all that'll matter.'

I stepped into the enclosure. The new world. Pristine. Protected. Cared for. Fixed Sunbeam's cage on the pole as Jay had instructed; lifted the pin on the door and nudged it open. The bird chirped.

Jay cooed back while still stroking the head of the budgie in his hand. A small smile lifted a corner of his mouth until he tightened his lip and stopped it.

Then the sunbird flew out, straight for the hibiscus at the far end of the enclosure.

'Attaboy,' Jay sank down. 'Watch him. See how he is measuring up the place? Give him a couple of minutes and then we'll let this one in.'

The bird in his hand cocked its smooth, priestly head.

Apart from the rustling in the box, no other sound disturbed the moment. Then Sunbeam sang out: a sharp high-tailed call.

'Okay. Now, let's get the others in.'

Jay stepped into the aviary and released the blue-black budgie from his hand. It fluttered around, almost drowning in the vast free space. Jay made a low, soothing whistling sound again until the bird finally found a perch.

'Bring in the box.'

I slid the door open just enough to pull the box in. The whole thing was rocking me with contradictory emotions, the earlier exhilaration punctured by spikes of guilt. I could see this was not freedom for the birds; merely the exchange of one cage for a bigger one. The fundamental nature of their lives had not changed. I could see from Jay's face that he did not share any such doubts; instead, it glowed. I put down the box and pulled open the flaps: all the budgies were huddled together.

Jay jerked his head at the door. We both slipped out and he slid the door shut.

'They need time. The box would have been scary, like sudden night. And now they have another day. A gift but a shock, no? That one I had in my hand saw there was no eclipse; he'll get them all adjusted. The light will make them feel safe.'

Jay was right. The lone budgie took off, making thin, indistinct sounds, and flew above the box in circles until his flight, lassoing the others, raised them, first one by one, and then the whole bunch in a whirl of colour creating a crescendo that seemed to envelop not only the cage but the whole of Casa Lihiniya and beyond.

By the time the garden darkened and the curving whoops and deep cries of wild birds drowned the sound of those in the aviary, we had dismantled the obsolete budgie cage up on the balcony – one of the first Jay had ever built – and made space for another fish tank.

Birds down there, fish up here. In Jay's world, you could pin the sun to a wall, hang the moon from the ceiling. You could make the world a safer place. Nothing was impossible.

'Wanna stay over tonight? Keep watch?'

I had not dared to hope before and now struggled to find the right balance. 'I'd have to ask my parents.'

'Is that a problem?'

'Dunno.' I hadn't told him about the row with them after the episode with the jeep.

'Call your mother. She'll be fine about it, I'm sure.'

After the Channa incident, my mother said that in her opinion Jay was a good friend to have, but for my father, overnighting at the Alavises' might be close to insurrection. From my mystery books I knew that in England and America kids stayed over at their friends' houses all the time, but I had never stayed overnight at someone else's house, except when we visited my father's lunatic fringe, as mother called them, on the coast near Beruwela.

Jay showed me the phone downstairs and I picked up the handset, careful not to disturb the arrangement of knick-knacks – a three-inch wooden Pinocchio and a litter of tiny glass dachshunds – on the small table. With every number I dialled I felt I was moving further and further from home, a river winding away from its source. Nothing to hold me back, only the question of how far I could go and the vastness of the ocean. No hint of the danger ahead.

'What?' My mother seemed to sense another irreversible change in the family constellation.

I said I was with Jay and would like to stay the night because we had to protect his birds.

'Where are you?'

'At his house. Just off Jawatte Road. Jay, you know, from Fountain Café.'

There was a pause as more ground shifted. She asked to speak to Jay's mother. I asked Jay.

'Sure. Why not?' He shouted for his mother, 'Telephone.'

Sonya appeared, shimmering, in a close-fitting maroon dress.

'Who is it, darling? Not that awful Mahinda, I hope.' She picked out a pair of tweezers from a pearly plastic purse. 'He's such a boomerang: every time you chuck him out, he comes back keener than ever.'

'Kairo's mother. He's gonna stay over.'

Her face relaxed. 'How lovely. For how long?'

'Just tonight. His mother is asking if it is okay.'

She took the telephone and spoke into it as if she was on film, the slender fingers of her other hand playing with the tweezers, wrist on hip.

'Why, of course he can. It would be lovely for the two of them.' She listened lazily as my mother must have gone through my nightly routine and then ended with a promise to meet up one of these days. She put the clunky handset down airily. 'There. All done. She was worried your sweetie won't be able to brush his teeth, but we have plenty of spare toothbrushes, don't we, darling?'

'I'll find one.'

'If not, give him one of my cotton pads. He can use his finger like that jungle boy. Now, you ask Iris to make you boys a nice omelette for dinner. I'm going out to the Mascarilla. I don't know what that father of yours is up to tonight but better stay out of his way. His whiskers have gone droopy and he is limping about like Dracula with a toothache.' Her lipstick glistened in the soft light of the table lamp as she leant towards me. 'Now, remember to brush those sweet teeth of yours and don't let our naughty Jay take you gallivanting over the rooftops instead.' Then she left, humming *Buona Sera* lightly to herself, tweezers clicking like tiny castanets in the scented air.

I asked Jay: 'Gallivanting over rooftops?'

'I go up to look at the stars. She thinks I'll fall off one day, but she's the one who goes gallivanting. Pater's gonna be furious.'

'Why? Can't he go to the Mascarilla?'

'You're a funny fellow.'

No, I wanted to say. More a bundle of nerves. Afraid to reveal myself. Afraid that the mask I wore could not be peeled off and that therefore I would live my whole life quarantined with my inner core forever knotted. No funnier than a telephone cable.

Iris was not pleased when Jay asked her to make two omelettes.

'You can't live on omelette, baba. Growing boys must eat rice. Chicken. Vegetables.'

'Make chicken then, but you'll have to catch one. We never have anything to eat in this house but eggs.'

'Tell your Amma to put on the order next time. They can bring chicken with her wine any day you like.'

'You are the cook. You tell her what you need.'

'I don't need anything if in this madhouse people only eat omelette. Any fool can break an egg.'

'Crazy woman.' Jay chivvied me. 'Let's go upstairs until it's ready.'

Up in his room, Jay brought out a tripod and then a big heavy metal tube.

'A telescope?' I helped him lay it down.

'If there is a man on the moon, you'll be able to see even the bumps on his nose with this. I have a moon chart. You can learn the names of the craters. The seas of the moon.' Jay checked the bracket and screws. 'We'll take it up on the roof after our victuals.'

'But what about the night watch? Shouldn't we start guard duty for the birds?'

Jay used a cotton swab to carefully clean the eyepiece of the telescope. 'Uncle Elvin gave me this. It's fantastic.'

Iris, the cook-woman, called out. '*Kaama lasstee.*' More of a wail than an invitation to dinner.

'Let's go eat,' Jay said. 'We'll do a patrol after that and see what to do.'

Two plates, each presenting a slice of charred bread and a harshly browned omelette riddled with red onion rings, cucumber cubes and green chillies bubbled on the big round table in the dining room. Two small towers of iced water filled to the brim stood next to the plates ready to douse the embers.

'I've never seen a round table like this before.' Effortlessly the dream shifted from a commando mission to knights in armour.

'Pater likes the Camelot idea, but we are never all here at the same time. It is an utterly pointless farce. They can't stand each other. Mater thinks she can play hell but he is going to really blow a fuse one day.'

Iris, one thumb hooked into the waist knot of her cloth, rattled the fruit trolley and asked if we wanted bananas.

'Nothing, no. Go, woman, scat.' Jay tucked in, urging me to eat.

She retreated to the kitchen, her tiny bare feet making hardly a sound.

'This is good. Thank you,' I called after her, trying to be more chivalrous and in that moment seeing what my friendship might offer Jay and why it should last beyond just cycle rides and pet projects. I could make amends for Jay's faults: his abruptness, scorn, temper, unexpected weaknesses. More than reciprocity, it gave me almost an advantage.

We finished eating and Jay stood up.

I used my napkin to dab my lips and dropped it on the table the way Jay had done, crumpled up, but then, before following him out, decided to fold it instead and place it neatly by the empty plate. Iris was not the mother, but I wanted her to think better of me.

The moon, still swollen from the adulations of the Poya crowds, let a silvery sheen seep through to the garden coating every surface in lunar breath.

'Let's check if the birds are all right.' Jay led us across the lawn. The cage was silent. The budgies perched in a line: motionless. Jay counted them all silently, folding his fingers one-by-one in several rounds.

Back upstairs, he said, 'They seem to feel safe enough.' He fastened a strap to the telescope and hung it over his shoulder. At one corner of the balcony, beyond the rail, he had a rope ladder swinging down from the roof. 'Time to go see celestial beauty.'

A moment later, Jay was over the railing and scrambling up in the dark. At the top, he slid onto the flat portion of the roof.

'Come on.' His face peered over the edge. A torch beam picked out the coir ropes. 'Grab it and step onto the first rung. You'll be fine.'

Of course, he was right: I would be fine. I reached for one of the wooden rungs and stepped out, grateful for the dark and that I could see nothing below. Keeping my eyes on Jay, I climbed. Near the top, Jay reached out and hauled me up – the first time, almost the only time, I felt his hand on me.

In the moonlight, the roof rippled never-endingly. Jay had constructed a wooden platform where he could set up the telescope on its tripod. He fixed it and brought the moon into focus and got me to look through.

'What d'you think of that?'

'Amazing.'

'Bashed about, huh? Hardly the White Goddess that Uncle Elvin claims.'

'I like it, dented like that.'

'This roof is one of my favourite hideaways,' Jay said. 'Everything is yours here. Daytime you can see the church that side, the Arabic garden over there and the sun worshipper in the house beyond our aviary.'

'There are sun worshippers in Tintin. He follows them to the Temple of the Sun, in Peru.'

'This one's French. From the embassy. She likes to sunbathe on her balcony.'

'In an "itsy bitsy teenie weenie, yellow polka-dot bikini"?' I half sang.

Jay could not suppress the small muscle curling at the edge of his mouth. 'No, actually topless. We'll come up one afternoon, you'll see. She usually does it on a Friday when the staff go.'

Clouds skidded across the sky rubbing out the stars.

'Hang on, we forgot the chart. I'll go get it. You stay here. Don't go near the edge.'

He swung his legs over and disappeared, leaving me alone in an arena of shadows monitored only by a bruised disc in the sky.

I never believed the stars governed our lives; at least, I don't think I did then. I am not so sure now. Everything seems to have a shape pulled and turned by an unseen hand. Perhaps the stars are its fingertips.

A light came on in an upstairs room of the house beyond the aviary. A woman opened the French windows and peeked out in a pale bathrobe. I tried to turn the telescope on her but couldn't lower the tripod enough to get the angle right. The light in the room went out as the woman stepped onto the moonlit balcony. She slipped off her robe and knelt on the floor; another figure appeared and melted down behind her. I could not make out anything more but found the ritual strangely thrilling: the glimpse of her milky face, briefly uplifted, before she bowed.

When Jay climbed back onto the roof, he immediately noticed the lopsided telescope. 'What happened?'

'Moon worshippers,' I explained. 'Kowtowing.'

'Who?'

'Over there.' Both figures had disappeared back indoors.

'The embassy lady?'

'Dunno. She was kneeling, and a man also.'

Jay studied me thoughtfully, but did not say anything. I hoped I had not committed an irretrievable wrong. Confusingly, my nipples ached.

'Here, check out the chart.' Jay unfolded a large map and shone his torch on it. 'Let's see if you can spot the Sea of Ventura.'

※

'What is this rain, rain, rain?' My mother pulled at the Venetian blinds that had once been her pride and joy. 'Is it never going to stop?'

'So, no drought then?'

'You can safely say there is no danger of that, son.'

It might have been the change in weather, but recently she had become less irritable. My father made up for it by being ever moodier.

'Bad form,' he grumbled. 'Churuchurufying non-stop until the damn road is flooded and that pain-in-the-neck Bandula comes around with another of his daft schemes for dykes, or waterwheels, or what-have-you.'

'He's your friend, no?'

'Thaththa's friends are all weird,' I said.

'Sometimes you have to make allowances. Even a pain-in-the-neck can turn into an old mate over time.'

'What's got into you?' She stacked together the cork tablemats and took them over to the sideboard. The desk-jotter – compliments of the Bank of Ceylon – had a page torn in half. 'You haven't lost another bet, have you?'

'Don't be silly.' He searched his pockets for his cigarettes. 'No racing today.'

'Why, is it raining in England also?'

Did rain fall differently there? Colder? The drops smaller? Could they rip leaves and buckle gutters in the Somerset and Suffolk I'd read about as they did in Havelock Town?

'Why not? They are not immune.' My father stood up and searched his trouser pockets again. 'Have you seen my cigarettes?

'You should stop smoking.'

'What have you done with them?'

'Nothing. I'm not your ayah. You want to smoke, you smoke. What has it to do with me?'

'Exactly.'

I don't know what my parents saw in each other to make them believe they could have a meaningful life together. Were such pairings totally random? Maybe the only choice you have is the choice of a friend. The person who becomes your best friend. Not what happens to them, or to you. I pocketed a couple of ginger nuts from the cookie jar and slipped into the garage where I kept my bike.

Our decrepit Ford Anglia – a yellowing white top with rusty brown edges – stood in the damp concrete box, the tyres ready to crack and the seats already split at the seams where the stitching had come undone. My father did not care. 'As long as it goes, what does it matter?' For my mother the problem was how to stop when the brakes were so soft. My brakes were also a worry – on my bike. The uneven rubber pads needed adjusting. From Jay I was learning that a touch of courage, a word at the right moment, a few drops of 3-in-1 oil was all it took to make a difference. As I finished tightening the brake cable, I sensed Siripala watching from the kitchen door.

'Don't go out, baba. You'll catch a cold.' He reached out. I shook his hand off.

Siripala grinned in a boxy sort of way. He grinned when he didn't know what else to do, a strategy of dazed help-lessness once but which had settled into sharper, more sinister angles as the months passed and the box emptied of hope.

He had grown up in a village in the south, a few miles beyond Kataragama, and had come to work in our house a year earlier. His schooling had lasted only for a few years, he said, mystified that I had to go to class after class. He proudly claimed to have left such impediments behind – left parents behind – but when I saw him at the beck and call of my father, I understood the fundamental flaw in the argument.

When the rain eased, I headed for Jawatte Road.

The air, heavy with moisture, reeked of wet leaves and washed bitumen; muddy rivulets and filthy drains gushed into each other at every junction. I rang my bell hard and fast, lifting my thumb with a ping. The old cobbler setting out his rickety stall at the corner of Thimbirigasyaya bared one of his rare red and yellow chewed-up grins as I took a low, fast turn. A bus, belching into gear, splashed and honked but I shot ahead. The main road was clear. I could get up a good speed on the long straight strip with its easy rise and fall. The dip near the Bo-tree and shrine had filled up and I sailed through, spraying water like a wild cat. Legs up, just on momentum. Until Jay had turned up, all my true companions sprang from the pages of adventure books, or from comics and films. I would conjure up deserts out of cereal bowls, prairies out of a patch of lawn, oceans out of puddles for them to explore. The men strong and of few words; the women permanently moistened and tantalising for reasons I could not work out. Friendship always an unspoken bond and love a fire that flared at the end of a story, not the beginning.

Near the racecourse, the Radio Ceylon building loomed. My mother was not there at that moment, but I could feel her earlier presence issuing from its mast like a phantom broadcast. I loved the building, the buzz inside, when she used to take me to see the Saturday stars and the faces behind *Kiddies' Korner*, the *Hit Parade* and the *Golden Voice*. But now, vaulting towards my teens, I only wanted to get to the playing field behind. I took the turn, deftly avoiding a lorry creaking round the bend with a load of cane chairs, and headed down the SSC – the Sinhalese Sports Club – road at the back.

Independence Hall, on Torrington Square, no older than me, pretended to be a monument of antiquity: a grand curved roof floating on ghostly columns that echoed the thousand-pillars of a legendary golden age. The national dream it tried to evoke had no effect on me; I had no passion for ancient kings nor the gods of any denomination. My heroes wore blue jeans, they danced to the tunes of Elvis and bounced along with John, Paul, George and Ringo. I rang my bell and started along the bund around the field singing 'I wanna hold your hand' at the top of my voice. Beatlemania in my part of town flowed solely from me: I felt I had a lot to make up for. Maybe I could persuade Jay to join me and together start a fan club.

Then, when I got closer to the hall, I saw I was not alone.

Standing by one of the stone lions guarding the hall, her bushy hair tied back behind her head, a proud red shirt tickling the shade, was a girl. She had her eyes trained on the main avenue leading to the square and thankfully not in my direction, but I wished I could be vaporised on the spot. Even from a hundred yards away, she must have heard me careering around, twisting and shouting like a lunatic from Liverpool.

Quickly wheeling my bike behind a tree, I pretended to fiddle with the brake cable and watched.

A few minutes later, Jay appeared coolly coasting hands-free towards her. Before I could warn him, the girl jumped down onto the road waving. Jay came to a stop. They spoke in a way that showed they knew each other. Then she got onto the crossbar of his bike, side-saddle, and he put his arms around her. He set off back the way he had come. He had not seen me. Probably could not see anything with his face buried like that in her hair.

The heart, I'd learnt, was the size of a fist: it pummelled the young dove I'd nurtured inside. As soon as they disappeared, I launched off, pedalling in the opposite direction: back towards the white-domed temple and the lanes where I often hid to numb my loneliness.

❀

The next day Jay called: his voice crackly, urgent, jumpy. 'Can you come over?'

'What's happened?' I asked, relieved to hear him, worried the girl had replaced me and ended everything: the night-watch rota, the sunset chases, the secret bliss I had found.

'We are under attack.'

'The bird cage?' I knew at once.

I put away my *Motor* magazine and rode over.

He was waiting at the top of the stairs, arms folded, face knotted.

'Who was that girl?' I plunged straight in.

'What girl? It's the cage, man. That's the problem.'

'In Torrington Square. You were going double with a girl.'

His jaw muscles loosened; his teeth appeared larger. 'That's Niromi.'

Not knowing what else to ask, I repeated her name. 'Niromi?'

'Listen, we have a real problem. Some animal has been trying to break open the aviary, going straight for the wire mesh. We have to lay a trap.' He uttered the word 'trap' as though it were one itself: short, sharp and sure.

'That thalagoya?'

'No, it's high up. Come, I'll show you.'

The damage was at roof level where we had put a sloping section of mesh – now bulging inwards in two cup-like shapes.

'You have a theory, no?'

'We have to observe and note down the lie of the land. Can you do that? Note everything you see?'

'Sure.' I had developed the habit of writing down all kinds of stuff in a secret notebook. My favourite detective solved cases by making thorough observations and then analysing the facts when she had the full picture.

I scribbled in forensic detail – the mysterious shape in the mesh, the ruffled leaves, the curled bushes – Jay walked around the cage looking for signs of greater danger, an idea forming. 'Let's put a decoy bird out.'

I used to do that with my army of plastic soldiers, the Marine Corps or the squad of commandos. Even the plastic bareback riders – chocolatey scouts – with their legs permanently splayed, I could lead into an ambush and then deploy the rest of their side to attack the unsuspecting enemy from the rear. But that was kids' stuff; putting a live bird out as a lure was taking the game to a whole new level.

As we headed indoors to get the trap, we came across Jay's father in his chair on the patio. Loose smoke obscured parts of his face.

'You boys have a problem?'

Jay hotfooted it inside without replying. I stopped. 'Funny business with the cage. Someone's been trying to get in.'

'That is funny.' Marty laughed. A fake, private laugh. 'Safer in than out, eh?'

'Someone's trying to get at the birds.'

'Those bloody budgies? Probably to shut them up. I could wring their bloody necks myself sometimes.'

'They have no necks.' The words escaped too soon.

Marty laughed again, quietly, impenetrably. His eyes shifted, half shielded, but his mouth curled beneath the wiry moustaches, unable to hide the sharp gleam of his teeth. 'You are a clever Dick, aren't you?'

'I mean they are tiny.'

'What is our friend going to do?'

'Set a trap.'

'Yes, you do that. Catch the culprit. We all need a mission.' Marty passed a hand over his face, waving away the smoke. 'It's a tough job, keeping things safe.'

Was he making fun of us, or working out a problem? I could not tell. I only wanted to escape his impending barbs.

Marty lifted the short transparent TarGard cigarette holder to his lips and took a long drag. Tar seeped through the slit in the gold filter to fill the sealed end of the holder. Black treacle. 'There comes a point, you know, when it just is not worth it anymore. You'll see, one day.'

'I better go.' I headed upstairs.

On the balcony, Jay had already uncovered Sunbeam's old birdcage and started reshaping the door.

'We'll do this like a fish-catcher, you know.'

'A what?'

'Have you not gone fishing? Set a *kuduwa* in a stream?'

'Never heard of fishing with a cage.'

'Oh, boy, you got a lot to learn. I'll take you one of these days. For now, you better just watch.' He undid some of the bars at the front and bent the thin cross wires to point inwards. 'The trick is to make the cage simple for the intruder to enter but difficult to get out.' He pushed his hand in, to show how easily it went through but how when he tried to pull his hand out the loose wires dug in. He had to push them back carefully with a wooden ruler to release his hand. 'How's that?'

'But what if the thing going in after the budgie is small enough to creep out again.' I never felt I was an intruder.

'It won't be tiny. You saw the damage. Anything that big will be trapped.'

'But what if it is too big to go in? Like a man?'

'How would a man make those dents? Anyway, if he puts his hand in, it will get scratched. There'd be blood. Even if he gets away, we'll know more than we know now.'

'And the decoy? Will it die?' What did it take to risk so casually a creature you held dear?

'Think: imagination.' Jay banged the front of an ancient chest of drawers, a dark piece of furniture that could have come from a pirate ship. The front panels were inlaid with pale elongated star shapes of Dutch cosmology, the bottom drawers heavy and crammed with junk. He rattled them and pulled out a life-size wooden replica of a budgie, painted yellowy green with shivering black lines around its head. 'Should do the trick, no?'

Downstairs, Marty had gone but I could still smell burnt tobacco in the air, much richer than the girly scent I had detected in Jay's room.

'Thank God, he's buggered off at last.' Jay pushed aside the empty chair.

'Your dad sounded concerned.'

'What did he say?'

'Just asked what had happened.'

'Oh, yeah. Like he cares.'

'Maybe he doesn't like your budgies much, but he hopes we'll catch the culprit.'

'Pater would like them all dead. All he cares about is himself.'

I found the disdain that distorted Marty's face uncomfortable, yet I did not think he was a bad man, just someone with a lot going on inside that I could not understand. But I was not going to argue with Jay, especially not on the subject of his father. Not now, when things were so fragile.

'You know what he said when I brought the first pair home?'

'That he didn't like budgies?'

'Said he'd wring their bloody necks if they woke him up in the morning. Can you believe it? That's why I brought more. And more. To see if he would wring all their bloody necks.'

'He says that but he's just joking, no? Pretending. He's never really done anything like that, has he?' But I couldn't stop myself imagining it.

'He's always got the air con on full blast anyway. Wouldn't hear even an elephant on the rampage.' Jay positioned the trap on a bird table he had put outside the aviary. We started back towards the house, Jay striding ahead continuing an angry argument of his own.

Harsh cawing grew loud above us. 'Wait.'

A crow swooped down onto the roof of the aviary. Swivelling its large black head, it took stock before dropping down onto the bird table to examine Jay's trap. Rather than squeeze into the opening Jay had made, it moved to the side closer to the decoy. Its broad, flat back tensed and expanded; then the massive beak plunged at the wooden bird through the wires. Since the decoy did not budge, it turned back to the aviary and arched its wings like a sorcerer; the budgies, clustered at the far end, started to screech. With another sharp cry, the crow took off and rose rapidly in the air, spiralling up as if in the grip of an inner tornado and then folded up into a bullet and hurtled down in a sharp dive at the cage. It banged into the wire mesh, making another dent between the first two, and immediately rose up in the air for the next attack.

'Jeez,' Jay whistled. 'He's like a Stuka. I've got to get that bastard.'

'So, it is him.'

'You watch him. I'm going upstairs.' He dashed back into the house.

The crow dive-bombed again and pounded the mesh, widening the dent. Two more crows circled the cage, cawing. The shrill alarm of the budgies inside rose. Jay had said to watch, so I waited and watched but I didn't know what I could do if the crow got in.

Then, as the crow reached its high point again, I heard the sharp report of an air rifle. The crow's wing juddered. The bird veered. Then another shot. This time the crow plummeted straight down and thudded to the ground, a weighted carcass cloaked in unflapping, lifeless, useless black wings. The cawing of its companions intensified. I checked the balcony. Jay was taking aim again. Another shot and a second crow dropped out of the sky with a hole widening in its head.

It frightened me. More crows appeared, circling. Their accusations, calls of retribution, filled the sky.

II

GALLINAGO

3

I didn't see Jay for a few days. Then one sleepy afternoon, as I lay cloud-watching a snow goose slowly evolve into a hazy white antelope, a bicycle bell rang furiously. Jay, trigger-happy at the gate, his face chock-full and radiant, called up.

'I'm going fishing. Wanna come?'

'In the swamp?'

'Outstation. Tomorrow. Two nights' rest and reparations at Uncle Elvin's estate.'

'Have to ask my parents when they get home.'

'Ask and come. Spend the night at my house. We shoot off at the crack of dawn.' He said, 'crack of dawn' the way he would if planning a raid. 'And bring a hat,' he added. Then he was off, standing on the pedals and whizzing up the road.

Estate. Outstation. Rainbow fish jumping. How could I resist? Only later did it strike me that there might be neither reparations nor recuperation; a fishing trip involved more deliberate deaths, and this time I would be the one doing it. Then the bigger shock: that was the draw.

☼

The recent downpours had not lasted; the town was sweltering. Downstairs, Siripala sat in the backyard chewing betel leaves – a practice expressly forbidden by my mother.

'You are not allowed that stuff in our house.'

'This is outside.' Siripala spat a mouthful of betel juice into the drain. 'In the village, people are warning of a catastrophe,' he added implying that was enough to tip the balance of acceptable habits.

'Is it the election?' My father had been going on about the possibility as a matter of national anxiety.

'No, baba, drought is coming.' He popped another wad of *bulath* into his mouth and screwed up his face. 'Little children will die.'

The cracks in his lips widened. Sly warnings and hidden threats bubbled in his reddish spittle.

Father came home before mother. Although there had not been another discussion on the demerits of the Alavises, and my father had not formally rescinded his veto, he had grudgingly accepted the first sleepover; I also knew that my mother had given a favourable report on Jay. So, as soon as he had settled into his armchair with his cup of creamy, sweet tea, I popped the question.

'Thaththa, can I go on a trip with my friend? Outstation?'

'Outstation where?' He put on his reading glasses and peered as if he expected to find the answer printed on my forehead.

'To Jay's Uncle Elvin's estate. Big place with fish and all.'

'That brown sahib?'

'Can I, please?'

'You like to see first-hand what their capitalist system does? How those absentee landlords suck the country dry?'

I couldn't decipher his expression.

'His Uncle Elvin is cool.'

'Is that so?' My father doubled up his newspaper into an oblong he could hold in one hand, close to his face, thus dispensing with the smears of his spectacles for a moment. The new budget announcements were progressive, he had told my mother in the morning, but the renewed focus on sectarian loyalties dismayed him. I was the least of his worries. 'Go then with your friend, *putha*, but never forget: he belongs to a class that only looks after itself. Keep a sharp eye.'

'I'm learning all the time, Thaththa. Jay is teaching me carpentry, astronomy, zoology.'

'I suppose you can't hold a fellow's breeding against him. After all he didn't choose his procreant, did he?' His voice took on a sympathetic lilt that made him appear oddly sanguine as if by yielding to me he had unexpectedly solved a long-standing dilemma.

The small, blue BOAC flight bag that one of my mother's foreign friends had left at the house proved perfect for the expedition: a towel, spare shorts and shirt. A change of underwear. Pyjamas. Toothbrush and toothpaste. My green plastic comb. All neatly fitted in. I did not bother with a book. Jay, despite his occasional big words, read only animal tracks, leaf fall and invisible fish trails in laughing water. I was going to be the same.

Then, at the last minute, filial deference mixed with rebel defiance overcame me and I slipped in the thinnest book I could find in the case outside the bathroom: *Problems of Life*. The blazing red title promised answers I could test out in the field. Although printed in Colombo, it was about life in the Soviet Union: a bonus.

My mother spotted the flight bag by the door as soon as she stepped in: 'What's all this about?'

'Boy is going on a trip.'

'What trip? He has badminton in the morning and then tuition.'

'Fishing trip,' I piped in. 'No tuition tomorrow. Holidays, no? And badminton doesn't start again for another week. Thaththa said I can go with Jay and his uncle.'

'Clarence, are you off your head?'

'Outstation with that young fellow you were so impressed with, and his uncle. Big trip for the boy. He'll see how badly the agricultural heart of our land is being squeezed.' He took a deep breath and steamed into political poetry: 'The salt of injustice may smart his eyes but it will sharpen the boy's mind. With luck, provide a very sorely needed political education.'

'Don't be an ass. Where is he going? Why? When?'

'What the hell? A quiz now?'

'It's all right, you two. Thaththa said, it will be good for me, no?' I was becoming an expert at stemming the back and forth of recrimination; born a boy who could be both conduit and valve.

'Child must know the truth. Understand how those plutocrats control the countryside. This time they escaped sequestration but by the next budget our comrade Krupke will have to go for real land reform, or else he will be out on his ear like a second-rate tsar.'

My mother ignored him and glowered at the flight bag. 'You have your toothbrush in there?'

'Have everything.'

'Will they pick you up?'

'Easier if I stay at Jay's house tonight, Ma, and then we can set off at the crack of dawn.' I looked to my father for backup.

'Good plan. Your mother can drop you on her way to her pogo club.'

She tensed up, drawing her sharp, troubled head back, perhaps already sensing the false promise of future accords. 'It's a dance class, Clarence. We do the cha-cha-cha.'

The gates at Casa Lihiniya gaped open. The porch light fizzed gently, dimming; moths shadow-boxed, a gecko on the wall revolved jerkily in a sporadic tailspin.

'With all their money, can't they even fix that bulb?' My mother raced the engine as if it might energise the fluorescent tube.

I slipped out of the car.

She tapped the inside of the windscreen and mouthed a goodbye. But when I headed for the outside stairs, she quickly stuck her head out of the window. 'Where are you going? The door is over there, child.'

'He has his own entrance, Ma.' I wanted her to notice the shortcomings of our low-grade rental house.

'There is only one front door. Don't be slinking around the back.'

Luckily, before another argument spoiled our parting, Jay appeared sweetly sparkling in the full beam of the Anglia's headlights.

'Hullo, Auntie. It's all right. Amma is expecting him. She's just getting ready.' Auntie? Amma? He definitely knew the language of charm.

It took the heat out of her face. 'You boys enjoy your trip then.' She backed out into the neighbour's gateway to turn the car around. 'Don't be any trouble, Kairo,' she called out as she stepped on the gas and demolished a knot of wayside kiss-me-quicks.

'She thinks you are a troublemaker?' Jay grinned, amused.

'Her mind is on other things. She's got a meeting to go to.'

'I wish she'd take mine also.'

'Your mind?'

'My mother you fool.'

I didn't divulge that it was a dance class. Or say that for me his mother was the top of the tops.

Inside, the centre of the sitting room was filled with camping gear: fishing tackle, pressure-lamps, a picnic hamper, bed rolls, a crate of cans, water bottles, hats.

'Everything but a tent.' Perhaps he had a wigwam on the estate, peace pipes, the stuff of a million daydreams.

'We have a bungalow, but we still have to take a lot of gear with us.'

At the back of the house, a separate building housed a pantry and Aladdin's store room; shelves and cupboards on every wall packed with tins and cans and boxes: prunes and peaches, spam and corned beef, crushed pineapple and halved apricots, cooked ham and lambs' tongues, five types of imported jam including raspberry.

'Early morning, you fill that polystyrene box halfway with ice from the freezer chest and bring to the front. Okay?'

'How come you have all this stuff here?'

'My father was in charge of supplies during World War II. You know, after Singapore we might have been the next to fall to the Japanese.'

'But that was over aeons ago.'

'Yeah, but you never know when another war might break out.' His grave tone suggested there might be a greater shadow over his life than mine because he was that much older.

Up in his room, Jay had already organised a spare mattress. I put my bag down next to it. Beyond the sarcophagi-like fish tanks out on the balcony, the night grew blacker as though the crows had gathered in force – in their hundreds and thousands – blotting out the stars and preparing to swoop down into the room and exact their revenge. They had Jay marked – and me, the accomplice. Even with a cupboard full of guns, we (and the innocent budgies, and Sunbeam) wouldn't stand a chance. It would be bloodier than the Alamo.

Jay patted the mattress. 'Should be more comfortable than the camp bed you had last time.'

From the floor, at the pillow end, I picked up an elasticated cloth band.

'What's this for?'

Jay grabbed it. 'It's a hair thing.'

'You can't put that in your hair.'

'Don't be daft. It's a girl's hair thing.'

I wanted to ask: how do you find out about girls' things, but I did not want to reveal the extent of my ignorance. Then I noticed a book by Jay's bed which surprised me even more than the hairband. A book encased in white leather with a brass zip running around the edges, except for the spine.

'You reading in bed?'

'Just looking up the story of a prophet. How he uses magic powers—'

'To protect the birds?'

'They'll be all right. I've reinforced the roof with more mesh and told Iris to keep an eye on it. She knows her life will not be worth living if anything happens to them.'

Another lesson on dispensability. I unzipped the Bible; it opened to the Book of Proverbs. '"The eye that mocketh at his father, and despiseth to obey his mother, the ravens of the valley shall pick it out."' The lines were not reassuring. 'Those crows, are they the same as ravens?'

'Same family.'

'You think they'll come back?'

'Those buggers?' Jay rattled a box of lead pellets. 'No way. Crows understand what a day of reckoning really is – for now.'

I woke at first light, hearing the metal gates shudder open and Elvin's jeep chug in.

Jay, already downstairs, had begun loading up by the time I brought the ice box to the front. Twenty minutes later everything had been tucked and strapped into place. Elvin reversed the jeep out onto the road and I squeezed in between boxes in the back. Jay shut the gates and took the seat next to Elvin. No one else in the house had stirred.

Within minutes we reached Borella and charged out over the bridge and onto the trunk road heading north. The wayside shops and kiosks, still lidded and boarded, barely blinked. As pale, milky light leaked onto the road, people began to appear shuffling out of the gauzy mist, wavering on bicycles, nudging wooden carts filled with coconuts or oil cans; some dressed in just a shirt and sarong, others wrapped in shawls as if they had migrated from the land of the dead; a few women, carrying baskets or pots, walked unevenly on the crumbling edge of the tarmac. Uncertain children followed seeking a steady hand. Elvin gunned the engine at each bend in the road and raced the jeep, scattering the last husks of dawn. His long, thin-boned frame shifted and his loose sleeves flapped in the wind; deftly changing gears, he skirted bakery carts, donkey traps, cattle-drawn *thirikkal* carts. The roadside tea *kadés* gave way to rice fields and coconut groves. Every so often we passed a team of buffalo ploughing a paddy terrace; squares of newly tilled mud in which a black-stockinged egret flapped its white wings, or a heron bent its pewter head in prayer. I spotted a gibbon scampering for the trees but before I could point it out Jay shouted, 'Hang on. Bumper-nickel.'

His warning came too late; the jeep hit a rut and bounced us a foot up in the air. Jay hooted, grabbing the dashboard rail.

Where the road divided, one sign pointed straight to Gampaha, another to Veyangoda hung loose on its post. The sun began to blaze. Elvin took the right fork and hammered down the empty road.

Jay handed out Iris's sandwiches and Elvin got him to steer while he opened his packet and examined the fillings at nearly fifty miles per hour.

'Are they all egg? What about that damn corned beef your father hoards in his war room?'

'Iris wouldn't dare touch those tins.'

'He really needs to move with the times, you know.' The wind whipped a scrap of greaseproof paper out of his hands.

My father was wrong to be so critical of Elvin; he was not a throwback. On the contrary, if anyone embodied the modern world of speed and the carefree, Elvin did.

Jay twisted around to hand me another sandwich. For a moment no one held the wheel. 'Soon you'll see the river and Lady Cynthia's *del kalava* elephants bathing by the rocks.'

He made it sound so normal but nothing that day was normal. Not him, not gleeful Elvin, not the speeding jeep, not the countryside, not the peacocks on the road, not any lady's elephants at bath time. By my watch, my father would be knotting his tie, listening to the news on medium wave; Ma would be urging him to hurry up. They would leave the house together and he would drop her at the broadcasting house before going to his office. All their oddities that irritated me at home became sadly normal in recollection – almost precious.

When the river slid into view – a glimmer of brown foam between the trees – things shifted into slow motion. An optical illusion that Jay or Elvin could decode in two ticks, no doubt, but neither of them spoke.

At the iron bridge, Elvin brought the jeep down to a crawl. Two elephants lay in the shallow water below, flapping their ears as mahouts brushed and scrubbed their backs. The bigger one raised his trunk and sprayed the other, seeding the river with what I imagined were its memories of slow migrations and ancient waterways. Clouds turned.

On the other side of the river, we drew up by one of the wooden kiosks lined with glass cases of brightly coloured sweets and roasted gram. Elvin honked the horn in a double burst and an anxious bearded man dashed out, almost tripping on his sarong.

'Sir, already here? Road repaired now?'

'Is there a message for me from Mr Tinki?'

He broke into a sweat. 'Have, sir, have. Will be coming, sir. Twelve thirty p.m. tomorrow. Said coming, for sure.' The last two words he repeated for emphasis.

A woman with a basket cocked on her hip crossed the road and stopped in front of the jeep fingering the lace on her blouse; her hair was pinned back with elaborate combs. Face bunched in small bundles, she studied the number plate for a full minute before shuffling away.

'What was she looking at?' Elvin asked the man.

'Just Alice, sir.' He tapped his head knowingly. '*Mallé pol*.'

'Right, we'll go then. I'll need some more ice tomorrow.'

'No problem. Ice, have lots. On the cycle, *kolla* will bring.'

Elvin put his foot down and the jeep shot forwards.

☼

The fields of gold swayed. Slow ripples of morning sun skimmed the grain, ripening the rice in waves. A man flailed in the fields, sowing what my father would inflate as small arrears of deferred hope. After a few miles, the paddy strips thinned out. Thick patches of heavy jungle crept up between squares of ranked rubber trees, regimental stripes of white gum flashed. Along the roadside, a narrow stream trickled from one cramped terrace of paddy to the next. Then, at the newly whitewashed stone markers of a culvert, Elvin brought the jeep to a halt.

Jay leapt out. 'Open sez me.'

Four separate stout bamboo poles, each as thick as a soda bottle, slotted into two posts to form the gate. He pushed the top one through and I did the same with the next, and so on.

'See you boys up at Villa Agathon.' Elvin honked the horn and drove in.

A long yodelling hoot rolled down the hill, quickly followed by a closer echo.

Jay replied with his own wild whoop.

The calls bounced back and forth.

'That's Gerry,' Jay grinned, slotting back the poles.

I helped him, marvelling at the balance the big poles seemed to contain in their length and the ease with which he adapted to plantation life. 'I thought it must be an owl,' I said, not sure if it foretold good luck or bad to hear one in daytime.

'No, that's his war cry, if we are playing Cowboys and Indians. I call him Gerry, for short. Otherwise he can be Cheetah and me Tarzan.'

Even then I felt that was not right, but could not work out what exactly was wrong. So, I said nothing. Jay was the Lone Ranger, I was Tonto. Jay was Batman, I was Robin. In the glorious new universe I'd stepped into, who could tell what was right and what was wrong and why it should be so in one place and not in another? All I knew for sure was that the world had instantly expanded to something much bigger than our small house in Grebe Road, my school, or the tropical seaside town I'd been born in.

A bare-bodied figure leapt over a heap of fallen coconut fronds and ran up, beaming, rising on his toes to sniff the air. He greeted Jay laughing like a child half his age, high and skittish and tumbling with a kind of inane delight. A skinny boy with large expectant eyes. '*Malu paninava.*' He lifted his hand in a small arc and beamed. Fish are jumping.

Jay pointed at the stream running by the road. 'That's where we catch guppies, but those jumpers he's talkin' about are in our lake. They are ginormous.'

On the way to the house to pick up the tackle, I carefully avoided the touch-me-nots and sleep-easies and the small scorpion holes on the sand path. Gerry darted ahead, picking mangosteens and tossing them excitedly in the air, juggling one, two or three at a time. The road curved around a pyramid of harvested coconuts before reaching the top of the hill. He sprinted shouting, 'Shortcut!' in English and diving through a patch of lime trees.

The only other person to be seen was a man, naked except for a loincloth, prodding a water buffalo down into a patch of mud.

'That's Buffalo Bill,' Jay grinned. 'Keep out of his way. He'll come up later for his bounty.'

I had pictured a tall villa with spacious verandas, ornate lattice-work and round red tiles; liveried servants with silver trays and gilded ornaments. Instead we came to a thatched bungalow with wooden shutters at either end and waist-high whitewashed mud half-walls in the centre. A hushed garden overshadowed by elderly trees stooping to catch the remains of forgotten kernels.

Elvin, settled into a planter's chair in the garden, his bare feet up on the extended wings that served as leg rests, greeted us.

'Have a thambili, boys. Straight off the tree.' He raised his glass at a spidery man standing a few feet away from him. 'Sulaiman, two more for Jay and his young friend.'

The man, slightly hunched with his hands behind his back, stepped out of the patchwork of a free-flowing bougainvillea. 'New friend?'

A small square cloth knotted at each corner covered the top of his head as snugly as a cap, but his shirt flapped long and loose over his sarong.

'First timer,' Jay told him. 'Kairo has never been on an estate before.'

'Ah, welcome to our *pol-watte*, Master Kairo.' A surprisingly bluish-grey eye blinked, slotting the parts of the head together again. 'You like thambili in a glass, or coming natural in the coconut like Jay-baba?'

'Same, please.'

'*Kolla*,' Sulaiman raised his voice calling Gerry. 'Two thambili, double quick.'

'How is your boy getting on?' Elvin asked as Gerry scampered away.

Sulaiman brought out one of his hands and opened his palm. 'Enough school. He learnt nothing. So now, only trying to teach him the business, one thing at a time. To count the nuts at the pick, check the trees after harvest, but he has no head for numbers.'

'I like that voice of his. The way he does that *hoo* as soon as we turn in.' Elvin pulled out a cigarette and lit it. He didn't offer one to Sulaiman.

'To hoot and sing is all he likes to do.'

'The yodelling bulbul,' Elvin whistled a tune. 'Puccini,' he winked at me.

Gerry came back carrying an orange king coconut in each hand. He offered one to Jay and the other, shyly, to me. I followed Jay's example, lifting it high with both hands and glugging from the hole punctured at the top. Afterwards,

I put the coconut down on the ground and used the back of my hand to wipe my mouth the way Jay did.

'Fishing, now?' Gerry asked, miming the words.

'Soon,' Jay replied, while Elvin dropped into a deeper conversation with Sulaiman.

'He's scary,' I whispered to Jay as we wandered down to the jeep.

'Sulaiman? Harmless, really. He's the superintendent.'

'I don't like police.'

Jay didn't laugh. He explained that the superintendent was the man who managed the estate for Elvin.

'You mean because your uncle is usually *absent*?' The word was my father's and smacked of his disapproval.

'Uncle Elvin comes every month. Sulaiman has his own house in the plot opposite and keeps the place in order day to day. He supervises the labour, like that fellow we saw with the buffalo, and Ivan the Terrible.'

'Who's he?'

'The watcher. Night security.'

To Jay the arrangement was perfectly natural. I could see how easily he could slip into his uncle's place one day: inherit this estate and loom over the shorter lives of less favoured people. The word 'plight' that my father had also used wriggled uneasily in my mouth.

'Is Gerry his son?'

'Yup. But Gerry is really an Apache. He has a cool toma-hawk. Let's go see if he's found the fishing tackle.'

At the back of the bungalow, Gerry had assembled the rods and set them out. Jay checked the equipment and okayed it.

On our way he told Elvin, 'We're off to the *wewa*. See you later, Uncle.'

'Good. Will you catch lunch for us then?'

'No Sulaiman special?'

'Tomorrow. We have guests coming tomorrow. Feasting will be then. Today we live the simple country life. Red rice and parippu. Fish, if you are lucky.'

Gerry lugged the fishing kit and a small axe in a sling; Jay and I carried army-issue canteens.

'What d'you reckon?' Jay asked when we reached the *wewa* – a large pond at the bottom of the hill. 'You like it here? That's huckleberry around the edge. Uncle Elvin brought back the seeds from America.'

'Cool. You have your own lake to fish in.'

'Might see a croc even.'

'What if we catch one? Like if it eats a fish that got hooked on my line?' From Tarzan's escapades, I knew that crocodiles have powerful jaws for closing, but weak muscles for opening their mouths. Like a boy Gordon Scott, would I have to hold the snout shut, while Gerry chopped off its vicious tail?

'That'd be funny.' Jay turned to Gerry, asking in Sinhala what he would do.

Gerry let out a hoot.

'Bigger danger is that water buffalo, no?'

At the water's edge, a white line of froth bubbled but the rest of the surface lay unbroken until the blue flash of a kingfisher skimmed over it. Jay shushed us.

'Crocs are amazingly good at camouflage,' he whispered, creeping up to a large spindly tree that had crashed down into the water and whitened like bone. 'If they are swimming, you'll see only the eyes. A pair of floating frogs.'

I kept close to him. 'We should have brought binocs.'

'Yeah. Next time.'

'Are we gonna put a line in now?'

'Sure we are. Jus' need to keep a lookout. The thing is to weight the line properly and put the cork float so the hook is suspended exactly at the right height for fish, not crocs.'

We searched the water for the arrowhead of a submerged jawbone while Gerry opened a small jar full of yellow jakfruit segments and baited the lines. Done, he crawled over and handed over the rods barely able to hide his pride.

Jay flung his line out. I did the same and watched for the float to bob back up.

After a while, I asked, 'Can't we cast the lines farther out towards the middle? Fish will be cruising in the coolest water, no?'

Jay half closed his eyes, head lowered, then abruptly handed over his rod. 'Hold this. I've got an idea.' He hopped over to the bags that Gerry had hidden by the trees and returned with a coil of rope and his bowie knife. He asked Gerry to find some banana tree trunks.

Gerry's face lit up.

Jay showed me how to wedge the fishing rods securely while Gerry ran off with his axe.

He returned with a banana log under each arm. Jay lined them up and started to tie them together; Gerry dashed off to get more logs. Jay wanted six in a row. He asked me to hold them in position while he fixed a couple of hard-wood branches cross-wise. Gerry fetched several ribbons of tree bark which he used as extra rope. Jay and Gerry had clearly built rafts before and worked like pros, pushing and pulling and securing the platform.

We all stripped off, because Jay said the banana sap mixed with water would ruin our clothes, before pushing the raft out and climbing aboard.

Gerry used a stick to punt the raft out; his thin chest swelled as he pushed, kneeling first then standing nude, not bothering to shield himself. I finally figured out what was meant by the word circumcised.

At the centre of the lake, the air was still. As we drifted dreamily between the occasional puckering in the water, I could make out at least half a dozen birdcalls ricocheting around the periphery, disconnected from the motionless trees, each a song in itself but also part of a larger concord. The three of us, naked on the raft, a similar mix of the isolated and the united. A cormorant skimmed across the water, followed by the kingfisher again, revelling in speed.

'Anything happening your side?' Jay asked.

'Nothing.'

'You had your eyes closed.'

'Only half, like you. I was listening.'

'You can't hear them bite. Keep your eyes peeled.'

'Can do it ultra-sonic-ally.'

The cork floats were still bobbing. No crocs. I was beginning to doubt their existence, even the existence of fish; of anything except a stirring of uncertainties and ever larger circles of uncontrollable pretence.

Gerry poked the water with his stick.

'You really saw them jumping yesterday?' Jay asked him in Sinhala.

'Jumping like mad, evening time. What else to do?'

'Maybe we should leave the lines in the water and come back after lunch,' I suggested.

'That's not sporting. The thing is, if you are here, eye on the line, then it's like your mind is in the water. It all becomes one thing. You are the line and the fish. If you catch it, you catch yourself.'

Gerry, watching the English language unreel from Jay's mouth, smiled to himself and scooped up some water to splash his front and drip wantonly down.

'What about him?' I wondered whether the three of us were indivisible too, like the fish and the fisher.

'It is no good just getting Gerry to watch it.' Jay stretched back and rested on his elbows; he pulled up one leg, raising his knee to make a triangle; his furled penis thickened and rolled sleepily across his other thigh.

'No. That's not what I meant.' I wanted to ask about the girl who had lodged herself on Jay's bike, between his legs. Would Jay bring her here, too, to float without a stitch of clothing? Could she do that? Then the moment Jay helped me up the ladder onto the roof to see the stars came flooding back.

Outside the bungalow, the garden had been turned into an open-air office: Elvin, primly balanced on the edge of a stern chair, faced down a massive ledger spread across a narrow table, his pen poised, a dart between his thumb and fingers. Sulaiman close by, hands behind his back again, droned out a list from memory weaving a web of monotony beneath the canopy of lilting bird whistles.

'They don't look happy,' I said to Jay as we made our way up the cart track towards them.

'Estate accounts.' He grimaced.

Sulaiman saw us and paused.

Elvin looked up in relief. 'Good catch?'

'Nothing yet,' Jay replied.

'What? All that tackle for nothing?'

'Fish aren't hungry at this time of the day.'

'You fellows are, I bet. Have to wait though. Must finish this damn ledger before we can have lunch.' He motioned to Sulaiman, urging him to continue.

We deposited our stuff and then Jay took me on a tour: first, to the kitchen with its open stone fire, then the newly built outhouse, the copra pits full of blackened husks giving off an evil smell and finally the cart shed. Behind it a sea of hundreds of fresh green coconuts stretched out: the 'pick' that had yet to be counted and recorded.

A hoopoe rolled its soft echoing hoots between the high branches; wagtails and shamas chirped, chivvying each other.

'I love this estate.' Jay closed his eyes and let the sounds envelop him. 'I love coming here.'

But what is it like for Gerry? I wanted to ask. Never able to leave; only ever seeing Jay come and go.

'How come you didn't bring the dog?'

'Garibaldi? He goes wild here. Fights too much with the estate dogs.'

By the time the ledger was done and lunch announced, the heat had curled the outer leaves of the pepper vines; the cardamom and turmeric had begun to nod.

Gerry brought a bottle of beer for Elvin and a jug of water for us. Sulaiman supervised the pouring, then stood guard at the far end of the table fanning himself with a brown file while we took our seats.

Lack of success in the fishing expedition did nothing to dampen Jay's spirits. 'You should put some game stock in that *wewa*, Uncle. The fish there are so sleepy.'

'Fish farming? Me? I should do fish farming?'

'Not farming. Sporting fish, like the trout upcountry.'

'The British put them in, no?' Elvin said.

Sulaiman laughed politely and muttered something about the demise of empire.

I remembered my father going on about fishing and farming being fundamentally in competition with each other and that it had to do with the caste system, a burden from the past; he had not brought the British into it.

'You'd like fishing, Uncle. We could have a fish-in.'

Elvin sipped his beer, gently rocking to settle the bubbles. 'You mean like that Marlon Brando business: salmon fishing and treaty rights in America? No thank you. We have quite enough demonstrations as it is in this country.'

'I meant an anglers club.'

'Tell you what – you get your father to sign up to my business proposition, and I'll make an angler's paradise for you and your young friend here.'

'Sure, why not? What's the deal?'

Elvin leant forwards and cupped a hand to the side of his mouth for a stage whisper. 'A shed full of chickens down the side of Casa Lihiniya.'

'Chickens? My father? That's crazy, Uncle.'

'Why?' He erupted in a coarse, deep guffaw, letting out a smattering of beer bubbles. 'Why crazy?'

'He can't stand even budgies. He won't use a pillow 'cos he hates feathers.'

'It's a pukka proposition. Broilers are going to be the thing.' Elvin amalgamated the romance of a gold rush with the blossoming of poultry farming in Australia featured in the *Sunday Observer*. 'This is his chance to come in at the beginning. Can you help me make him see that? Imagine a hundred chickens in your back garden. Money for jam.'

'Chickens outside his bedroom window will drive him nuts. You want to drive him nuts, Uncle?'

'I'm offering him an entrée. We are family, no?' He pushed a large oval dish of pebbly red rice towards me. 'Come, come, help yourself, son. You must be starving. Must not let your friend's lack of commercial perspicacity lead us into malnutrition.'

'Isn't this the place for chickens, anyway?' Jay asked. 'Not in the middle of Colombo?'

'Now you are on the job, son. At last, putting that brain into gear instead of reacting ideologically, which seems très à la mode. Let us pursue this through a proper logical dialogue. You see, it is not only about chickens.'

'Broilers, is it?'

I couldn't help asking, 'What's a broiler?'

'Good,' Elvin hummed approvingly. 'Good, you are learning to ask questions as well. At last, we have hope – a younger generation that might have some intellectual curiosity. Socrates would be pleased. Our Villa Agathon here might yet live up to its name.'

'Kairo is a great one for asking questions, Uncle,' Jay said proudly before replying to me. 'Broiler means especially reared for cooking. For eating.'

'Aren't they all?' Raising myself, I looked over the half-wall. The doomed future of the two chickens pecking their way around the guava tree seemed obvious.

'No. Those hens, for example, we keep for eggs,' Elvin said. 'Their lives are charmed by fecundity.'

Jay repeated the word, 'Fecundity,' and laughed.

'Trouble is these country chickens are not a good business proposition.' Uncle Elvin considered the bowl of glistening okra. 'You are right, Jay, the broiler is the thing. Fattened and near to the oven. And where are the new ovens?' He drew a question mark in the air. 'In Colombo, of course. Fancy gadgets quickly ordered before our famous socialist government imposed those import restrictions. Now the problem is that our eager Colombo ladies need something decent to roast in their American ovens.'

'But everyone eats chicken already.' Jay spooned some yellow mush onto my plate. Gerry watched from the back steps, a puckish twitch around the edge of his lips.

'Not tender, succulent, oven-ready cock-a-doodle-dos. These scrawny peckers are only good for a slow-cooked curry.'

'Chicken curry here is always fabuloso. We'll have it tomorrow, no?'

'Thank you, Jay-baba, thank you.' Sulaiman bowed. 'You'll like this grill-fish also.' He had wisely not relied on our fishing prowess.

Elvin used the blade of his knife to lift the flesh off the fishbone in one clean slice. I had never seen anyone do such a delicate operation with such ease. 'Sulaiman has special ingredients for his pot here that your regular Colombo housewife cannot get hold of, isn't that so, Sulaiman?'

The superintendent shuffled back bashfully, eyes locked to his feet.

'Anyway, point is: we'll have the chicken right there, five minutes from the kitchen. With our plan, Mrs Fernando, or Mrs Kanagarajah, or even blooming Mabel Rastiadu can decide on Sunday morning to make Maryland chicken for lunch if her heart desires, and bloody well do it with the freshest of the fresh!' He tapped the plate with the knife in his hand.

'Real American fried chicken?' I asked.

'Roast or Russian. She can do chicken Kiev for Madam Butterbean, I don't mind, as long as she pays the right price. We'll even have a VIP capon for those who'll cough up some of that convertible currency they all hide under the mattress. Foreign exchange: dollars, sterling, francs, lire – anything and everything – except maybe not the rouble.'

I could see it, even if Jay could not. An expanded version of our aviary and a flock of white chickens slowly turning into black-market dollars.

'And why, Uncle, would Pater be interested in making money out of chickens when he does very nicely out of cardboard and paper? Why are you, Uncle, when you have all this? Land and crops that you understand and love. Isn't coconut enough?'

Elvin exchanged glances with Sulaiman.

'Fair point, Jay. But you see one cannot afford to be complacent. You must not put all your eggs in one basket. And your mother and I were thinking, your father needs the diversion.'

'Is she involved? Since when has she had a clue—'

'No, not involved like that. But don't scoff, she's a helluva smart lady. A heart of gold too.' Elvin paused to rearrange his argument. Jay waited nonplussed for the explanation, but Elvin returned to national politics instead, dismissing the domestic. Or pretending to. 'The point is – there are some highly undesirable plans afoot in the intemperate dash for socialism we see in this country. We must have a strategy to deal with them, son.'

※

At the chicken coop Jay poked the wire, testing it. 'It's not good. I don't like it.'

'He did say he'd stock your fish, if you helped him.'

'Yeah, but I can't be talking to my father.' Jay cocked his head and listened as a fast, frantic hammering echoed from farther down the hill, piercing the weave of lighter warbles. 'A woodpecker.' He pulled a catapult out of his pocket. 'Let's go find it.'

'To kill it?'

He squeezed his eyelids like a crack shot. 'No, why do you say that?' His long fingers twanged the catapult. 'This is to get it to fly. Gotta see it fly, man: the *undulation* is the thing.'

We followed a line of plain grey trees, searching the mopheads until we heard the hammering again. I spotted it first – a green bird with a small red tuft on its pointy head attacking a tall cotton tree.

Jay sank to his haunches. He picked up a small coconut seed the size of a bird's egg and settled it in the pouch of the catapult. Then, raising his arm, he took aim, drew back and let go; the missile flew and hit the trunk below the bird with a penetrating crack. The bird jumped and seemed to hang for a moment in the air.

'Watch,' Jay said.

The bird flew, a swift green line wafted on an invisible wave, dipping and rising, dodging more enemy fire, arcs of green and yellow, arias of friend and foe.

'It's like it really bounces. You want one in the aviary?'

Jay's head tilted, taking in shafts of light and timber. 'No, actually. He needs miles of space to fly like that. Anyway, I want species you wouldn't otherwise see.'

'What about Sunbeam?'

'I know.' He blew out his breath noisily. 'That's a problem. I didn't think at the time. Jus' wanted him. You live and learn.'

'So, let him go now.'

'Can't. I'd miss him. And now he's used to the cage. Domesticated.'

'Is that what it means? My father goes on about "pernicious domestication".'

As we talked, we found ourselves drifting towards the main gate.

'Uncle Elvin plans to go into the broiler business like some American tycoon, but look at this – doesn't even bother to fix a proper gate here.'

'I didn't realise he's a businessman too.'

'He should stick to what he understands: coconut, rice, fruit crops. Trouble is people get funny ideas. Like my dumb parents. What is it with them?'

We climbed over the bamboo poles onto the culvert.

Jay turned back towards the house, cupped his mouth with both hands and did his whoop.

The stream flowed heedlessly as tiny fish flickered against the current to keep their place.

'Boat race?' Jay asked.

We marked twigs with knotted grass and threw them into the stream on one side of the culvert, scattering the fish, and bet madly on which would get through to the other side first; again and again, shifting starting points and finishing lines each time. After a while, Jay did his whoop again.

This time, Gerry called back. Jay beamed: 'Watch out.'

A few minutes later, Gerry appeared carrying a shark-head wicker basket under his arm.

'What's that for?'

'Don't you recognise the *kuduwa*?' Jay laughed. 'It's our fish-trap.'

'Like that birdcage for the crow?' Easy to enter, impossible to exit.

'If we go farther up, there's a stretch where the stream goes wide,' Jay said. 'The little fellows all collect there.' At the point where the paddy fields started, the stream took a sharp turn. 'You see how it's channelled? To irrigate the rice fields, they use these really old-fashioned sluices. I reckon there must be a more efficient system.'

'Like what?'

'I'm working on it.'

We walked single file along the wrinkled mud ridge squaring the paddy. Towards the middle, out of sight of the road, the light purply haze crackled with popping grain and the heated, translucent wings of drowsy dragonflies and gall midges. I believed I was in a stream too, separated from Jay and Gerry by panes of solidified air with someone looming over us lowering a giant invisible cage – a *kuduwa* – to fish us out and preserve our peculiar childhoods forever.

At the katchati patch, Gerry knew exactly what to do. Without a word, he took the jar out of the trap and scooped some water into it and placed it on the ground. Then he hitched up his sarong above his knees and stepped quietly into the stream, scarcely disturbing the lazy duckweed. The water came halfway up his shins. He bent down and laid the trap with the large ekel-toothed mouth facing the flow of the water, wedged in where the stream narrowed in a low gurgle and then stood over it on guard. A kingfisher darted behind him, flashing its sharp blue wings.

Jay slipped in upstream and started wading towards the trap. He gestured for me to join him where the stream was wide enough to walk two abreast. I rolled up the hems of my shorts, unnecessarily, and slipped in, toes curled. Then made my way slowly, stirring the water with my feet as if they were wooden paddles.

As the stream narrowed and we neared the trap, Gerry lifted it out with a great whoosh. Sure enough, there were half a dozen or more small guppies and fantails flapping inside. He opened the back and gently shook them out into the jar. Then we did the whole operation again.

After the third time, Jay announced, 'Mission accomplished.' The jar was teeming.

☀

Later in the afternoon, while Gerry fixed up the bedrooms for the night, the two of us strolled back to the *wewa*. The sun hung lower in the sky, the water darkened promisingly. A light wind plucked at the treetops, rippling the palm fronds.

'Listen,' Jay cocked his head to one side. 'For me, that is real music. From our native harps: a thousand coconut lyres hanging in those branches. Uncle Elvin should bring my mother here: then she'd understand what I mean by the songs of the wind. It's so much better than any instrument. It's like the sound of our globe itself turning.'

I was not sure I liked the word 'native' but I had to admit the sound in the trees flowed easily in a kind of natural music with a chorus of birdsong threading a hundred different melodies between the rustle and thrum of the leaves.

We cast our lines in several spots but had no luck anywhere.

Eventually, Jay reeled his line back and took the bait off the hook. He chucked the fruit in the water. 'That's fishing. Sometimes you get lucky, but most of the time you just wait.' Not wanting to wait any more, we packed up and headed back.

Near the bungalow, at the well, we found Elvin astride a tiny kitchen stool in his swimming trunks. He had his hands on his bare knees, shoulders hunched, braced for a calamity.

'Hello,' he bellowed.

A wiry woman in a damp cloth and blouse was hauling up a bucket at breakneck speed behind him. She hid a red-stained smirk when she saw us. A moment later Elvin yelped, spluttering under a deluge of water. The woman stepped down from her wooden platform and dropped the empty bucket back down the well. The smack of the metal and the splash took long seconds to emerge; she hauled it up again for the second pouring.

'Ah,' Elvin cried out, this time ready to enjoy it.

As she went for the third bucket, he asked Jay if we had been out swimming.

'Wading, Uncle, in the stream.'

'Have a well bath then. Pukka thing to revitalise the brain.'

He got hold of a bar of red soap and started lathering himself, singing Belafonte. The woman soaped his back and beat it with the edges of her lean hands in karate chops; then, when his shoulders eased, poured several more buckets of water on him.

Surprised at the strength hidden in her small frame, I asked Jay, 'Who is she?'

'Never mind. Wanna try a well bath? I'll do you first, and then you can pull the bucket for me.'

Elvin dried himself. The woman coiled the rope around a peg and melted away through a curtain of flowering ginger and long-leafed turmeric.

We undressed down to our jocks, in case she came back, and Jay got me on the stool first.

'You like it?' Elvin asked.

I managed to splutter, 'Fantastic,' before another icy-cold bucketful knocked the breath out of me.

'Have one of these every day and you can live to be a hundred.'

'Is that what you want, Uncle?' Jay let the rope of the bucket run through his fingers. 'To live to be a hundred?'

'Good God, no. Otherwise I'd have to be here every damn day, wouldn't I? Longevity is thoroughly overrated. Give me a good cigar instead any day.'

After dinner, we lingered out in the garden with only an oil lamp and a string of candles for light. Sulaiman joined but he still did not take a chair, leaning back against a wall instead, lifting one leg and bending it behind him so that his foot was flat to the wall and ready to propel him forward if the need arose. His extended fingertips drummed slowly, measuring the flitter of night insects between his hands before he caught and crushed them.

Elvin, sprawled on his planter's chair, gurgled softly between long soporific breaths. Moonlight serrated by coconut fronds whitened his bare feet splayed out on the smooth wood of the leg rests. He took a sip from his whisky-soda and eased back his head in preparation for the kind of lecture men go in for after a glass or two of alcohol. But when Jay went to get his new power lamp, Elvin beckoned me over and spoke quietly and directly — not as if to an audience.

'Look, son, you must get our friend to be a bit more... you know?'

'More what?'

'More...' He waved his glass, sloshing some drink into the sand, searching for the word. 'More cooperative, you know. He is too much like his father.'

'Really?' Jay would not be pleased.

'Same damn foibles, father and son.'

'Foibles?'

'That's the thing.' The corner of Elvin's eye caught some sharp yellowish light. 'He may not like it, but sometimes he acts just the same. He won't take the wider view. You have to learn to take the wider view, otherwise you don't know where the hell you'll end up with your foibles.'

'Are you talking chickens again, Uncle?'

'No, no.' He took a long evasive sip. 'Definitely not. There is a heck of a lot more at stake than poultry, boy.'

'Kairo,' I reminded him.

'What? Oh, yes. Right. Good. You stick to the point. A sound mind and steadfast. You'd make a good lawyer, son.'

No one had ever praised my abilities so grandly before. It stuck. A legal eagle. A chink shifted and I saw a future of closely printed papers, words underlined, a hint of theatre. Would I be alone? I wanted to ask more questions, but then that look which I had anticipated earlier settled in his eyes and Elvin started to describe his boyhood, his thwarted ambitions, his recognition of the duty he owed to the land of his birth and the need for perpetual self-interrogation. He stared at his glass as though it were a crystal ball.

At that point, Jay came back with a large lantern. He trained the powerful beam at the tops of the coconut trees, the yawning silent lyres, and beyond.

'This can reach the stars,' he said. 'What d'you think, Uncle?'

'Good. Very good. Where did you get that utterly glorious searchlight?'

'Pater brought it from Bangkok. You should get one for Ivan. Superb for the night watch.'

'That's just it. That's why he must come into this business with me, son. He has connections, no? Reaching out to South East Asia, the Far East. He has that entrepreneurial spark, if only he would use it properly.'

Jay shone the torch on Elvin's glass. 'How much of that stuff have you had, Uncle Elvin?'

'The point, as I said, very much is the family, Jay. The chickens are secondary. That empty underused space, doing nothing, is – how shall I put it? – risky. If you don't use it, you might lose it. The government is obsessed with land use and land reform. They don't like big gardens – or large private estates. We must get him to take some action. Will you do it?'

'Uncle, if you can't, how can I?'

'You see, Jay, we are at a crucial moment. Colombo is…' he paused. 'Colombo is at a crucial stage of development. Land is at a premium. Only once in a hundred years do you have a moment like this to get it right; we must get it right for us. It is our obligation. Use what we have from the old world to get a proper foothold in the new.' Putting his glass down, he pressed his thumb against the centre of his forehead, summoning the forces of his formidable ancestry. The rattan chair creaked: softening, stretching. 'We need to close ranks. It would be good to have your father on side. Good for him – and you too. It's in the family interest. We need to move with the times. Then, one day, we might even go back into your great-grandfather's business of producing a first-class local liquor. Now there was a man who knew how to take advantage of an opportunity. Nothing wrong with that, you know.'

'My father is not interested in family or arrack. He has enough trouble with my mother. He threatened to dump her.'

'Never. Your mother?' He took a sip. 'I prefer Scotch too, but…'

Gerry slipped away and was swallowed by the dark edge beyond the circle of candles. As he disappeared, the crackle of cicadas swelled up, fracturing the night. I wanted to follow Gerry, slim and elusive, among the trees, out of hearing and leave behind the family problems of the overloaded.

Later, when we crawled into our separate beds, cocooned in mosquito nets – us two boys in one room, Elvin in the other – the intense darkness muffled my wants.

The night was still, thick and deep. Jay's thousand green-stringed lyres swaddled. Not even a whisper ruffled the trees even though the earth was spinning and every leaf breathing. The only sound came from the drone of a poison-pronged insect circling the cotton mesh and the sudden whine as it tried to drill through the net. None of it bothered Jay in the next bed; his breath was even and steady. I lay rigid, tense and too alert. I was convinced we were more than what we seemed; that we were boys whose bodies were dross that would one day be discarded, dry sloughs from which we'd escape and find ourselves more lasting shapes. I wanted it to be so. Unable to sleep, I pulled out the slim pamphlet I had stolen from my father's shelf and hidden at the edge of the mattress where the net was tucked in. We each had a small silver Eveready flashlight issued for emergencies. Huddled and shielded by a pillow, I clicked mine on and started to read the dense pages. Luckily, in the small white circle of the torch beam the tightly packed print loosened into words of mystifying appeal: *liquidation … monopoly … drunkards*. The thin, prematurely yellowed paper had the surprising smoothness of a comic instead of the raw, rough grain and rasp of a homespun schoolbook. The pamphlet had been printed and stitched two years earlier, a half-mile or so as a bat would fly from our house on Grebe Road, but the words and sentences could have come from my father's mouth any day of the week. The problems described in the pages were hard to grasp at times but the arguments proved comforting. If the night had not been so unsettling, I would not have read more than a few paragraphs before nodding off. Instead I got through almost all the pamphlet, from a rant against vodka to a hymn on the virtues of cinema, before falling asleep with the flashlight warm under my chin.

At dawn a diffused grey light softened the treetops; the threads of night spiders snapped. A groggy cock crowed. I woke to find Jay already in his khaki shorts, fitting fat orange cartridges into an ammunition belt.

'Ready to shoot?'

'A shotgun?'

'Time you learnt,' Jay said. 'Thing is, make sure the stock is tucked well into your shoulder, otherwise you'll dislocate it. Or it'll kick you in the face and break your jaw.'

'Maybe I'll just watch.' The pace was too dizzying.

'Joking. It's only a four-ten — the smallest bird-gun. Even a girl can handle it. Just a matter of technique. We hunt snipe today. *Gallinago*. Fast birds. Zigzag from right under your feet. You have to pull the gun up fast, bang.' He simulated the action. 'Aim ahead. Where he will be, not where he is.' He showed me how to load the gun and passed it over.

'What are these?' I asked fingering the dozens of notches on the wooden stock.

'Crows,' he said. 'On the other side are the snipe I've bagged.'

Ten minutes later, we were heading down to the paddy fields. A low morning mist, wispy, untroubled yet by the warming sun, masked the hillside in cotton rags.

'Stick to the same speed as me as we comb through the paddy, okay?' Jay lowered his voice. 'Safety, you understand? Keep the line. You'll hear the whirr when they take off. Always shoot straight ahead. Don't swing and get me by accident.' He smothered a laugh, but I didn't see anything funny in the possibility.

As we crossed the stream, sunlight brightened into a grainier yellow, burning off the night's remaining fluffs and the mirror dew on the lower ground. In the distance, the wrinkled green edge of the estate released its dawn minstrels: coppersmith barbets, thrushes, minivets.

Leaving our sandals by the main sluice, we stepped into the field of golden paddy guarded by a limp scarecrow, a hundred yards away, and a pair of vagrant bushlarks squeaking in the rushes. I knew, even then, young as I was, that this sense of contentment could not last. Maybe carrying a real shotgun in my hand for the first time, and knowing what it had done and could do, cast a pall. Or maybe my father's warnings, the polemics in his book, were beginning to unsettle me. Tranquillity could only be temporary.

'Make lots of noise,' Jay called out. 'We have to flush the blighters out.'

I carefully inserted a cartridge into the breech, as Jay had shown me, pressing it in from the brass edge of the base, wary of setting off the charge even though I knew the primer — a tiny pink button in the centre of the shiny base — needed a hammer blow. With my thumb I slipped the safety catch off and cocked the gun, determined to keep my hand steady. I didn't think to question why we were hunting these birds.

'Stay in line.' Jay started moving, the gun pointing down but firmly locked into his shoulder, finger hooked around the steel trigger.

I did the same and kept to a parallel path; the pressure of my finger against the metal tightened all my veins. My whole body hummed taut, ready to explode. I zeroed in on every sound in the field, from the squelch of the mud underfoot to the lisp of the grain. Would I see it or hear it first? The sudden whirr of wings that Jay had mimicked by blowing through his lips and fluttering them. Why would the zigzag birds – the *Gallinago gallinago* – come here? They could go anywhere in the world. Why would they come here and get shot? Of course, they didn't know they would be shot. And if they were in my patch, the chances were they would not be hit. But why doesn't instinct take them somewhere safer? Out of the reach of boys with guns. Would my father, a zigzagger himself, have an answer?

Then, a rush of wings. A second later – the bang of Jay's gun.

Next, I had my chance. Another whirr, a brown flash, then an explosion in my hands. I had no idea where the shot went, or whether I had even got the gun pointing up. It did kick my shoulder though, hard.

'Good shot,' Jay called out. I let out the breath I hadn't known I was holding in, relieved I had not swung round in my excitement and shot my friend by mistake.

'Did I get it?'

'No. But good try.'

We had another couple of chances each, and I felt I was beginning to understand the procedure, and how deep an instinct I had for this pursuit. An irreversible connection grew between the hunter and the hunted – a line from life to death.

'So, how?' he asked when we had climbed out of the rice.

'I'm getting the hang of it.'

'A shotgun is easy, yeah?'

'Yeah.' My shirt was stuck to my skin. My shoulder ached. I could have spent hours more in the paddy, unthinkingly sowing hard, round pellets of lead in the slowly blistering air, forgetting to question anything. I stroked the gun. 'But why are we doing this? You like birds, no?'

'I love them, that's why,' Jay said as though that clarified everything; that death was a gift to give, a kindness to creatures smaller than himself who had lost their way, or were frightened of winter.

Near the bungalow, we found Gerry clearing out the hen house.

'Find the eggs, did you?' Jay tossed him an avocado he had picked off a tree.

'All found, but lunch hiding in the bush. One with the green feather in the tail.'

'Man, you gotta flush him out. Go down that way, and we'll scare him from the other side.'

The cock sprang out and skittered across the sand, Gerry caught it by the foot and took it squawking up to the kitchen yard where Sulaiman patrolled the border with his hands hidden behind his back.

Gerry offered him the bird; Sulaiman grabbed it by the neck. His other hand swung out with a machete. He sliced the head off with one stroke and let the bundle of frantic feathers fall. The headless chicken spun around spurting blood and then ran around the yard blindly, bumping from bush to tree. Although we had been hunting and fishing for the table, it had all been in a fantasy. For all Jay's talk, we had brought nothing back. Now, something had been killed specifically for us. I'd seen creatures die before, like the crows that Jay had shot, but this was one that we were going to eat. I did not have the words, back then, but I knew that the world was being turned inside out. Soon, I feared, it would disappear and I would be left floating in emptiness.

Gerry picked up the carcass when it had stopped flopping and dropped it into a basin of water, releasing a cloud of scarlet plumes. A flock of jungle babblers sounded the alarm and took to the air.

'Wanna pluck it?' Jay asked, revelling, for the first time I felt, in my discomfort.

I moved away and glanced at Sulaiman. I asked him: 'Is that like a ritual? What you did?'

Sulaiman sheathed what could have been a smile as he wiped the blade of his machete. 'No, Master Kairo. That is just what we do here on the estate when we need to feed our visitors, as instructed by the boss in the house. Not a religion. You must not rush to judge, not knowing the man nor his faith.'

Back at the bungalow, breakfast was ready; I made do with roast bread and jam and a slice of papaw, having no stomach for eggs.

Afterwards, on the front steps, Jay showed me how to clean the guns and oil the barrels with a plumb line and sponge. In the hot sun, the smell of burnt cartridges and linseed oil seeped deeper into my fingers as I tried to focus on the mechanics, as yet unclear about what I liked and what I disliked.

'How's about a drive? We have a cool contraption all rigged up.'

'Sure.' That would be safer. Ever since I first picked up a motoring magazine at Mr Ismail's bookshop, I had wanted to drive. To go as fast as I wished, in control of everything. Fully grown up. Primed. Knowing for sure all those things I was so unsure of as a boy.

☼

The vehicle turned out to be a small two-wheel hand trac- tor no bigger than the motorised lawnmowers I'd seen in American movies, or a wheelbarrow with an engine. Gerry lugged it out of the shed and Jay poured a pint of kerosene into the gleaming red pot that was the fuel tank. He set the throttle at the third mark and pulled the choke out full, then wound the starting rope around the flywheel and yanked it. The metal wheel turned but the engine did not catch. He adjusted the throttle and choke combination and tried a couple more pulls without success.

'This works, no?' he asked Gerry.

'Not working now.'

'No one fix it?'

'Your uncle can fix it, father said. So to wait. We have the buffalo for paddy, cow for cart.'

Jay pulled off the caps and tops near the motor and blew into the crevices the way he blew into the nostrils of the estate dogs to get them excited. Then he tried turning the flywheel again. Not a spark.

He asked Gerry to get the toolbox and some newspaper and, when he brought them, immediately started stripping the engine carefully, adjusting the jaws of the spanner to each nut, unclipping wires, prising off the heat shield, dismantling the outer flange. Gerry and I followed the operation, fascinated, until Jay got stuck on four screws that had seized up.

I suggested oil.

Jay applied a drop of kerosene with his finger; it made no difference. He kept at it and after ten minutes managed to get a couple of the screws off; enough to reach the fuel pipe, but not to remove and clean it.

Gerry's solution was to twist a piece of newspaper into a long thin probe; it wasn't firm enough.

'We need a pipe cleaner,' Jay said. 'Kairo, go ask Uncle Elvin. He's bound to have one.'

Elvin was not in his chair in the garden, nor in the bungalow. I checked the cookhouse where the same silent woman as the previous day crouched on her haunches in front of a stone slab, systematically scraping the green ridges of a long drumstick of murunga. Watching the ritual, I began to see that this might be the drudgery that the Soviet pamphlet railed against, the household chores that it claimed enslaved women. The passages had not seemed relevant in the circle of my flashlight; at home Siripala did the cooking and a dhobi man came to do the laundry. Never my mother. We had no servant woman. But then, I remembered, even in our Grebe Road house the person who cleaned the bathroom was a woman. She came from outside and hardly ever spoke. Head always lowered, her wobbly front only loosely covered, she'd crouch and scrape the floor tiles, peeling back my confused thoughts with the rasp of her brush.

The cook raised her eyes. I asked if she knew where the others were — Elvin and Sulaiman. She moved her furrowed head slightly, implying she knew nothing beyond her stone slab and the chipped saucers of turmeric and chilli powder, karapincha and rampe, next to it. Then, yielding, she wagged her chin and suggested the pond.

At the water's edge, Elvin, listening to Sulaiman, raised his hand and made a gesture that could signify a million acres, or a galaxy, or surrender, or possibly one of those moments of hollow fabrication that plagued the grown-up world.

This was probably the wrong time to be asking for pipe cleaners but I ran up to give the mission more urgency than a faulty two-stroke motor.

'Uncle, Uncle Elvin.'

'What? What's happened? Ambush? Snipers?'

'We need a pipe cleaner. Jay said you might have one.'

'You boys started smoking already?'

'Jay is cleaning the engine.'

'The jeep?'

Sulaiman immediately knew the problem and jumped in: 'The Landmaster, sir. Not functioning. On the list to discuss, sir, down at the bottom, after we deal with the pineapple trenches.'

'What's the problem?'

'Wilt, sir. In this particular case, water level is not the problem. We must spray fenitrothion or carbophenothion every three months, if you are agreeable, to have any hope of a crop next season.'

'Not the pineapple. What's wrong with the hand tractor?'

'Oh-oh. Won't start, sir. You pull and pull but it doesn't make even a fart.'

Uncle Elvin didn't laugh, so I explained. 'Jay says we need a pipe cleaner.'

'I'm afraid I don't have one, son, although I agree they are extremely handy things to have around.'

Sulaiman clasped his fingers together in front of him. 'Maybe can get the new model, sir. One with crank-handle.'

'Let's go have a look.'

Jubilantly, I sprinted ahead to tell Jay that the cavalry was on its way.

'He'll know what to do. He's forever taking apart engines and putting them together again. You should see him work on that vintage Bentley of his. It's fan-tabulous,' Jay said.

I was amazed at how he had dismantled so much of the tractor motor without any qualms and spread the components out like jigsaw pieces on the newspaper. I wanted to learn how to do that too: proceed without fear, do whatever needed to be done without hesitation.

I monitored every move as Jay handled the engine parts – peering at the gaps, blowing dust off, easing the catches, checking bolts, braces, belts – completely absorbed by the task at hand, pride and elation pumping in tandem.

Elvin arrived, Sulaiman in tow, and nearly swooned: 'That's neatly laid out, son. Definitely a budding engineer, I'd say.'

'I've watched you, Uncle.' He moved the grey, dented manifold into line. 'One hand on the wheel, the other holding the spanner.' Jay pulled out one of the rubber hoses and squeezed the end.

'That's good. You need to be able to use both hands in today's world. The future definitely needs two hands to be grasped.'

Sulaiman's tempered laugh turned into a cough, which he smothered quickly with the cloth he whipped off the top of his head. He then quickly smoothed the material and fixed it back, tightening the knots on the corners of the improvised skullcap with both hands.

'Problem is the darn fuel pipe. Can't get the thing off to clean it.'

Elvin crouched down next to Jay and examined the bare bones of the motor; they had a bond that I feared I might never be able to match.

'Pipe cleaner is a good idea, son, but right now we need an alternative.'

'We tried a twist of paper, but no good.'

Elvin rested his face in a bracket made with his finger and thumb. 'We need something long, thin and flexible.'

The moment he described the need, I saw the solution. I pushed a dried coconut frond, one of Jay's fallen tree harps, forward with my foot. The spines of each leaf of the frond curved obligingly. 'An ekel?'

Elvin slapped his knee. 'That's it, sonny. You got it.'

Jay picked up a needle and tested it but it broke.

'You need one that's not so brittle. Try a greener one.'

I found him a fresh leaf and stripped most of the blade off, keeping a tiny piece at the end like the sponge rag on the plumb line we had used to clean the gun barrels earlier. I broke it into a manageable size and handed it to Jay.

'Brilliant,' Elvin said. 'That should do the trick.'

Jay inserted the flagged end into the pipe and wiggled it, biting his lip as he dug further in. At first nothing happened and I started to sharpen another ekel. Then Jay let out a triumphant whistle and a tiny stream of kerosene began to trickle out.

'Bravo.' Uncle Elvin clapped him on the back.

Jay jabbed the ekel in again and more crud streamed out. 'I still don't understand why it didn't even splutter when we cranked it. Even with no fuel it should still make the sound, no?'

'Has someone been messing with the innards?'

'What do you mean?'

'Had the engine been opened up?' Elvin turned to Sulaiman. 'You try to get it fixed at all?'

'No, sir. I told the boy to wait for you.'

Jay rubbed the tip of his nose. 'Come to think of it, the cover nuts were easy but the inside screws were sheared like someone had tried to force them.'

'Must be from before, sir. We had a lot of trouble at first but has been working fine the last two picks. Boy said suddenly it won't start.'

'Check the wiring, Jay, and then put it all back together.'

Twenty minutes later, it was ready for another go. Jay got Gerry to wind up the flywheel cord and pull. The engine burst into life. Gerry and I climbed into the trailer while Jay took the driving seat – a bicycle saddle fixed to the front of the box. He grasped the handlebars with both hands and revved it.

As we rattled down the hill, Elvin shouted after us to collect the ice from that *kadé* and save the poor fellow with the gunnies a journey.

At the main gate, Gerry leapt out and pulled back the poles expertly. Jay slowed down to take the turn but as soon as we were on the main road, he opened the throttle.

'Wait for Gerry,' I shouted, but Jay just laughed.

Gerry threw the poles back in place and sprinted after us. Within a hundred yards, he'd caught up and jumped on, out of breath but exhilarated by the challenge. I didn't approve of the way Jay messed with him but then all I knew was that there was a lot I didn't understand; the *Problems of Life* pamphlet, with its theories of consequences, even though written by a champion of the downtrodden, was of no help with someone like Jay.

We rode into the small one-horse town, crowing, converting the ceremonial white flags of a local funeral strung along the roofs of the shops into victory bunting. At the shop where Elvin had ordered the ice, Jay slowed down and Gerry hopped off and spoke to a small bearded man seated idly on a crate outside.

Jay chugged up to the telegraph pole and turned the vehicle round, veering right across the empty road before coming to a stop in front of the shop.

Gerry had disappeared inside with the man. They reappeared dragging a large, heavy, square jute sack, which they heaved into the trailer, immediately cooling the air around.

Wiping his face with the flap of his shirt, the shopkeeper spoke rapidly to Jay. 'Message came for our *mahaththaya*. Mr Tinki coming for lunch today, as planned, but the other gentleman, Mr Percy, has been called away and can't come. He will see sir on sir's way back to Colombo tomorrow, for sure. Mr Tinki will fix up everything when he comes. Telephone is ready and waiting, please tell.'

The shopkeeper was not a privileged 'bearded boyar', nor, despite the urgency in his voice, a 'revolutionist', as described in the pamphlet. Nor did he seem to my eyes to be landlord, worker or peasant. Could he be what my father called a representative of the petty bourgeoisie? A trivial man. Having delivered his message, he shifted his gaze to a marigold wreath propped up precariously by the roadside as though there might be an issue of self-interest to be resolved in that too.

As we eased off – Gerry running alongside to reduce the load – I asked Jay if I could have a go at driving. The powerful desire not to be just a passenger any more was irresistible.

'You know how?'

'Same as a bike, no?'

'Yeah, but it's all in the handlebars: throttle and brake. Wristwork, no footwork.'

Jay stopped in the middle of the empty road and let me take over. I caught Gerry watching us exchange places, an expression of longing on his face.

'You know what I really want?' I shouted as the engine chugged up to full power.

Jay reached over and adjusted the choke. 'Yeah?'

'To drive a car.'

Back at the bungalow, while Gerry dealt with the ice, we rushed to give Elvin the message from his lunch guests.

'Is that so?' Elvin's face sharpened. 'Damn nuisance. I was relying on Sulaiman here to go over the bloody details once we had the plans settled.'

Towards midday, a small, blue bug Fiat putt-putted up and sighed to a stop near the bungalow; Elvin placed a hand on the bubble top and peered in. The car rocked.

'So, Tinki, why alone?'

Mr Tinki stepped out, a furtive man, unable to see over the dome of the car. Although he had a discernible paunch, he seemed unlikely to make much impression on the pot of chicken simmering in the kitchen.

'You got the message, Mr Elvin, I hope. Very sorry but the fellow got buggered by the minister.'

'What?'

'All ready to come, but then minister got wind of our plans and asked for a full briefing.' He pulled at the awkward tie around his neck.

'So, he'll demand a cut as well.' Elvin slapped aside a fly. 'It's intolerable.'

'Not to worry, sir, we can do the needful with our Percy tomorrow. If you stop by Ambepussa, on your way back, we can easily sort out the lot over a lime juice or two, no?'

'I don't much care for this stop-start business. Once we set the route, we should stick to it. Who the hell drinks lime juice at a time like this?'

'Definitely.' Mr Tinki shut the door and made a clumsy gesture with his timid hand. 'No ambush, sir. Just short call at the rest house to dot the T's of the paper I have brought for your eminent perusal. I will arrange, for sure, a nice cool beer instead.'

'The I's.'

'Sir? Not to worry. No one to spy. Very safe.' He moistened his lips, swollen with so much talk.

Elvin fanned the air. 'Cross the bloody T's and dot the frigging I's. Excuse me – that was uncalled for, I know. Anyway, at Villa Agathon we must hold no grudges. All love and the brotherhood of man, no? Come, have a drink. Hot journey?'

'Oh, *harima* hot, sir. Today is so hot-hot.'

Jay had melted away. No sign of Gerry either. I was not brave enough to do the *hoo* signal to call either of them. The fishing stations were too far. So, I settled down to watch for them by the shed, from where I could see all the different paths that led to the house and was close enough to hear the shout when lunch was called. At home, I spent a lot of time on my own. I was not afraid of being alone; only afraid of taking a false step on the wrong ladder.

The morning's snipe-shooting expedition confused me. The birds were life-sized, yet absurdly unreal. My shoulder, still sore from the recoil of the gun, admonished me both for trying and for missing. I could not keep my thoughts in one place. The kill-count notched on the wooden stock ran into the dozens. No doubt Jay had failed to down a bird that morning only because he had used a single-shot rifle instead of his regular buckshot bird-gun. What was he trying to tell me?

Between the slow whoosh of palm fronds, the random punctuation of birdcalls, a high, long hoot reached out followed by a shorter one. Gerry came running in its wake, heading for the house. I called out to him: 'What's happening? Where's chief?'

'Coming.'

'Where d'you go?'

'Jus' running.' Gerry pulled at his banyan, twisting and knotting the puny shoulder strap in his fingers.

Elvin called out. 'Hey boys, ready to eat?'

We returned to the bungalow and divided up as before: Gerry to the back to help with the dishes and I right up to the front steps.

'Where's the captain?' Elvin asked.

'On his way.'

'I hope you've worked up an appetite. Sulaiman has put on a feast, but the fellow with the big mouth can't make it. There's a heck of a lot for you two boys to polish off.'

The visitor, Mr Tinki, tapped the table and half sniggered. 'Wanted to come very badly. But, what to do? Minister called, tcha.' He stopped abruptly, unsure of how to proceed.

The atmosphere was not conducive to small talk and clearly there had not been much meaningful conversation since his arrival.

Sulaiman took charge and served out the food, plate by plate, starting with the diminutive guest. By the time Sulaiman had fished out a drumstick, Jay appeared.

His hair was all tousled and strands of straw and grass stuck out from it.

'What have you been chasing?' Elvin asked.

'A pig.' He grinned.

'Where?'

'Down by the papaws near H block.'

Sulaiman quickly said, 'I'll get rid of it.'

'I had a trap. All worked out. Should've got him easy but fellow evaded. Slippery as hell.'

'How were you going to catch it? I'd like to see that.' Elvin chortled.

'You should breed pigs, Uncle. Put a pig farm here.'

Sulaiman collapsed into a coughing fit. Uncle Elvin scraped back his chair. 'Get your father some water,' he instructed Gerry who was watching, appalled, from the back steps.

Jay started to expand on his vision, but Elvin stopped him. 'Forget bacon, son. Let's stick to chicken for Sulaiman's sake. Now eat.'

Mr Tinki gingerly picked up his fork and spoon and hummed, bucked up by the prospect of a feed.

'*Athin kanna.*' Elvin urged him to eat with his fingers.

Mr Tinki dug in gratefully and asked, between mouthfuls, feeble questions on coconut cultivation and paddy.

Elvin, on top form, pontificated with pleasure, moving from the Green Revolution, which sounded much less risky than my father's red one, and high-yielding rice to the competition in international agriculture. Mr Tinki truncated his questions in retreat from the efficacy of crop diversification to the price of fertiliser. Sulaiman came back, his chest narrowed and his arms tightly folded, having survived a battle for his breath outside.

'Can you imagine being at the controls of Gemini 3 when it's launched, Uncle?' Jay asked.

'Quite heavy on the hands, I imagine, but neater than the Soviet Voskhod.' Elvin laughed, happy to enter the space race.

'No, can't be. Everything is weightless up there, no?'

By this point, Mr Tinki was completely lost. He sank further into his seat, head lowered and in hand-to-mouth combat with the curried cartilage on his plate.

Sulaiman took the momentary pause to gently bring Elvin back to the more pressing problem of crop irrigation on their own patch of planet earth. 'Sir, need a decision badly on the water problem we were discussing.'

'Certainly. But I don't understand why you are so pessimistic, my dear fellow.'

'The signs are not good, sir. We've seen beehives close to the ground. Large wasp nests. It does not bode well. Should prepare for a drought next season.'

'But we've had so much rain, the *wewa* is full, no?'

'Not retaining the water, sir. In a real drought it will soon go dry. Leaks, no?'

'But the pick was good, you said. Plenty of coconuts this time. Surely a sign that the water table is high?'

'Only for now.' Sulaiman's face grew graver. 'If we see the weaverbirds nesting early, or the crows reducing their hatching, then it is inevitable. Water level will drop. I recommend a second reservoir with a full lining. We can siphon the water we have from this one if we act fast. Then line the old one also for next season.'

'Nothing is inevitable, Sulaiman.'

'If it is the will of God.'

I took my plate to the washbasin. Gerry, back in his houseboy role, collected it and when I had finished washing my hands with water from a pot, handed me a towel.

'Don't you ever eat?'

'No need.' He seemed crushingly shy of any direct attention, no sign of the ease with which he had stood naked on the raft. In the shadow of the house, his hand had gone limp. None of the eagerness that had earlier thickened his playtime giggles remained. I sensed another gulf – one which dismays me more than ever now.

By the time Jay had finished and left the table, Elvin was becoming exasperated with Sulaiman's dour prognosis. 'Anyway, if the weather is going to confound us every time, all the more reason to diversify. I'd like you to spend some time in Colombo overseeing the poultry operation. Once we get going there, we can branch out here also and supply towns like Kurunegala. You have to think ahead.'

Sulaiman assembled the unused cutlery from the different places around the table and made a small arsenal in front of him. As he sorted the forks from the knives and the spoons, occasionally tugging one of his long earlobes, Mr Tinki edged closer.

Jay, behind me, whispered, 'Let's go. They are after us.'

'Who?'

'Choose, cowboy, choose.' He puffed out his cheeks to hide the dimples. 'You shape the enemy in your head, but Gerry can be a mean son-of-a-gun.'

My journey from home to the estate bungalow – Villa Agathon – had been already as fantastical as a trip to Mars or Moscow. It hardly took a blink now to relocate myself to a mythical ranch of rawhide and tumbleweed and turn geckos into iguanas.

'What are you?' I asked, playing for time.

'Jesse James.'

'Why Jesse James?'

'Because he robbed from the rich and was a friend of the poor.'

'You a Robin Hood?'

'I've got hold of a stagecoach carrying a load of gold and I'm taking it to my hideout. I've got to cross danger land.

Gerry is going to ambush me. Somewhere down by the Lake of the Wandering Pig. He likes to do the war cries. You are the sheriff on my trail. I've got to kill you both.'

'Why kill us?' The configuration was wrong.

'Follow my trail, you'll find out. I'll start from the bathing well, but I get a five-minute head start. I'll have the air rifle and you can take the BB gun.'

'No gun for Gerry?'

'He has a bow and a bunch of arrows. If he wants, he can use his *bata-thuwakkuwa* also. Actually, a bicycle pump will spit paper pellets out harder than that hopeless bamboo pop-gun, but he'll be all right.'

'You and I will be shooting air guns?'

'Don't worry. You won't get permanently killed. We'll use gandapana berries for pellets. Only stings. Just don't aim for my face. Anyway, I'll get you first. You get hit – splat – you are out. Dead for three minutes. Okay? We play this all the time.'

Gerry would have known nothing of Apaches, or the Comanche, or any of the great peoples of America. He certainly didn't read Westerns; no cinema in the town nearby to bring the Magnificent Seven cantering in; he had nothing to hang this misguided fantasy on. What could he make of Cowboys and so-called Indians? Was there even a Sinhala term for either that didn't just mean local cattle kids and tea-estate workers from India?

The tiny peppercorn-shaped gandapana seed-berries that Jay wanted grew in clusters of a dozen or so in a knobbly ball the size of a fingertip. For each berry to work as a pellet, it had to be slightly wider than the calibre of the gun barrel, plump but still hard and not yet ripened from green to purple. Jay demonstrated how to use them by rolling the cluster between his fingers to separate the seed-berries and picking one to press into the barrel where the lead pellet would normally go.

'No repeater action,' he said. 'You have to load one at a time. Means you have to aim fast and shoot fast.' He began to harvest the berries and separate them.

'Aim at what?'

'We'll have hats. So, hit the hat.'

'I didn't see his hat.'

'Gerry has a headband. He can be hit anywhere. But he'll be attacking me, not you. I know where to shoot him. We are enemies until one of us dies. Then we reincarnate, after the count, and continue.' He poured a palm full of seed pellets into a small round tin in a drumroll of hard rain. 'Also remember, we only use the guns at twenty paces or more. Otherwise even a seed could injure you. Close-up, we have to fight with our hands. Frontier judo.' He handed the tin over. 'Now, go back to the bungalow and give me a five-minute lead. Follow the trail – but watch out, sheriff, or I'll get you before you even begin.'

Elvin and Sulaiman were poring over a large chart spread out on the lunch table. Mr Tinki had left. Sulaiman drew a circle with his sharp finger. 'Sir, this is the ideal spot for a second *wewa*. Can connect the two in one cut and manage for sure the water properly.'

'Damn expensive business.'

'But then, sir, we can beat any drought to come.'

'What is the point if we might lose the land anyway to those jackasses in parliament hellbent on wrecking the estates?'

'Won't wreck this one, sir. If they want land, we have plenty of useless acres on the eastern side we can release. Give those to the land distribution commission, if it ever gets going, and we'd actually be better off.'

'That may be,' Elvin conceded temporarily. 'But before their redistribution nonsense, we need to become experts at our distribution. Fresh meat distribution. That is what you and Tinki must focus on. Work out a first-class system, like the Americans. You should see how they do it.'

I wanted to hear more: America, Elvin's plans, Sulaiman's forebodings – learn from them both – but Jay was out on the trail and the clock was ticking. I slipped into the bedroom and collected my hat: floppier than I liked but extra brim meant extra protection. To beat an ace shot I was going to have to move fast. I knew I could – move fast and shoot fast. His girl Niromi, cowgirl or not, sure could not do that.

I counted the minutes and at five, stepped out – BB gun in hand, heart tight, raring to go and mete out true justice in the Wild West of coconut canyons.

Elvin spotted me. 'Hunting again?'

'Jus' playing.'

'When you see that boy of Sulaiman's, tell him I have a message for him to take into town. A telegram.'

I did not explain that Gerry was incommunicado, waiting to trap Jesse James and scalp invaders.

Halfway down to the main gate, I saw that my quarry had gone off-road, ripping ground cover and pepper creepers, daring me to follow. The motor had been turned off.

Taking up position by one of the kumbuk trees, I loaded the BB gun and cocked it, safety catch off, keeping a few extra berries loose in my breast pocket. In every outlaw story there comes a point when you find you can trust nobody. You find your friend is as good as dead; you are on your own.

※

In the still air, the shrill alarm of a cricket spooked my horse and I made my way towards the pond on foot. At the bund, the laughter of light on the water, half in love with muddy chaparajos and sudden puffs of gun smoke, made me drop my guard. The first phut of the air rifle skimmed flat and indecisive; a few seconds later another shot plucked a leaf off a pond-sniffing guava an arm's length away. I couldn't work out the gunman's position. If only we had tracer bullets like in a war comic: long white arcs trailing across the sky, thickening into clouds to feed the dreams of carefree days and make a new world out of an afternoon's make-believe.

Then, ten yards ahead, by the water's edge, a dry coconut frond sailed through the air. Gerry's war whoop followed. No glint of sunlight on gunmetal that shone in the pages of my favourite Westerns; nothing gleamed under the coconuts. No white Stetson, nor bent eagle feather.

I raised the BB gun. Jay was right: the gun made the game real. No need to imagine a bullet reaching out to the target;

no one would have to pretend to be hit, or argue against it. If the aim was good and I shot straight, Jay would be hit. There will be no need to negotiate. The green splat would be proof. He'd be dead. That was all I had to do: make him dead. The point was to shoot straight, not pretend, and be somewhere almost real. The idea was liberating.

Jay's rifle had telescopic sights, cross-hairs; mine had a simpler V and ball, but that was enough. I was learning to believe in natural gifts: how to still the mind, let every sound, smell, waft of wind, press the outer layers of the senses and reveal the state of things. To live, as Jay urged, in one universal breath from now to infinity. Slowly, his beaming face came into focus: the high cheekbones catching the sun, glistening, his fringe mussy and wavering below the hat, his tongue peeping as he searched for us. I closed my eyes in a marksman's prayer, tasting metal, a hint of the corrosion that lay ahead in the journey out of a shell into a world that would mingle light with darkness, doing with undoing.

Then my hat was hit – smack in the middle of the crown.

'Got you, asshole,' Jay's exaggerated Wild West shout echoed. 'Out for three minutes.' His motor spluttered into life and he set off.

Downed, I counted the seconds, furious not to have fired a single shot.

Gerry let out another whoop and hurled a branch, leaping out onto the open ground where we had abandoned the raft: in plain view, his half-length sarong flapping. I could have splattered that easily, probably even hit the headband, if Gerry froze for a second, but the three minutes were not up. With another whoop, Gerry plunged into a grove of cardamom plants and orange trees.

I retrieved my hat and discovered a hole in it. Could a gandapana seed, a berry, do that? I counted the final thirty seconds and set off after the other two.

Although the sound of the motor provided enough of a trail, I kept checking the ground, converting the indentations in the sand into hoof marks and searching for two horses up ahead instead of a hand tractor with a baby horsepower rating. Country lore was not the point. What thrilled me most was the single-mindedness of the pursuit. Nothing could detract from the fullness of the moment, a pleasure that would stay with me forever. The thrill of hunting: the search for a memory, a word, a friend, a spark of hope in a careless world. Chases that would sustain me when nothing else could.

Then, the motor ahead stopped again. The air settled. No birdsong. No wind. No intrusions. The strings up in the trees were zipped and hushed. The silence grew immense until a bird, unable to bear the emptiness, pricked it with a sharp, long, fluttery trill. Another followed, and another. A chorus of new birdcalls rippled from tree to tree. Among them was Jay, teasing me for not being able to tell one kuk-kukuroo from another. No doubt Gerry could; he must listen to them every day. He would know them all. The trills, the chirps, the warbles, the squawks. Maybe Gerry was doing birdcalls too. The two of them in cahoots. This was, after all, their game. Gerry would know exactly where to run, where to do his war whoop, where to shoot his arrows and where to fall dead. For he must. Jay could not be the one who is hit and falls. It dawned on me then just how far this game surpassed any I had ever played at home.

I took the next bend low. The small hide on stilts at the edge of the paddy fields twenty yards down promised an advantage. A woodshrike flew ahead. The twang of a bow. An arrow flew in a slow curve and fell short into a clump of copperleaf. A moment later Jay's air rifle fired three shots in quick succession. Could he reload and fire so fast with gandapana berries? Without lead pellets in the automatic feeder?

I saw Jesse James shift his position behind the *cadjan* screen of the hide. A moment later, the rifle was firing again. I rolled over and took cover behind a walrus tree. Jay had not spotted me. I took aim and fired, forgetting the rules of engagement, hoping to hit Jay anywhere I could. All I wanted was to hit him. Smack, smack, the gandapana berries exploded against the tightly woven coconut fronds of the screen. Jay turned his fire on me, snapping one of the branches nearby with a shot. I found a better angle; this time the berry-bullet burst on the post close to his face. Jay ducked. I ran towards the next tree, but was hit by two fast shots, one in the arm that stung like hell and the other in the hat again. 'Down,' I yelled and fell, playing dead. The green splodge on the hat and my arm proved that Jay's last two shots, at least, were definitely seed-berries.

Jay fired some more at Gerry who dodged and danced from tree to tree. Then Jay did his own war cry and leaped down from the hut. With a howl, Gerry retreated. Jay chased him into the bushes, and emerged moments later with the abandoned bow and a couple of arrows. My three minutes of being dead a second time were almost up.

'Truce, we need some time out,' Jay announced, examining the bow. 'He never does it properly,' he complained. 'See? The string has to be a lot tauter, I keep telling the fool.'

'Now what?'

'You join my gang. No more sheriff. I'm going to show him how to really use a bow and arrow.' He had a pistol tucked into his belt.

'You have two guns.'

Jay patted the handle. 'This? Nice repeater, but no pressure. Only good at point-blank.'

'But that's not fair, is it?'

'I'm an outlaw. It's not about being fair.' He pulled out his bowie knife and cut off the pointy end of the arrow and split the end open.

'Now what are you doing?'

'Like a blunt pencil, this. Useless. It needs to stick in when it hits something solid. You know, like in the movies. Thud – and there it is, quivering in a tree trunk by his head.'

He opened a small brown case strapped to his belt and pulled out a small packet of fishhooks, pins and nails and some twine.

'You putting barbs?'

'Don't want to torture the bugger.' He picked out a couple of slender narrow-head nails. 'This is what we need.'

He fixed one of the nails to the split end of the arrow and wound the string around it to hold it in place with an inch of the metal point sticking out. 'What d'you reckon?'

'Looks mean.' I hesitated. 'Were you using real pellets back there?'

Jay laughed. 'Just one or two to fizz things up.'

'You got my arm, not just the hat.'

'Let's see.' Jay quickly brushed away the flecks of green pulp still on my skin with his fingertips. 'That's a berry mark. Didn't hurt much, really, did it?'

He fixed up the second arrow and then tested the bow, putting his foot on one end and flexing it and tightening the bowstring several notches more. 'I've shown him how to string it so many times, but bloody fool just doesn't get it. He could never be a real Geronimo.'

I didn't see Gerry as any kind of fool; only a boy with no choice. Did he even know we had paused the game? Might he be stealing up right now? 'We track him, or what?'

'That's it. The tables are turned.'

'Does he know that?'

Jay's mouth broke open into a coarse, haphazard grin, as he did his Jesse James drawl: 'What matters is that it is time for us to nail him.'

He strapped his air rifle to his back and carefully slotted the string of the bow in the notch of the arrow and held it in place between the fingers of his right hand; the shaft and the bow he gripped with his other fist, along with the second arrow. If determination was the route to victory, Jay was assured of success.

'What happened to the *bata-thuwakkuwa* and his tomahawk?' I asked as we passed Gerry's last stand.

'The dickhead just dropped everything and ran. That's no way to win.'

I no longer knew where the boundaries were, but I followed Jay along the path up to the cowshed where Jay said Gerry always ended up.

'You draw him out and I'll show him what an arrow can do.'

Jay grinned and I grinned back, unable to resist, entranced by the sleek, modernised arrow, the plastic fletches primed to guide it to pierce the veils of boyhood dreams.

An alu kobeiya flapped its broad wings and took to the air, and soon a chorus of panicky birdsong ricocheted high to low.

In Jim Corbett's jungle book, to flush a tiger out of hiding you should create a line of sound combing across the scrub. Then the tiger thinks a giant claw is scraping the land and doesn't see that at any point it is just a single man moving in, banging a drum; one man that it could tear to pieces with ease. To flush out a boy with nothing to defend himself would surely hardly compare, especially Gerry who did not understand the earnestness of our fantasies.

I gave a war whoop.

Our prey leapt out, over the back wall, into a banana grove. I stole around the side of the shed.

A moment later, Gerry appeared again, peeping from behind a carriage of green bananas.

'Over there,' I said to Jay who had come up and crouched down behind.

'This'll scare him shitless.' Jay pulled back the bowstring taut and then sprang out with a roar and let the arrow fly, aiming at the carriage of bananas.

Gerry jumped forwards instead of back and yelped as the arrow got him in the leg. He crashed into the bushes.

'Damn fool,' Jay swore. 'Why'd he do that?'

We ran up to Gerry. He lay on the ground, baffled, holding the arrow stuck in his thigh. A red stain bloomed in his sarong. His face had darkened where he'd been hurt as he fell; his left eye thick and bloody.

Jay snatched Gerry's headband off and hitched up the boy's sarong. 'Here, put this quick around your leg.' He pulled out the arrow and tied the headband tight around the puncture. He swore again, under his breath. 'Damn. Better go back to the house and put some Dettol on it.'

'In the cart?' I asked.

'Nah. It's only a small thing.' Jay let go of the end of the sarong. 'Can walk, no?' he asked him.

Gerry was trying hard not to cry. His bad eye fast swelling up in fat rolls, the flesh turning crimson; the socket looked buckled. 'Can't see,' he moaned.

Jay gave him a hanky to cover his eye and started to pull him along; I followed a few steps behind. The sand exposed a trail of red blobs. I felt sick. All the lonely dread, which over the last two months had ebbed away, rose again, breaking the veneer of camaraderie I had carefully fitted to our joint enterprises. Gerry let out a whimper as he half hopped, half limped along, but Jay seemed not to notice. The trees sagged, mute. A solitary hornbill arched its wings.

Up at the house, Jay made a cold compress for the eye and dabbed antiseptic on the wound. As he was dressing it, Elvin turned up.

'What the hell are you doing?'

'First aid,' Jay said. 'Wounded, no?'

'Bloody hell. Who's going to take my telegram to the tom-tom shop now?'

That night, Gerry was confined to the kitchen where he was told to rest while Ivan, the watcher, was drafted in to help with the evening chores. I fretted over the spectre of blindness, or tetanus – the thing that led to lockjaw and death by slow star vation. Gerry suffering for our misdeeds.

When we got under our nets to sleep, I asked Jay if he had brought his Bible.

'I found what I was looking for.'

'What?'

'Elijah. A lonely prophet, like Moses, and a fighter for God. Jews, Christians, Muslims, all call him the herald.'

Something in Jay's voice made me feel relieved. 'Moses...'

Jay pushed his face close to the net. 'Seriously, I wanted to know who Elijah gave his mantle to, and how.'

'Like a crown?'

'A cloak. But really, it's his powers; magic powers that part the seas, get ravens to bring him food during the great drought. The day his life ends, he vanishes in a whirlwind, giving his mantle to his disciple, Elisha, who then has to fulfil the things that have to be done.' He paused, relieved by the retelling.

'In Russia, it is the people who have the power to change things.' My father's pamphlet seemed to offer a much more practical programme. A safer world.

By nine the next morning we were ready to head back home. The jeep packed with the same paraphernalia we had come with, minus the provisions – anything we had not consumed, we left for Sulaiman and his family and Ivan the watchman. Gerry didn't turn up to help. Sulaiman said he was still complaining about his eye.

'He wasn't shot in the eye, was he?' Elvin asked.

'When he fell he says a branch got him just there and now the boy can't see a bean.'

Elvin made a tsk sound. 'You better take him to hospital this afternoon when you've finished that other business. Use the tractor.'

'Can't we take him to a doctor now?' I asked.

'There's no room in the jeep, son. Can't be going up and down, I have an appointment to see Percy and that clown today.'

I didn't want Gerry going blind because of us. 'He can squeeze in the back with me.'

Elvin paused, measuring conscience to pragmatism. 'Bundle him in then. Sulaiman, you hang on to the back plate. I'll drop the two of you in the town but I can't be waiting, you understand? You'll have to sort it out from there, eye or no eye.'

'Yes, sir.'

Not far from the bridge we found a house with a red cross painted on a board but the doctor was out on a call; we left Sulaiman and Gerry to wait and drove on.

'Helluva thing to do, son, crippling that boy. Fellow usually runs behind us down the road hooting, no?'

'His fault. Jumped straight into the line of fire. Never learns what's what.'

Hearing them, I felt a growing sense of both guilt and betrayal.

'So, you boys catch any fish in the end?' Elvin honked the horn at a bullock cart on the road.

'Got fantails for the aquarium. Big jam jar full.'

'That's good.'

'What about you, Uncle?'

'Trouble is I can't tell whether I am the fisherman or the fish, but someone is definitely hooked somewhere.'

'Mr Tinki?'

'Small fry. Have to wait and see.'

At Ambepussa, I saw a sign to another medical centre and sickened again at the picture it brought back: the gross, mangled eye, Gerry whimpering. We turned into the rest house; Elvin parked under the flimsiest of trees.

'So many bloody trees here.' The bonnet steamed. 'Do we need to roll the top on?'

Jay studied the trees above the jeep. 'Nothing's gonna perch there.'

Up at the rest house, Mr Tinki paced the veranda clutching a spoon; a man twice his size burped loudly in a brown lounger, finishing off a bowl of porridge.

'You boys go and get yourselves a cream soda,' Elvin said, heading for the showdown.

Jay went in search of a waiter; keen for some time on my own, I wandered into the terraced garden.

Down a level, I discovered a cell cut into the side of the hill and secured by thick, black iron bars; inside, shredded poles of bamboo had been scattered on the floor. In the far corner, a dark, furry bundle swelled into a small black bear that ambled slowly towards me. I inched back.

Jay, who had followed me, saw the bear and immediately started to croon; he slipped his hand in through the bars and tickled it behind the ear.

'Don't do that. He'll bite your hand off.'

Jay slapped the bear's snout as it swivelled its head, baring its fangs. 'Fellow just needs a cuddle. Some affection.'

The bear took a swipe at him, but Jay's hand was swifter and out of the cage. 'See? Just wants to play. This isn't the life for a bear, stuck in a cage.'

Back in the dining room, our sodas and a plate of rolls were already out.

Each bubble in the soda seemed to me as extraordinary as the highs and lows of the trip: sparkling one moment, empty the next. Nothing, yet everything. Would I ever be able to describe the world I had been in, or what had happened in it? A bear?

'Wanna play Battleships?' Jay asked.

'You have graph paper?'

'We can make squares.' Jay picked some paper and a couple of pencils from the bar and set about drawing lines and positioning his ships. 'Just three ships. No aircraft carrier.'

I had sunk a cruiser but lost a submarine by the time Elvin came over.

'Who's winning?' He placed a hand on Jay to steady himself.

'Draw,' Jay replied. 'You?'

'Buggers don't understand the American mindset, but we are getting there. I feel hopeful.'

'Got your beer?'

'Oh yes, at least I managed a couple of beers.' Elvin slid forwards and then stopped himself. He patted his stomach. 'Pissoir first and then we'll hit the road, Jack.' He chucked the keys of the jeep over to Jay. 'You boys get started. Reverse the damn thing and get it pointed in the right direction, will you, Jay?' He hiccupped and ambled off.

'He lets you drive?'

'Sure. He's the one who taught me.'

We got in the front, and Jay started the engine. 'Tough old bird,' he said, and reversed the jeep expertly. He did a demonstration of the gear changes; he showed me how to coordinate hand to foot, and explained what the different levers were, including the four-wheel-drive stick.

'I know all that. I've read hundreds of test drives in the mags.'

'Yeah, but to learn properly you must do it – step by step.' He killed the engine. 'Look, sit here and do a run-through without the engine on.'

I followed his instructions, learning the way Jay said was best: watching someone who knew what to do and then trying to do it better.

When Elvin returned, I hopped out and he climbed in.

'Like to take the wheel, son?' A sleepy grin spread across his face.

'It'd be the best thing.'

'Our friend here will teach you, I'm sure.'

Jay brushed aside a leaf that dropped on the dash. 'Just need one of your cars, Uncle, and he could be an ace in no time.'

Before we set off, Elvin asked Jay to put the roof on. 'So bloody hot already.'

Jay unrolled the canvas and showed me how to fix it. We kept the sides open.

'All sorted?' Jay asked his uncle.

'What?'

'With those two.'

Elvin's eyes drooped. 'These chaps these days, they want so much and they always want it straightaway.'

'Like what?'

'Never mind what they want, what they need is patience.' He jerked the jeep into gear and took the turn out of the drive slowly. The jeep drifted over to the other side of the road where a massive lorry was looming. He heaved the wheel and swerved back just in time. 'Damn lorries,' he swore. The oncoming traffic swung in and out of the way but Elvin did not notice. He hung on to the huge steering wheel and moved his body before his hands whenever he took a bend. Within half an hour, his head was dipping regularly. Jay asked him more questions, cajoling him, prodding him.

'Wake up, Uncle Elvin, wake up.'

'I'm awake. Don't worry, son. I can drive this bloody thing with my eyes closed.'

He gave the jeep another spurt of juice. Even on a straight road the vehicle kept veering from side to side like a drunk in search of a wall, scaring the occasional cyclist that had to wobble out of the way, or a dog that would retreat, barking crazily. Luckily, the number of big, bushy hay lorries had dwindled. But at the point where Elvin woke himself up with a snore, Jay insisted he stop the jeep.

'All right, we'll stop. We'll stop. You drive then. Let me close my eyes for a tick.'

Jay took control of the wheel and steered the jeep to the side. He pulled the handbrake to bring the jeep to a halt. We moved Elvin across and Jay took his place. Only then, with Jay back in the driving seat, did the muscles in my chest finally loosen; the breath I had been holding in eased out in relief.

III

LIHINIYA

4

At our house, we never ate meals together as a family: breakfast rumbled in shifts, lunch drew pairs at best, and dinner became a series of tumbled snacks between six and nine, snatched after a shot or two of liquor at the sports club in my father's case, or an excursion to a dancing class in my mother's crammed timetable.

So it did not bother me that neither parent was in when Jay dropped me home after we had unloaded the jeep at his house. The front door had its usual cloth-covered brick propping it open; the disruptions were all in myself, not my surroundings. Having had nothing to eat since the stop at the rest house, I headed straight for the kitchen.

The larder boasted only a can of pilchards and a tin of peaches but the kitchen reeked of oil; the wall near the cooker shone, coated like flypaper, usually an indication that Siripala was currying favour and his fried tin-fish cutlis were in the offing.

'*Ko cutlis?* Where?' I called out.

A gecko chuckled.

Siripala peeped in. 'Cooling. Your thaththa likes them cold, no?'

I found the bowl of small, oval fishcakes, crusted in golden breadcrumbs, hidden behind a lump of hardened Gouda and a bowl of cemented tapioca in the fridge.

Siripala brought a plate. 'Two cutlis, baba?'

'Three.'

'Stringhoppers also? Pol sambol?'

My father's comfort food.

'Is Thaththa in a mood?'

'He put another bet and the horse came first. So now, everything tops.'

'Got his winnings this time, did he? So, why stringhoppers and all?'

'Have to build up merit when you can, baba.'

Some would be handy for me, too, having been out with the enemy. I took the plate and plonked down on a footstool to eat.

My father came rolling in, head full of cheers from the club. 'Did the nobs not feed you in their dacha then?'

Siripala panicked and asked whether he should put the stringhoppers out on the dining table. Mollified by the prospect, my father cocked his head, weighing the options. Then, remembering a parent's obligation, he ignored the servant and asked, more solicitously: 'So, what did you learn from your trip, son?'

'Not a school trip. Went just to see—'

'I know, I know. With our very own Oblomov. So, what did you discover about the landed sloths of this country?'

'We went fishing.'

'Ha! You had to fish for your supper?'

'Caught guppies for the tank. Jay has an aquarium in his house. Lots of tanks. Angel fish even.'

'My God.' He struck his forehead. 'What a world we live in.' He turned to Siripala. 'You made fish cutlis also, no?'

Siripala unveiled the bowl.

'Not guppies, I hope.'

I washed my hands and started for the stairs.

'What's he got out there, your Lord Elvin? Some big *walauwa* mansion?' He tried again, doing his best to show a genuine interest and rein in his instinct to mock.

My mind raced between the urge to retreat to the pile of comfort books upstairs and the chance to challenge my father's prejudices. With all that had happened on the estate, I had hoped the gap between us might be lessening, but now found I had to defend Elvin and Jay from his jibes instead. I had no wish to diminish him; I wanted him to know more about the wider world and not be misled by ignorance.

'Not a big house.' I swung the kitchen door back and forth, a punkah heralding the winds of a rebellion or, at least, a shift in perspective. 'Only a mud hut.'

'Don't be silly.'

'A bungalow. Jus' two rooms to sleep in and an open veranda-like thing to sit. No electricity or anything. Not even tap water.'

My father gasped, acting appalled. 'What? He hasn't even brought electricity to the area? Thoroughly use-less fellow. Does he have no sense of responsibility? Land reform doesn't go far enough. It should reduce estates to fifty acres, not two hundred and fifty.'

'I read your book.'

That stopped him. 'Which one? When?'

'I took the one called *Problems of Life* to read on the estate.' The words gushed to mask any misdemeanour. 'Translated from Russian.'

'My Trotsky?' The news pleased him. 'Why didn't you ask me, son? I could have guided you to something more fitting for the trip.'

'Was fitting, Thaththa.' I squeezed another drop of boyish bravado out. 'I read the whole thing in one go.' Skimmed it, I should have said, skipping from one spotlit passage to another.

'Good. We must study the good comrade's words together then.' He allowed some levity to creep in, hoping, I suppose, to draw me closer. 'Tell me, what other mischief did you get up to besides reading misappropriated books and fishing for your dinner?'

'Played this and that.'

'This and what?'

'Cowboys and Indians.'

'With coconuts?'

'Guns and bows and black bears...' I hesitated, unsure how much to reveal of what had happened. Luckily, he returned to his hobby-horse warnings.

'Actually, not cowboys but landlords are the problem in our country. The poor peasant cannot survive because the bosses sit in Colombo creaming profits from the countryside.'

'Sulaiman is the boss and he lives there. The biggest worry is the drought – he says it is sure to come.'

'What boss?'

'Superintendent.'

'A minor member of the petty bourgeoisie, son.' He ran his fingers through his thin hair, evidently thinking thoughts too complicated to explain in one breath. 'Drought is not what they really fear. Disorder, a dent in profits, possible revolution – these are the things that your dubious friends are anxious to prevent.'

✺

The next day, I cycled over to the milk bar imagining not the deserts of Arizona, or the cacti of New Mexico, but cinnamon gardens and coconut groves instead; rain-filled ponds and muddy rivers where dashing brown-skin warriors courted gold-tinged princesses with lances and poetry. A fantasia where Gerry, healed, comes to the city for the first time and is bewildered by the mansions and stately boulevards, the racecourse, the radio station, the milk bar, the garden enclaves where the poor and destitute only encroached in single file. I would be the one to show him around then; I'd become the guide, rather than the guided.

But it wasn't a star-struck Gerry that I found at the milk bar; instead, the boy from Fountain Café, hunched over an upended bike, spinning the back wheel and trying to refit the chain. I had not spoken to him again since that day he'd been cornered; the barrier between the language streams at school – Tamil, Sinhala, English – may not have been physical, but it might as well have been. I should have tried harder to cross the divide, but at the time it had not struck me as important; there were gulfs between me and all my classmates, none of which I had any desire to cross. The only chasm that mattered to me was the one that might open between Jay and me.

'What's wrong?'

'Keeps coming off.' He bent the metal chain guard and moved the pedal backwards slowly.

'This isn't a garage, boys.' Mahela leant forwards across the counter. 'Don't crowd out the place. Need customers, not grease monkeys, no?'

'How's about a Chocolac?' I replied and peered at the upturned bike. 'Nice machine. Is it new?'

'Shouldn't have this problem.' The boy turned the pedal again and demonstrated how the chain scraped the blue metal guard.

'Can't you shift that piece?'

Then Jay swooped in, a rush of feathers, wind-borne, ringing his bell. 'Channa, no?' he asked, coming to a stop inches away.

Channa let a small smile escape, pleased to be recognised. 'Yes.'

'So, what's the problem?'

'Chain trouble,' I intervened.

'Those new bikes from that Kelani factory – one knock and completely out of alignment. Dodgy Soviet machinery, I bet.' Jay undid the small toolkit that hung behind his saddle and picked out a spanner which he used to loosen one of the nuts. 'Now, do your side, then tap the spindle in.'

When Channa had done that, Jay gave him a washer to fit before tightening it up again. After both sides were done, Jay told him to turn the bike the right way up and lift the back wheel off the ground. He worked the pedal; the chain moved smoothly.

As Channa climbed onto the saddle, a sleek black Wolseley pulled up. A man smoking in the back seat put a hand out and tapped a slug of ash off a cigarette. His thick finger summoned Channa. 'Oi, come here. Ronny Kanagaratnam's boy, right?'

Channa slipped off his bike but stayed put.

'You tell your damn father to be careful, stop poking around.'

The man puffed out some smoke. Then he addressed Jay. 'You should know better than to hang around with his kind.'

Jay moved in front of Channa. I wasn't sure what to do.

A milk delivery truck turned in and stopped right in front of the car. The Wolseley driver gave a blast with his horn. Mahela shouted, 'Reverse.' Engines raced, more honking and protest. Mahela came out weighing a wet sponge in his hand. The man in the back seat of the car quickly rolled up the window. As the argument between the drivers heated up, Channa slipped round to the rear of the car. His expression – pulsing between pity and cunning – made me think we should scram before things got a lot worse, but then the car, revving up, backed out and with a wild swerve took off down the road.

'What have they got against your father?' Jay asked.

'Writes for a paper, no. Right now, a good journalist has enemies everywhere.'

'Why?'

'Who knows? My father says everyone is against him: government, the big newspaper bosses, the monks, the gangsters, the unions.'

'Should have ripped his tyres whoever that man was.'

'He won't get far.' With a bashful smile, Channa lifted his plastic water canteen. 'In the rumpus, I emptied *this* into the petrol tank.'

'Attaboy!' Jay put out his fist into the centre between the three of us; we two instinctively did the same and all our fists met.

'The three musketeers,' I murmured. I had never been in a gang before.

'Right.' Channa stepped back, lowering his head.

'You don't know the musketeers?'

'Sure, I do.' His mouth turned firmly down at the ends.

'You boys want your Chocolacs? Fresh batch.' Mahela slid the milk drinks to the edge of the counter. 'Or back in the cooler they go.'

'Now, now.' We trooped over.

Mahela laughed, back in his role of milkman. 'So, now you are three?'

'Yeah, three for one, one for three,' Jay chanted. 'We are the brotherhood.'

'All for one, one for all.' I couldn't help correcting Jay on the crucial point of allegiance.

'Is that so?'

'D'Artagnan says it. He's like the fourth Musketeer but it becomes their motto.'

'Okay. So, now it will be ours.'

'Motto?' Mahela asked.

'We will be inseparable,' Jay explained. 'Bound together in one endeavour.'

'That's good,' Mahela collected the empties. 'Good if you boys can stick together.'

'All for one, one for all,' Jay repeated.

'Who is the one?' Channa asked, glancing at us. 'Which one?'

'You tell,' Jay said.

'We have to defend each other.' I spoke solemnly, passing a flattened hand in front of me like a noble blade. 'Look out for each other. If anyone thumps one of us, then it is the same as all of us being hit. Together we are always stronger than we would be on our own. We all take the rap for what happens to any one of us. It's like... equality.'

Channa shook off his Batas and drew a circle on the ground with his bare toe; a faint, uneven, doubtful circle.

That evening, at home, my misgivings grew. Could we really stick to the motto, if we had not all been thrilled by the book, or the film? Could we be inseparable, if our fathers lived in such separate worlds? If Gerry, surely a musketeer too, could so easily be abandoned?

In the late afternoon, the leafy trees on the lane leading to Casa Lihiniya wilted a little, listless from the long heat;

the occasional gust from the ocean stirred the suburbs with brackish air but offered no relief. I chucked a stone at a marooned lizard, hoping to see it scuttle. The future for all of us seemed fraught to me, but the slogans on Galle Face Green and the communal chants on the perimeter of Beira Lake of recent days, which bothered my father so much, did not disturb the grand house at the end.

The gates and the glass doors beyond were open. Music tinkled out. Inside, Sonya plucked at a harp lodged between her knees, her slender hands rose and fell and the flight of notes formed what could be a sonata for the moonlight to come, or a falling star. Her eyes firmly closed, she eased her head, crowned with a hive of curls, from side to side, lapped by the rising melody.

When she opened her eyes, her lips, bubblegum-pink, also parted: 'Oh, it's you again.'

The simplest of words failed me.

'You like the harp? Come, I'll show you how to play it.'

A fragrant soda, sharper than perfume, laced her clothes. Her hands – frighteningly frail – moved lightly across the perpendicular strings, nearly vanishing with the music despite their smooth, manicured physicality. I could not understand how such slender fingers could thrum the strings so effortlessly and cause such tremors in me.

'Do you play an instrument?'

I made a weak, sorrowful croak and watched the veins on the back of her hand rise and mark the delicate, cinnamony flesh.

'Would you like to learn?'

'Yes.'

'You know, it is a beautiful thing to be able to make a sound that pleases the heart and soothes the soul.'

She could do that without moving a finger.

'Can Jay?' I asked, finally stringing two words together.

'Not Harpo, is he? I wish he'd learn the violin, I'm sure he'd love it. Can't you just see him standing tall and handsome and playing Carnegie Hall one day, but he won't even try a note. All he likes is to play with his bow and arrow.' She released another string of notes, pleased with her cupid joke.

'We have no instruments in our house,' I confessed, embarrassed. 'Only a record player.'

'Maybe *you* should try the violin. You'd need to practise regularly, but you could do that here. We must have Jay's Strad somewhere around – just a copy, you know. He'd be pleased to see you playing it.' She patted the divan. 'Sit next to me, darling. I don't bite.'

I perched on the edge and gripped the firm piping on the velvet cushion.

She took my right hand and placed my fingers on the strings. Her curved glossy nails scraped only the uppermost layer of my knuckles but it felt as though the whorls of my fingertips themselves shifted as a result, like the contours of the earth after an eruption. 'Use the first three fingers. Try.'

I managed to twang the burning strings, one after the other, and smiled at her in surprise.

'Lovely. You'll have long, strong fingers when you grow up. Perfect hands.'

Enthralled, I plucked the strings again. How could Jay not wish to learn from his mother?

'Now, run along and find your friend. He's hiding in that zoo of his.'

I wanted to ask when we could have another lesson, but she was already distracted by some other murmuring in her head. Swallowing hard, I added, 'Aren't you going to play some more?'

'Not now, darling. I have to get ready to go out.'

When my mother needed to 'get ready', it meant she had to dab some powder on her face and pin back her hair. Possibly change out of her beige Kundanmals slacks into a chiffon or georgette sari, depending on whom she was going to meet. I could not imagine what Jay's mother could do to get more ready than she was, even to woo Hollywood.

'Why?' I didn't mean to be so bold.

'We'll have another go next time you come.' In her lips I could detect some amusement, but her firm jawline quickly stopped the drift. She played a light glissando. 'For today, just remember the red strings are your anchor lines.' She pronounced the last two words with difficulty, slowly untangling them in her mouth. Then she stretched up on tiptoe as if she had an irrepressible urge to dance. Pulling a white cotton dustcover over the harp, she glided to the open-stepped ultra-modern staircase. A moment later, she floated up and away, a freed note herself seeking a secret boon I had yet to divine.

Jay, enthroned on a stool inside the aviary, had budgies chirping on his shoulders and knees. On a towel wrapped around his right hand, a large grey parrot balanced, regally rolling its head at him.

I stuck my nearly long fingers into the tiny hexagonal spaces of the mesh. 'Whatcha doing?'

'Making friends,' Jay whispered, lips tight.

'That's a massive parrot.'

'Comes from Kenya via the pet shop near the eye hospital.'

His mother and her harp faded in the echo of Gerry's injury.

The parrot squawked out a greeting. 'Hail-lo, Jomo.'

'He can really talk? I thought that was just in books.'

'He talks.'

'Jomo,' the parrot repeated.

Jay stroked the scalloped grey feathers. The bird lifted its wings and spread them the way my father sometimes rolled his shoulders at the dining table.

'What's his name? He should have a name.'

'Sinbad,' Jay replied, quick as a flash. 'Traveller, story-teller and ship's mate.'

The parrot mimicked him, breaking the name into two: 'Sin-bad.'

Jay eased the parrot off his arm onto a wooden stand and then slipped out of the enclosure. 'He's going to be a good friend.' The tone of his voice was as much of a blow as the suggestion. 'Their life span is much the same as ours. And when they mate, it's for life.'

Up in the sky, I saw the bats had started out in formation. I wanted to tell Jay, but hesitated; things had moved on.

'Tomorrow I'm going to see a bird breeder,' Jay added. 'Wanna come?'

'To get a mate for him?'

'To get some info. I don't even know if he's really a cock. Could be a hen.'

'You can't tell?'

'It's not like boy and girl. You can't just unzip and look.'

'He must be a he.'

'Anyway, I'm going in the morning to see one of Channa's older cousins, an expert. If you wanna come, be here around eleven. Okay?'

'Channa's been here already?' This time the arrow entered my chest and nicked my heart; it hurt even more than the stab I felt every time a red-eyed koha called, whooping like Gerry.

※

At home my father, obscured by a screen of newsprint, flicked a finger at an item in the international section. 'I see your Beatles have made a film.'

The idea that popular music had become news both irritated and intrigued him, especially in a world so close to Armageddon, but he must have hoped it might provide a lure.

'What's the use? It won't be at the Majestic for ages. Everything comes here two years after everywhere else in the world.'

He seized the opportunity. 'You see, son, this is the problem of the economic relationship we have with the capitalist world.'

'England?'

'Yes. The Labour party might get in by a whisker at the next election there, in England, but Harold Wilson's economic programme will not change that much: it is not socialism. It is up to us in the underdeveloped world – the deliberately underdeveloped world – to fight for justice everywhere, including in poor England.' He folded his newspaper, discreetly hiding the race sheet inside, as he zigzagged from one bee in his bonnet to another.

A car honked outside, alarming the house sparrows bickering in the gutters.

My mother hurried in with a plastic folio case under her arm and clattered up to her room. My father swiftly shoved his betting slips and pencil into the drawer of the bureau and picked up the Ceylon *Radio Times*.

When she popped back, she announced grimly, 'The school problem is going to get a lot worse.'

'Surely, it can't. Not worse.'

'Government put out a new plan today.' Her voice faded. 'It's shambolic.'

He chose a mild rebuke over commiseration: 'Why doesn't your radio have a proper political debate on air, instead of *Poetry for Pleasure* every week.'

She did not rise to it; instead, she unveiled her own plan. 'So, I've arranged for a new tuition master for Kairo.'

'Another one? What on earth for?'

'The child needs an education, Clarence. That useless fellow you found never turns up. Have you not noticed?'

I had heard her conspiring with her custard-toting friends about how to harness the scarily efficient breed of tutors crawling out of the woodwork as the school system creaked with the weight of progressive reform.

'There you are, then,' my father said to me with noticeable relief. 'Your mother has you sorted.'

'I'm fine anyway.'

'Have you even looked at those schoolbooks you got the other day?'

'Which books?'

'The Sinhala readers. You really need to get up to speed.'

'Okay.' Meaning I knew I needed to, but also, like my father, giving a general positive note that might suggest I had complied without quite fibbing.

'You start tuition next week with the new tuition master. This one will help you with your Sinhala *and* your mathematics.'

'What about geography?' My father asked. 'History?'

'Maybe *you* should get some tuition too, Clarence. They won't take excuses forever, you know. All government servants have to pass the national language proficiency test.'

'Thaththa is always doing maths. Calculating odds, no?'

'Never mind all that. The point is you too will need to improve your Sinhala, even if your father thinks he can dodge it. You must do well next term in the class tests, or it will be a real mess. You are a big boy now. Time to get serious.'

※

The afternoon sun splintered in the trees as I cycled down the middle of traffic-free Jawatte Road, side by side with Jay.

'Your uncle said land reform is what will happen.' I did not know then what the phrase meant, except that it involved redistributing things with great difficulty and a reconciliation of disparities. 'My father says it's like the panacea.'

We were on our way to see Elvin.

This time we strolled in through the front gates and up the long drive with borders of dishevelled hedges and pale, lanky temple trees, circling the large garden sunk in the middle to form a shallow, bare, brown soup bowl. Only the Austin Healey, gleaming under the porch, seemed cherished and poised. I let my hand brush the creamy curved bonnet and absorb some of the sheen from the rubbed wax as we climbed the steps to the long veranda.

Jay led us through an ornate doorway into a vast room of swaddled furniture and muffled chandeliers.

'Does he live all alone here?' In Bolshevik Russia a family would be billeted in every corner, easing conscience and muting extravagance.

'He's single, but you'll find all sorts of cadgers dozing about. Hangers-on. He's a soft touch.'

We cut through to the east wing veranda. Elvin, bent over a wooden table with his back to us, was crooning a Sinatra song to himself.

'Uncle,' Jay called out. 'What's you doing?'

He did not seem surprised to hear Jay. 'Studying, my boy. Studying. That is what you should be doing as well, and your young friend, instead of shooting the staff with bloody arrows.' A red puddle of tangled fur at his feet erupted and rushed at Jay.

'But no school, Uncle. It's the holidays for the rest of the month.' He gave Garibaldi, twisting and wagging around his legs, a fond slap.

'With all these bloody socialist strikes, they may never open again.' He examined me over the tops of his thin horn-rimmed spectacles.

'I have a tuition master,' I blurted out. 'For mathematics and Sinhala, and a science book to study, so I'll be ready for the class tests.'

'My word, you're thinking ahead, boy. You tell Tarzan here about the virtues of civilisation. Can't live in the trees forever, can you? This tutor of yours, good fellow?'

'Don't know. Only next week, he'll come.'

Elvin chuckled. 'I like it. You reserve your judgement until you see the arse, right?'

'My father got me a tutor once,' Jay caught the dog by his snout and massaged his teeth. 'An idiot. I chased him off.'

'Shot the fellow in the backside, did you?'

'That was an accident, Uncle. Anyway, Gerry is always getting himself pipped. Just bounces back.'

'Not so bouncy this time. Apparently, he still can't see straight.'

Another hidden layer of conscience prickled. 'He's not going to go blind, is he?'

'His other eye is fine.'

I had stopped believing in God – but not completely. I still found myself praying for sweet dreams and ice cream, and feared at being so selfish. The verse from Proverbs hovered over me.

Jay peered at the paper laid out on the table. 'Is this your chicken shed, Uncle?'

'I need a mathematics wizard.' Elvin pointed a school-masterly finger at me. 'Some serious calculations are required. You see, the recommended size is forty-one foot by four hundred and ninety-three. But that is for America where they can process twenty-five thousand chickens at a go. Here, a mere two thousand will be our target.'

'Two thousand chickens?' Jay exploded. 'You said five hundred last time. Now you want my father to have two thousand chickens in our garden?'

'No, just five hundred on your site. We have plans for another three locations dotted around in city farms for the initial phase. Two thousand birds total in due course. We intend to supply the top-notch restaurants from the Capri to Mount Lavinia as well as the oven-ready housewife, as it were.'

'You'll have them here by the stables also?'

Elvin blinked. 'Here?'

'You have the biggest garden in town.'

'Ah, yes. We'll have the breeding unit here.'

'How many birds?'

'Obviously not as many as in the coops – a hen lays more than one egg, no? – but it will be the central hub with incubators and a nursery for the chicks. Also have to garage a small fleet of vehicles and things of that sort.'

'Vehicles?'

A small gathering of cross-hatches tugged an eyelid into a sly wink. 'It's an elaborate business. The logistics, the buildings, the space. A lot of calculations for our young friend here.'

'Can't do x and y, or anything like that.'

'Don't undervalue yourself, boy. Modesty is only becoming in a genius.'

Jay flicked through a report on a poultry farming conference in Australia, rust-marked by the staples which had been fastened in three places on the side. 'What about the slaughtering? Who'll do that?'

'Good point, Jay. I've asked Sulaiman to look into that. You see, you must have intermediaries and partners. That's the way business works. You understand, Jay, don't you? You should. Business is in our blood. This government does not comprehend the real world the way we do.'

'So, you are helping the government?'

'For mutual benefit.' Mischief puckered Elvin's generous lips. 'You see, I discovered that as a new commercial enterprise in this field – integral to the government's modernising programme – we will be allowed to import new vehicles.'

'Is this whole thing just to get an import permit for another car?'

'Of course not. I've already got a new one coming. I've ordered one of those Lotus kits nobody knows how to stop because it is a car you make yourself.' Elvin stretched out his hands in parallel lines to demonstrate straight-talking seriousness and engineering gravitas. 'We all deserve decent, nutritional, modern food. And my friend, Wilbur, will provide it. If we can improve the average age of the vehicles going down Galle Road, by the by, what's the damn harm in that? Can't leave it just for those ministers to bring in their braggy, bloody Benzes only.'

Jay wasn't listening. I could see he was figuring out something more important.

'Uncle, never mind the cars, it's the land you should be worrying about. Have you not seen the signs?'

'What signs? You sound like that halfwit Cassandra on Bullers Road spouting doom and gloom like there will be no tomorrow.'

'Those weird signs popping up in all the empty areas, like near that abandoned golf course and even in front of Kairo's house, saying trespassers will be prosecuted.'

It was news to me. I didn't like the idea that he'd passed by without telling me, whether with the girl or not.

'Well, if it is private property that is perfectly understandable.'

'Uncle, you gamble, no?'

'A flutter now and then. On the Grand National for sure. Sometimes the Derby. Some of us still have a soft spot for England.' Elvin's stern lips relaxed knowingly. 'So, what? You are talking in riddles, as usual. Think logically, Jay. And then, once thunk, speak sensibly.'

'What if I told you some gangsters plan to turn Colombo into Las Vegas?'

'Flashy Cadillacs and leggy girls?'

I made a mental note to read the article on Las Vegas, the new boom town, that I had seen in my father's *LIFE* magazine.

'Uncle, imagine awful casino joints all over town like they are building in the middle of the racecourse.'

'Your young friend here assured us that it is a socialist planetarium they are building there. Solemnly scientific, not hedonistic.'

'Someone is after every plot of unbuilt land.'

'We must reach for the stars, my boy. You hear that Arthur C. Clarke programme on the radio? Fascinating. Gambol, not gamble, is the name of the game.' He consulted his watch. 'I reckon it is about time for a little drinky-poo. A Las Vegas sundowner?'

'Be serious, Uncle. Soon there will be nowhere in Colombo for the wildlife, Uncle. What'll happen then?'

'We'll have a different kind of *wild* life?' He smoothed the papery crinkles around his mouth.

'It's not funny.'

'Tut, tut. You are becoming rather prudish, my boy, at an age when most young lads become rather more lascivious. What does our young Adonis say?'

'Kairo.' Growing firm, resolved, I reminded Elvin.

'Ah, yes. Kairo. Well?' Elvin pushed back his chair and stretched out, cracking a joint or two magnanimously.

Jay launched in, breathless: 'You've got to move fast. It's a competition for land, no? You need more than our garden. Get Pater to buy the next-door plot for a future extension. And you, Uncle, buy every other wasteland in the neighbourhood so that the Las Vegas gang can't grab them. Put broilers in one or two and keep the rest natural for jungle fowl.'

'Jungle fowl? What on earth for?'

'For the future. Remember our watchword, "There'll be no life without wildlife," Uncle.'

Elvin slipped off his large leather loafers and rubbed his feet together. They were pale and sensitive, rarely used unprotected. 'And where's the money, dear boy, for this sudden land grab of yours?'

'You are rich, no, Uncle?'

'Rich in character, my boy, but short of cash. It doesn't grow on trees.'

'But it does, Uncle. Coconuts, no? Sulaiman probably nicks half the crop for himself.'

'Ouch.' Elvin winced, feigning a hit. 'I suppose he may be a bit of a thief, but he is a reliable thief. And now he'll need all the money he can pilfer for that liability of a son – if the bugger really goes half blind. You are also forgetting what the die-hard leftists in charge of this country covet. Owning more land is not sensible in an age of envy, son.'

'Why?'

'Soon, they'll be confiscating private property that exceeds some arbitrary level – no doubt to suit the land minister's own prime holdings. Luckily, Wilbur's scheme will circumvent that. You see, son, the thing is to focus on the point of owning the land. The smart move is to exchange it for something less conspicuous. An invisible asset that can generate a profit.'

'Chicken sheds are hardly invisible.'

'You have not grasped the nature of the enterprise, Jay. You see, we will not *own* the sheds, nor indeed the land. The company will take over the lot and build the sheds and do all the stuff to get the thing going with pukka ideological credentials. Manage the whole damn thing as a sort of hybrid cooperative and get all the pesky licences. Your father merely has to exchange a slice of his utterly untended garden for a percentage of thoroughly managed shares – the same as I will.'

'Pukka what?'

'It is a tad complicated but, as I told your father, shareholding is the trick. If you study Marx properly, you'll see he was all for it. There will be no political impediment if the wording is right. Even our cabinet ministers are doing it: look at that textile mill everyone is talking about. Safe shareholdings producing dividends. In our case, chicks and eggs galore until the Day of Judgement – when, by the way, the judge will be an uncle or a nephew of someone we know anyway.'

'But why does your Wilbur need you? Why doesn't his company just go buy some land in Kirillapone or somewhere, for next to nothing? He doesn't need you — or my father.'

'As a matter of fact, he was on the verge of doing precisely that, but I spotted an opportunity to join in the bonanza. I must say I made rather a good case; convinced him of the economics of proximity – the value of being close to the dining tables that matter. The marketing angle was the clincher: if the fowl come from the best addresses in town, who could resist the snob appeal? It would be like ordering your capons from Kensington Palace.' He sniffed the air for the aroma of a classy roast, or the sundowner that had not yet appeared. 'You see, son, you must take advantage of your advantages, otherwise some other blaggard is bound to do it from under your feet. Having a few hectares to spare is no insurance these days. The future will belong to the entrepreneur. We must get your daddy-o on board.'

'You said my mother thinks it's a good idea?'

'Definitely.' Elvin brightened. 'Your mother and I see eye to eye on this.'

I saw a small stone in the argument Jay had been building crumble, but it did not faze him.

My father often complained that the rich were able to organise things to their benefit in ways the poor could not even dream of; he loathed the inequity of it.

※

The next day, cruising down Elibank, we passed a new building site. The plot had been stripped of all greenery and filled with heaps of sand and a concrete mixer.

'Bloody hell,' Jay swore. 'More trees gone. A pair of massive pied hornbills used to nest in that garden. Old Madam Konovsky must have conked it. We've got to act fast or soon only those damn crows will be left.'

'But down our road, no one will build in that jungle.'

'Of course they will. We must protect whatever we can. I need the old man to get hold of Bertie's plot next door: the twenty perches there are a great wild habitat now, but it's just what these people want.'

'*Who* want?'

'Come with me. He'll listen if you're with me. He says you are a good egg. Both he *and* my mother think so. I've heard them talking about you.'

'Me?' The idea of Jay's parents talking to each other about me was hard to picture. I had never seen them in the same room together; they functioned as an optical puzzle where if one became visible, the other disappeared. 'What? Like in a conversation?'

'In a row about me. You know how he sneers. And how she can mock him. That's their idea of a conversation. You were a moment of truce. Sometimes they completely lose it. Last night was a humdinger. He smashed a bottle of gin. He gets so angry when he's with the booze.'

'Attacked her?'

'They can really chuck stuff at each other. If they are stuck together, they both drink like fish and then fight with whatever they can grab. You wouldn't believe it. I had to clean the whole bloody mess up – gin and spaghetti all over – after they buggered off.'

I didn't know what to say. The quarrels at our house were not battles; I never had to scrape bolognese off the walls.

At Casa Lihiniya, we found Marty facing the round dining table on his own, knife and fork primly aligned on his plate. A tiny gilded coffee cup to hand. No sign of any ketchup spilt.

'So,' he sampled his coffee with the exaggerated calm of a man who had regained full control of his circumstances. 'This fellow rope you in to build another playpen?'

'Sort of.' My catch-all reply that revealed nothing but usually satisfied a grown-up's requirement of a verbalised response.

'Chicken shed,' Jay added, keen to establish the terms of engagement. 'Going to measure up for the chicken shed that you and Uncle Elvin are planning to build.'

'Hold on, son. What planning? I am not agreeing to that preposterous idea.'

'You don't want chickens?'

'Your bloody budgies are bad enough. I told him, I don't want his blasted chickens.'

I saw this might be where I could usefully step in even though I didn't know if broilers were hens or not. 'You'd have fresh eggs every day, Mr Alavis.'

'Who do you think is going to be poking around all that muck looking for eggs every morning in this house?'

'But you like eggs, don't you, Mr Alavis?'

'We live in a town. A town that is halfway to joining the twentieth century. There is an egg marketing board whose job is to provide eggs for us. If my desire was to hunt eggs,

I'd live on a farm – outstation where people grow nuts and go bananas. No, grow… Never mind. Point is: in my house, I expect to wake up to the hum of air conditioning and fridges, a cup of coffee – in proper Limoges china preferably. Not bloody cockerels with their doodle-dos and broody bloody hens popping eggs out of their bottoms, or any other damn hanky-panky.'

'So, you don't want chickens anywhere near the neighbourhood?' Jay asked innocently.

'You've got it, my boy. Your fish are fine, a few budgies chirping at the far end of the garden I'll tolerate because you are, after all, my son. But five hundred chickens, oven-ready or layers, I flaming will not.'

Jay pulled the long, curved lobe of his ear. 'In that case, you'd better move pronto and stop their plans for next door.'

'Bertie's backyard?'

'Uncle Elvin's business partners have their eye on that patch too. They'll be putting chickens right there in no time, Dad.'

'Bertie is a *flâneur*. Couldn't care less about a business proposition from Elvin. Now, if it was a Martini at the poolside or a brandy egg-flip…'

'That's the thing. Couldn't care less, so he'll let them do whatever they want if he is just given a case of smuggled champers, no?'

'Did Elvin say they intend to go in with Bertie?'

'If you won't let them in here, then that's the obvious next option. Won't be tea and roses next door. If you want to keep them out, you'll have to talk to Uncle Bertie first and buy that strip off him before they do. It's the only way.'

Marty eyed his son with cautious admiration. 'You are thinking very…' he pressed in his upper lip with his forefinger, flattening the bristles of his moustaches to coax out the right word. 'Yes, very astutely. Elvin says sell, but you might well be right, son. This could, in fact, be the time to buy. Extend one's holdings when all around you men are losing theirs.'

'If you want something, you have to make it happen.'

'Right, son.' Marty beamed. 'That's exactly it. You don't know how happy I am that you can see that.'

☀

Cycling over to the milk bar later, Jay made his bike rear, like a stallion, pulling up the front wheel. 'He's all talk, the old man.'

'He was impressed. He said you were right.'

Jay dismissed the idea with a wave. 'He hopes I might be useful one day for his business, that's all.'

The trouble with fathers was that they were always scheming. We lived on an island close to the equator, but our fathers were icebergs: all shiny and smooth on top but with jagged edges lurking out of sight. Jay's father, like mine, only exposed a fraction of his cogitations, assuming his contempt could be masked by sarcasm. Except, this time, the praise had sounded genuine; perhaps Jay should have been more generous in return.

At the milk bar, Channa occupied one of Mahela's new picnic tables, leg pumping up and down in excitement.

'What's the news?' Jay asked.

'You really wanna hear?'

'Come on, tell.'

'My dad's going to go to England,' Channa blurted out.

'No way. How? Embargo, no? No one can get an exit visa to go anywhere.'

Mahela slid the chocolate drinks onto the counter. 'No, no, no. We are not yet the Soviet Union. If you've already stashed money abroad, or if you have a sponsor, you can go. And some people have all the luck, no?'

Channa glowed, lit from inside, his shiny round face a luminous paper lantern.

'What's the scheme?' Jay asked.

'Not his scheme. British Council selected him to go on a study tour.'

'But he's way too old to study.'

'It's a tour where you get to learn stuff for your job. He might go for a whole year and he said we'll be able to visit him. In London and Manchester and Nottingham.'

'Sherwood Forest?' Spellbound, I waited for more place names.

'Yes. Everywhere. After that, my dad says, he won't have any problem. He'll have a special qualification no one else here has.'

Jay circled Channa, studying him from different angles, piecing together a puzzle that had unexpectedly changed shape. 'How will you go?'

I wanted to tell Jay everything did not always fit neatly together. Sometimes extraordinary things happened. A light appears, a new star, and it changes the way things are forever. He of all people should know that.

☀

'Could some people really have all the luck?' I asked my father, taking a chance on another full-blown lecture. Mahela's casual fatalism bothered me. 'Like, how come we don't have an estate?'

'So, that little pamphlet has piqued your interest after all, young man.'

'Is it the fault of the British?'

'Were you not listening the other day? Nationalisation is simply a restoration to pre-British common ownership. You see, in 1841, or roundabout, those crafty buggers Arbuthnot and Mackenzie expropriated the best agricultural land in the name of the crown and put it up for sale — only thing, they gave themselves the first bite.'

'A land grab?'

'Precisely. Bought huge tracts for peanuts.'

'But Jay's uncle is not one of them.'

'One of his scheming forebears would have been a colonial lackey and been rewarded with a piece of this or that.' He ran a finger along the spines on his bookshelf. 'I have a book here on plantation economics and the colonial enterprise.' He pulled out a mustard-coloured tome and opened it. 'The British knew that their future prosperity lay in places like ours.'

'You want me to read *that*?'

'Perhaps not yet.' He shut the book and put it back. 'I'm sure I have another Young Socialist pamphlet that might be more suitable. I'll find it for you after my bath.'

The phone rang while he was in the bathroom. One of mother's friends invited her to make a fourth for a game of bridge.

'Righty-ho. I just need to pick up some groceries from Premasiri's and then I'll be over.' She sang a French song about regret as she quickly jotted down her shopping list.

'Have you ever thought of a trip abroad, Ma?'

'I'm going to Colpetty.'

'British Council is sending Channa's father to England to do a study tour. If they do it for newspaper people, they must do it for radio people too.' I waited for a moment, before adding, 'Then I could come too.'

'Your father would not approve of me going like that, especially not with the British Council.'

'Why? To get a trip like that would be a sign of major good luck. He'd say you hit the jackpot, no?'

She smiled kindly. 'Doing well is not a matter of good luck, *putha*. Channa's father, Ronny, is a charmer — especially on a dance floor — but he is also a doer. Your father believes that luck is a substitute for hard work but chance is more likely to lead to an accident, not fortune.'

I could not accept that. She was wrong. Already, from what I had seen, I knew good luck existed and that my father's faith in it was not misplaced. Accidents had nothing to do with it.

'But don't you want to?'

'What I want, child, is a fair chance. For you and for me. That's all. And that darn earring. Where did it go?' She rummaged around the brass prayer bowl that collected all the mini-paraphernalia of our household: keys, jotters, pencils and coins. She had the knack of reducing all the world's problems to a single action within her remit. She found the tiny moonstone stud and smiled triumphantly. 'Anyway, I'm off now. Tell your father I've gone to bridge – if he remembers to ask.'

By the time he came out of the bathroom and called for her, she had left. I told him she had gone to play cards.

'At least she hasn't gone over to Voice of America.' He dug out his thick, webbed brown sandals from under a cupboard. 'I'm popping over to the club for another spot of Russian roulette, or whatever the heck they are playing at today. You should get on with that declension and conjugation business. At your age, it's the best thing you can do. Learn the lingo of the day.' He did not say mother tongue. It was not an oversight.

⁂

Wanting a night ride, I cycled over to Jay's house at full speed, dynamo whirring, cycle lamp blazing. The roads were empty. The sky pleated and starless.

At Jay's house, the gate yawned open; I did the two-note signal and climbed the outside stairs to the balcony.

He had his Dansette on low: I recognised the haunting hit single about not letting the sun catch you crying. Gerry and the Pacemakers.

Jay lay stretched out on a bench in front of a tank studying a brazen angel fish as it flashed its silver side in the moonlight.

'What's happened? Didn't you hear me whistle?'

Jay inclined his head slightly but said nothing. I was used to that – Jay thinking; when ready, speech would flow.

In his stillness, the admiration I had felt for him in our early days returned; disquiet always quickly faded in his presence. This evening though, Jay himself seemed to have faded. He rubbed his eyes with his knuckles like a child.

'Why are they called angel fish? They don't have wings. They can't fly.'

'With those fins, they look like angels?'

'How angels? You see how they poke each other. So aggressive. Flat, one-dimensional, aggressive triangles. A piece of swimming geometry. They should be called angle fish.' He sounded more angry than heartbroken.

'Sounds too much like *angler*.' As I said it, I saw that language – the organisation of words – was infinitely more interesting to me than geometry, algebra and arithmetic. I wanted to understand the meaning of words I had begun to notice: equality and dignity. The meaning of love.

Jay reached for a small pencil torch and switched it on. He shone it on the largest of the angel fish.

'You know, swimming like that in a tank, the poor bugger looks bloody nervous, like he doesn't know what might be lurking behind those rocks. Such a safe place, but he doesn't know it. So dumb.'

'In the wild, it isn't safe. Like, in a lake he could be swallowed by a croc any sec.'

'They come from the rivers of South America. Yeah, I guess it wouldn't be safe there. If only he knew the waters have changed. The situation has changed but he's still stuck, living with his ancestors' fears. Look, he thinks that leaf is a gourami ready to gulp him, so he takes it out on the smaller fellows. It makes him feel safer, scaring the others. I wish I could make them *all* feel safe.'

'Isn't that what you are doing for them? And for the birds?'

'But I can't. I can't make it really safe, that's the problem.'

The light caught his face as he put the torch away, his eyes smaller than usual, inept, the skin puffed up round the edges.

'The crows haven't tried anything again, have they?'

'Sunbeam is dead.' Jay's voice was hardly audible. 'I found him keeled over.'

'How dead?'

'Dunno. Guess it happens. Maybe God takes those he loves sooner.'

'That's love?'

'The love of God; that is what we must climb up to, Uncle Elvin says.' Jay spoke softly but determinedly. 'You bury the dead and learn to live.' He meant learn to live with loss and the inexplicable forces that shape a life, although I did not understand it at the time.

'Will we bury him in the garden?'

'I've done it already.'

I swallowed my disappointment and waited patiently for Jay to conjure up again the small yellow augury that had flashed so dazzlingly on the day we first met.

'He weighed like nothing in my hand. Breath all gone. Just feathers and tiny bones. Could have just crushed him like a piece of paper.'

I feared then that soon I would lose my friend too. Even at that tender age I had a suspicion of worse to come: unfocused, unbearable loss. A child who knew so little and yet was so sure of inevitable grief. I wished for strong, buoyant words then, the most buoyant words ever known. Words that would make some sense of the growing confusion of our lives.

When Jay finally spoke again, his voice was tentative; his words devastating. 'I need to be alone.'

I climbed down the concrete steps to the bikes and untethered mine from Jay's. I pushed off without bothering with the lamp; the wheels hissed in the dark. The huddle of fireflies halfway down the lane dispersed, blinking in disarray. I took the long way home, finding comfort in movement.

At the roundabout, I stopped. The roads were empty. I had not seen the girl who'd ridden with Jay since that day by Independence Hall but he had, no doubt, and it troubled me more than I could understand then. If only I could hold Jay back from stepping out of our world – my world – into that adult world that seemed so full of recrimination and regret. A world so messed up that it mistook death for the love of God.

The glass bowl of the streetlamp swelled with unnatural light.

5

At home, despite their bickering, I began to see my parents had a much stronger bond than I had thought. Their arguments were not as bitter as those described by Jay. They stuck together, disconnected from any extended family; no living grandparents, uncles and aunts rare as pink hippos. We were ultra-nuclear in a national maze of creeping family trees where genealogy was the number one protocol. Hunkered down, my father preferred comrades to relatives but relied mostly on an idealistic future. My mother found release by immersing herself in a world of microphones and mellow voices, a musical fantasy that stretched from the *Caribbean Beat* to the *Latin Quarter*, and letting off steam at cha-cha-cha. Her ability to flit between separate worlds appealed to me; I wanted to be able to do the same.

Wearing a fresh Fred Perry shirt and a clean pair of white shorts, I turned up at three thirty on the dot at her tea-break, as I used to do before Jay entered the scene.

'How nice,' she said and steered me proudly through the double doors. 'Come, *putha*. We have new regulations now but you can explore the archive room.'

On our way, we met Lazlo, the famous émigré guru of the gramophone.

'You like to be on the radio, like your Mummy?' He stooped over, leaking odours of minestrone and Old Spice.

My mother laughed in a way I hadn't heard before: lightly, frivolously. 'I'm not on air, Lazlo.'

'Not yet, Monica.' The bleak grey eye winked at me. 'What about music? You play the guitar?'

I surprised myself as well as my unsuspecting mother. 'I'm going to learn the violin.'

The archive room was locked and so, after a quick glimpse of the inside of studio three, I left.

Outside the building, a girl hugging a satchel and humming to herself blocked my way. Recognition turned to distaste. 'You're the one who goes cycling with Jay, no? What have you been saying to him about me?' Her yellow dress wrinkled around her chest in narrow feathery lines.

I forgot strategy and went defensive. 'Nothing. I've done nothing.'

'You're just a boy. You know nothing.' She soured each word before spitting it out. 'Don't spoil everything.'

Her warning made no sense. 'I'm only a friend.' I did not want to argue – and that *was* all I was.

'You are not a girl.'

I did not want to be a girl. I wanted to be a man; a hero who saves the world from evil, catastrophes and villains like Liberty Valance.

'He loves me. He will marry me.' She twisted a thin silver band of flux wire around her finger. It had been coiled into a flower-ring.

Danger steamed off her: beads of perspiration, incensed cheeks, bubbling lips. I wanted to tell her she didn't know what she was saying. Jay was a free spirit and would only tolerate another free spirit with him. Not someone who just hitched a ride, however weirdly she moistened her eyes. I wanted to add, for good measure, that marriage was an instrument of a retarded state – my father said so, and he should know.

Instead, I said: 'His mother won't let you.' I don't know why I mentioned Sonya, nor how I found the courage to taunt Niromi. The moment the words flew out, I regretted my mistake.

'That crazy woman? She belongs in a loony bin.'

I wished she had not said such a thing, and that I had not made her say it. I should have kept my mouth shut. It would become my principal policy in times of trouble.

＊

At a quarter to six, back home, my mother called me downstairs. A sourish man, inclement even in posture, togged up in a long national-dress tunic the colour of curdled milk, stood glowering at the dining table, pressing his hands on it, testing it.

'Here is your pupil,' she announced.

The man straightened up. 'Ah, so you are the *podi kolla* who needs improvement? Good. All encouraging to see nicely put out books.'

She had laid them out neatly on the table, together with a fresh, new blue exercise book.

'I'll leave you two to get on. There's a cup of tea on the table for you, *gurunanse*, and a lemon puff under the net.'

'All fine, madam.' The tutor, reeking of Vick's vapour rub, inspected me.

'Anything else we need, our little scholar can do, no?'

I braced myself. The bad feeling I had doubled.

'So, trouble with mathematics, correct?'

'Not trouble.' I reckoned I had forty-three minutes left.

'Oh? So, let us start with a little test then.' He pulled out a piece of paper from a large brown envelope.

To play the imbecile might be my best option. If I could do nothing at all, then the tutor would have to start from the basics, and that would mean I could coast for weeks, pretending. I did my best to frustrate him by loading every page of the blue exercise book with basic errors and gibberish.

After he had thoroughly checked out my father's bookcase, he proceeded to investigate the stack of newspapers, grunting. 'What is your best subject? What are you good at? Anything?'

I went for what had to be most aggravating. 'Art. And English.'

'Playing with crayons? English for what? The *suddho* have gone. You have a lot to learn. We better start with improving your mother tongue. You have your *Kumara Rachanaya*?'

I pulled one out of the Sinhala primers my mother had put on the table. 'Will we study Tamil also?'

'Don't joke with me, *kolla*.' He picked up the wooden ruler and twirled it in his hand. 'Right, do the chapter one comprehension exercises while I have a look at your maths.' The sighs and chortles that followed gave me more satisfaction than I had hoped. 'You really are a chronic case. Not surprising your mother has taken remedial action.'

At six thirty, my mother peeped in.

'So, you can help him, *gurunanse?*'

The tutor sniffed. 'Once a week for now, madam, is best to do. Tuesdays, if you don't mind, because I can go straight on to Mr Wilbur's house afterwards where also I give tuition.'

I pricked up my ears.

'Not to the Selvarajahs?' she asked, puzzled.

'No, no, not those people, madam. Mr Wilbur has that big house right at the top of Grebe Road. Such a bright boy, his son, Anura. So, I'll come same time again. Prompt corrective action is required if your son is to get anywhere.'

☼

The school holidays were coming to an end; I tried to slow the hours by fantasising about the end of the world. I cycled over to Casa Lihiniya every day, sometimes more than once, but Jay was never there. No one was there. Jay would not have gone back to the estate without telling me but with Niromi on the loose, I feared anything could have happened. Mahela at the milk bar had not seen him for days. Then, one afternoon, at the Fountain Café, I finally found him at one of the outdoor tables, neck sunk, his hands clasped together, idle. A green glass sundae bowl with leaf patterns stood empty, forlornly empty, in front of him and two spoons licked clean.

'Where've you been?'

Jay barely acknowledged me. He arranged the spoons neatly next to each other, backs upturned and wide-eyed.

I sensed bad news. Gerry? His mother? Niromi?

'The nesting kondayas are now gone.'

'Those birds next door?' Bad news, but in some way the best news: we were back on track.

'Yeah.' Jay started to massage one of his fingers.

'Is that a new ring?'

'Let's go,' Jay ignored the question. 'We should have another chat with Uncle Elvin.'

We used the back entrance and parked the bikes by the garages.

Like two scouts we dropped down and wriggled to the side of the house; I recognised Marty's voice, pitched higher than usual, on the veranda. Then Garibaldi bounded up and Jay had to clasp his hand over the dog's nose and stroke him behind the ears until he settled by him in a soft, whiny circle.

Marty's voice grew intense and urgent. 'Cut and run, Elvin, cut and run. It's the only way.'

'Can we not find a middle ground?'

'I have examined the issue very seriously. If I don't do it now, I will be the one who goes mad.'

'What about your obligations?' Elvin asked.

I rose to take a peek, but Jay restrained me.

'She will be provided for. The boy will be fine. So, it's up to you. I'll be fine too, as long as I don't have to hear any more talk. You know how she…'

'Do you know what you want?'

'I know what *you* want.'

The air thickened the way it does before a cloudburst. Jay made a gesture with his hand: *vamoose?* Not the right time for a chinwag. The dog whimpered, sweeping the ground with his tail. We slipped back towards the stables.

The telephone in the house began to ring.

We collected our bikes and set off.

'What were you gonna talk to him about?' I asked as we cruised towards the radio station.

'Just an idea.'

'What idea?'

'Stuff I need to figure out.' He flicked into a higher gear.

Ahead of us a two-tone Holden turned into Coniston Place. I didn't recognise the driver, but next to him, head thrown back, I saw Sonya laughing, carefree, in what inexplicably seemed to me the saddest light of that day.

'Look, isn't that your mother? Wanna catch her up?'

'Nah. Let's do that downhill race.' Jay didn't even bother to look.

The realm I had entered with Jay was making me increasingly uneasy. Whatever might be happening to the town, the trees, the birds, Jay's parents or mine, was not as worrying as what was happening to me.

☀

The rains became erratic, spluttering without abating for three days. Siripala did not speak again of the danger of a drought, but he blamed the Russians and the Americans for pricking holes in outer space and causing havoc. The big news on Grebe Road was that the Selvarajahs had their garden flooded.

I stayed in and reread my mystery books. Whenever a female character came into the frame, she would be transformed into Niromi; I could not work out why she kept growing in my mind.

My father took to pacing the dining room. Rain hadn't stopped his sport – in England the weather was surprisingly fine, he said, and horses madly raced to the summer's end – but his local bucket shop had been raided in a government crackdown on illegal gambling.

'The government says they intend to build a socialist state, but how can they if they pander to the religious lobby at every turn? The only problem with a bet on the horses is that the monks, who can't tell a horse from an ass, despise the idea and our lazy politicians rely on them to deliver the majority vote.'

'Are there no monks in Russia?' I asked surprised.

'In Russia, even Stalin didn't stop racing. I'd love a punt on the Soviet Derby, if that damn fool Siripala could put the bloody money on the right horse. Aniline, for example – one helluva Russian horse. There is nothing anti-socialist about a bit of fun. The point is that the turf club and the bookies should be open for anyone, like the cinema.'

'I heard they will be.'

'What, open the doors at the Turf Club? Where did you hear that?'

'Not that, but some people are planning to open casinos like in James Bond, I heard.'

'You heard? Is that what your new friends are up to now? Fixing up a Monte Carlo in Cinnamon Gardens?'

☼

On Sunday, my mother emerged from her room in a new sleeveless green polka-dot dress with a large, droopy bow at the side.

'Come, Kairo, time to go.'

My father looked up from his paper. 'Where are you two off to?'

'To see his music teacher.'

'A budding pop star now?'

'We have to find what he is good at. Before school starts again, I'd like him to have a go at the violin at least. He has expressed an interest and Mrs De Souza is a virtuoso.'

'Is that so? What's she doing in Colpetty then?'

'Giving tuition. Speaking of which, you better start *your* Sinhala lessons, Clarence. You really must make an effort. It's no joke. People are getting sacked.'

'Insisting on language proficiency is not the way you build unity, or even national pride – whatever that may be. If the government hopes to bring people together, it's going about it entirely the wrong way.'

'It's your job, Clarence. You can't risk it. If you think you can get one in the private sector instead, you better get a move on before things change there, too.' She picked up the car keys from the brass prayer bowl and marched out.

All the way over to Mrs De Souza's house, she kept mis-judging her gear changes. Every time she shifted, shoving the gear stick angrily, she'd race the engine and the clutch plate would shudder, shaved paper-thin, the cogs almost snapping as the car heaved closer to total disintegration.

'Ma, just lift your left foot gently as you press the accelerator with the right.'

'So, now you know how to drive? How, child? From a comic book?'

'Jay can drive.'

'I'm sure he can, but you just learn the violin, and leave the car alone. It's not a toy. Don't just fool around like your father.'

Mrs De Souza's house, a modern brutalist building, squatted at the end of a dead end. My mother stopped the car in the centre of the lane. 'Shouldn't they have something more artistic than that growing outside?' She pressed the entry-bell button lightly, twice, dismayed by the lone snake gourd hanging off the wall between the grey blooms of mildew.

A man with opaque eyes opened the door.

'Madam coming,' he muttered and led us into a musty room.

I had expected a professional musician's house to be more like Casa Lihiniya but this one had no glamour. I wanted to tell my mother we should give up and go but she was undeterred. She crossed the room examining the certificates framed on the wall and making sudden turns in an effort to stir the stagnant air. Only the score open next to a vase of lilies on the coffee table seemed to have any life, the notation wriggling on the nets like tadpoles. The prospect of having to tame them made me queasy.

Then Mrs De Souza appeared. She steamed across the room straight towards me. The water in the glass vase bubbled into a brown froth below the rotting leaves.

'So? Your ambition is to play the violin?'

No. Not any more – but my mother was not going to let me say that. I glanced at her for guidance, and then nodded politely.

Mrs De Souza was not impressed. 'You'll need a stronger neck than that, boy.'

I could tell she was one of those people you could never impress. She made a diversion and stopped at the sideboard. From under it, she pulled out a violin case and hauled it over as if it concealed a machine gun.

'Let's see if you can hold it properly, at least.' She shoved the case into my hands.

I put it on the table and opened the lid, feeling a twinge of disappointment: no gun inside after all – I would have known how to handle that. The long neck, the plump chest, the curves of the body were more voluptuous than I had expected. I undid the felt tabs and lifted the bow in one hand and the violin – so light – in the other, fearing things would end badly. Mrs De Souza started to groan. Her head began to quiver. I had a choice but I needed to act fast: put the violin back down or tuck it under my chin and aim to hit her right between the eyes.

Then she spotted someone come into the room behind me.

'Thank God, you are here,' she cried. 'Come and show this oaf how to pick up a violin. Come, Niromi, come.'

I spun around at the name. I should not have spun. The bow hit the lilies. The vase toppled. The foul water drenched the score. Mrs De Souza blew her top. My musical career was over before it had begun.

'Get out, you stupid, clumsy prat.' She turned to my mother. 'Get this animal out of my house, right now.' Her nose flared. 'Damn fool nincompoop.'

I expected Niromi to join the attack but instead she quickly moved to rescue the score. In the process, she managed to catch my eye and gave me a fleeting smirk of sympathy. I did not know why we had to have secrets, but she planted one in me that afternoon that has lasted longer than almost all the rest. For the first time, there among the fallen lilies, I grew jealous not of her, but of Jay.

My mother rose to my defence, deploying the full Radio Ceylon tones of the broadcasting heavyweights she admired: 'Really, Mrs De Souza.'

I mouthed a silent thanks to Niromi while my mother bundled me out.

'Her music must be awful, if her language is so vulgar,' she huffed, safely back in the car. 'Narrow escape, son. Thank God.'

⁂

The next day, Jay was at our gate ringing his bell with an urgency I had not heard before.

'Come down, will you?'

'What's wrong?' Fears of Niromi flashed in my mind, or the possibility that Gerry had died. 'Is it Gerry?'

'He's okay, now. Jus' come, will you?'

By the time I got down to the front gate, Jay was vigorously pumping extra air into the front tyre of his bike, although that could not have been the problem that brought him to me.

'Puncture?'

'Might be the bloody valve.' Jay worked the bicycle pump some more, then tested the tyre by pinching it. Impatiently, he wiggled the valve before unscrewing the connecting hose; then, licking his finger, he smeared the tip of the valve with a film of spit to see if it formed a bubble.

The small temple tree in the corner swayed in a gust of hot wind. A praying mantis on the garden wall pressed down while a line of beady ants on the top bar of the gate wavered, their tiny antennae measuring danger in the air.

'Is it okay?'

Jay fitted the small, black dust-cap onto the valve. 'My father has gone,' he said tersely.

'Where?'

'No one knows. Bloody disappeared. Didn't come home last night.'

'Must be one of those parties.' My mother often complained about the drinking parties that my father and his friends – men of a certain paunchiness – went in for these days. Shindigs that carried on into the small hours with the slap of dominos and carrom strikers punctuating the bawdy tales of rowdy raconteurs.

'They had another massive row. Then he buggered off. The Gymkhana Club is where he usually hides.'

'What do they say at the club?'

'Useless. My mother called. Nobody knows a damn thing. Iris was the one who raised the alarm this morning. He never misses his breakfast. Two-egg omelette every day at the eight o'clock pips, without fail.'

'Maybe he's with your uncle.'

Jay struggled to keep his mouth tight and thin. 'We tried his phone. No answer. Come with me, let's check out his place.'

☀

Elvin was in the smaller garage applying a chamois leather to his Austin Healey.

'Boys, you just missed a fine ride,' he greeted us. 'Want to do some polishing instead?'

'Was Pater with you?'

'On a joyride? Would he ever?'

'He didn't come home last night.'

'Another tiff with your mother?' Elvin raised an eye, more amused than concerned.

'But he's never gone AWOL like this before.'

'Not never. When you were little he was always storming off.' He folded the chamois and gave the bonnet another wipe. 'Don't worry. Your mother will reel him back soon enough.'

On our way back to Casa Lihiniya, Jay swore. 'Bastards. Both of them. Uncle Elvin knows more, no?'

'He'll tell your Ma, won't he?'

'You think we all live in a cage?' Jay asked. 'A cage you can't see.'

'Imprisoned, you mean?'

'Nobody cares fuck all.'

Marty did not turn up that evening. The next day Jay, searching his father's room, discovered that the roll-top desk had been left unlocked. The drawers had been emptied. The blue cardboard suitcase with the expandable metal hinges that was usually stored above the wardrobe was missing and also the snazzier Sea Island cotton shirts Marty had collected from his trips abroad. Jay pulled out all the drawers. 'He hates her. That's what. He hates her and hates me.'

The news of Marty's disappearance spread quickly through Colombo's networks of clubs and card tables. My mother was concerned about Jay but my father said that people of that ilk were always one step ahead. 'Must be dodging something.'

'I heard he has set up in Thailand,' she told him in a tone that suggested a wider conspiracy. 'Another woman.'

'The farther away he goes the better,' he replied. 'It'll take seven years before the tsarina can claim he is as good as dead and get control of all that ill-gotten wealth.'

'Ill-gotten? How can you say that? The poor woman must be in a state. Dilini says he had no money left anyway. He's left her in the ditch. Serious debt.'

'Rubbish. Poor, she is not. True, the misdeeds of his forebears are not her fault but she married into the pot. Those

Alavises, I heard, come from a pedigree line of rogues. The grandfather was the worst kind of feudal caste-clot turned capitalist. Ill-gotten is the kinder way of putting it. How do you think they got all that money? Working in the post office?'

I thought it my duty to interrupt: 'Maybe he's been kidnapped?'

'With his suitcase, you say?' my father sneered, once more bungling the opportunity to engage across the generations.

'Gangsters might have come and got him to pack his bags for a long journey.'

'Enough Perry Mason,' my mother said. 'Instead of those ridiculous detective stories, you better get on with your algebra for your tuition master tomorrow.'

My father tried to repair the damage. 'Don't worry, son. Your friend will be fine. These people have a way of turning any obstacle into an advantage.'

'Isn't that your ambition too, Clarence?' my mother shot back at him.

I left them to brew another useless row and cycled over to my haven – the bookshop on St Kilda's.

***

Mr Ismail, squeezed into a corner, his hair unsprung in places, used both hands to gather the pencil shavings strewn like dazed birds into a neat pile on his desk. In front of him, studiously ignored, a parcel of books lay unwrapped, the brown paper flattened and folded back and held in place by a bottle of Parker ink.

I slipped past him into the alcoves where the World War II comics and W. E. Johns paperbacks were shelved.

Mr Ismail sensed my hesitation. 'What are you looking for today, young man?'

'Don't really know.'

'Thank goodness. If we always knew what we were looking for, we'd never find anything new, would we?' He paused, his gaze shifting between the books and me. 'The thrill of the unexpected, if it is truly uplifting, is hard to beat.'

'You've discovered something, Mr Ismail?'

The smoky lower edges of Mr Ismail's face – his chin and jawline – were speckled with grey as though a recent fire had razed the surface. He pressed his fingers to the place a few inches from his mouth where the rough deepened.

'I have just realised I've been labouring under a serious misapprehension all these years. I've always assumed that people are driven by a curiosity at the heart of their being. That when they come here, to my book room, they are curious about the world and are keen to find out things.' He rubbed the corner of his mouth, lifting it even as his large eyes sank lower into his empty cheeks. 'But I find now that is not entirely true. You nibble at everything to find out the truth only when you are young. The adult mind just wants to forget, or escape.'

'Has something happened?'

'Yes,' he said. 'This sad revelation has come, like a kick from a mule, thanks to Mr Jonathan Wright, my vagrant American customer en route to a posting in Mindanao.'

'He'll come back.'

'Look at them,' he said and then wagged a finger. 'Or perhaps you should not.'

They were not totally unfamiliar: Harold Robbins, for one, I recognised from my father's bathroom shelf.

Using the tips of his fingers Mr Ismail pushed the pile away. 'I knew from his first visit that he had a taste for the racy, but I had hopes that his Peace Corps rucksack might have had room for an essay of Emerson's, or some Thoreau. Maybe even the sermons of Dr King, or Thomas Merton, or Black Elk – why not? But look at what he has carried all the way from America. You can see from the back covers that he bought most of them in a New York bookstore, except for those two from London and San Francisco. Thank God for Allen Ginsberg.'

'Maybe he hung on to his favourites.'

'Alas, no. He said this was the sum total of his being, although not in so many words. He wants to arrive in Mindanao a new man.'

The idea that these books had been transported from San Francisco, New York and London by hand was exhilarating to me and compensated for any disappointment Mr Ismail suffered over the content. I understood of course that most of the books in Mr Ismail's shop came from other places, but it had never struck me that a specific book might have travelled by ship or plane just as a person did, like the mysterious Jonathan Wright himself, to bring peace to troubled minds. What Mindanao, wherever that was, did not apparently need, could be my ticket to a new world.

'Can I get one? Maybe this?' I picked up a small, square, black-edged book and opened it to a poem celebrating a green automobile.

'I've never had one of these City Lights editions here before. I can't let it go just yet. In any case, you may be too young for that.'

I checked the bookshelf of older books and recognised the name Engels from my father's favourites.

'What about this then?' I pulled it out, intrigued by the title – *The Origin of the Family, Private Property and the State* – hoping Mr Ismail would cheer up seeing that curiosity still lived in a youngster's mind and that I had a browser's golden touch.

'Interesting choice. A subject we all ought to understand, young and old. An early edition, I believe, and Mr Engels' last book. I suspect quite heartfelt, beneath the academic veneer. I suppose any book needs a slice of the heartfelt to keep it afloat.' Mr Ismail counted the coins I handed over. 'I have to say, if not for you, my little bookworm, this valiant ship could very well sink.'

I smiled politely at the weak joke, but as I pedalled away, the worry that it might be true grew in me.

☼

Term began and I fell into an anxious routine in which I would drop by Jay's house before going home after school almost every day, unsure of what to expect and what to hope for. Although Jay had said Gerry was all right, his injury preyed on my mind too.

I didn't see Sonya, but Jay said his mother was becoming increasingly distraught with every additional day of Marty's absence. 'She is going nuts. Completely nuts.'

It made no sense to me back then. Marty and Sonya seemed to have no real need of each other; why would she care about his absence when he impinged so little on her life? I had no understanding of the compromises by which the adult world found its temporary equilibrium, whether between partners, lovers, families or tribes. In any case, I was more interested and pleased by the fact that Jay wanted to confide in me. 'What about you?' I asked.

'She doesn't understand he's walked out on her. Just proves he is the bastard I always reckoned he was and she is plain stupid to think that she's free but he is chained.'

I had not fathomed, in our boy's world, how deep an anger Jay had for his parents; even at that point I did not grasp how forcefully it would shape both our vanishing childhoods.

Elvin was the one who had explained the situation to Jay. Marty had called him from Singapore to say that he had put the formal matters regarding a divorce into the hands of his lawyers; he had asked Elvin to look after the family – Jay and Sonya – until a proper settlement was agreed. Although he had, as Jay put it, funked a showdown, all the temporary arrangements had been meticulously planned.

Not until the third day after Elvin's revelation did I see Sonya. She emerged from her room, clutching a bottle, and headed for the patio. Her hair was not good. Approaching a large pot of anthuriums, she stretched out a hand, unsteady but determined, and snapped off the long stamen of the biggest flower. Then she saw me and the moment of triumph receded. She screwed up her face. 'Don't you start pointing your damn finger either.'

'Are you all right, Auntie?'

An awkward scuffle broke out around her mouth and she drew breath. 'Much better,' she said. 'I'm much, much better now.' She spoke with the conviction of a person who had seen her chances slip permanently out of reach.

She stumbled and I caught her by the arm. Her perfume was that sweet, yeasty one that I had noticed before, but stronger this time – enough to make me almost gag.

'You want a drink, sweetie?' She lifted the bottle and examined it. 'Oops. Maybe not.'

'That's okay, Auntie. I'm looking for Jay.'

'Me too. Just like his father. Here one minute, gone the next. What are they up to?'

I said I would go have a look in the garden, by the bird cages.

'Try upstairs. Ask that bloody parrot. Seems to know more than the rest of us all in a pie.' She poked at her loose, awkward hair; nails lustreless, peeling. Those veins that had seemed like decorations when I first saw them had puffed up. 'You know, Kairo, the thing is they don't understand what I've had to go through. If my father was alive, he'd never have let them behave like this. He would have got them into line. He appreciated my intelligence. "Not just a pretty face," he'd say. He wanted me to study and become a doctor or a lawyer. I wanted to, you know. To be somebody. Not just a nobody. But my mother wouldn't have it – so old-fashioned she thought pleated slacks were made in Sodom and Gomorrah and spelt the end of civilisation even if it was Katharine Hepburn who wore them. If only he hadn't gone and died first…' She sat clumsily on a patio chair and looked at me dazed, suddenly unsure of my allegiance in her private war. 'You never say anything, Kairo. What are you waiting for? Don't wait so long you miss the bus.'

I climbed up to Jay's room. I wanted appreciation too. For anything. From her and from him.

Sinbad called out from his new perch, 'Hail-lo. Hail-lo, stranger.' Then he added, 'Niromi, Niromi, Niromi.' He twisted slowly on his perch.

Two of the tanks were empty.

'What's going on, Sinbad?'

'What pot apricot,' he squawked and raised his wings in a slow, solemn shrug.

From the balcony, I saw Sonya crossing the garden and heading for the aviary: her shoulders bunched, head slung low. At the cage, she fumbled with the padlock; despite Jay's precautions, she had a key. Once inside, she grabbed one of the sticks Jay had left by the pond and started swatting the air. Then she advanced on a cluster of budgies. Luckily the aviary was big enough for them to scatter out of her reach. After a couple of jabs at the birds, she yelled at them and two flew out of the door she'd left open. She followed them and started poking the branches of the neighbour's pomegranate tree with the stick.

'Auntie, the door,' I called out. 'The cage door is open.'
She did not even look up.

I raced down to the garden and across to the cage. The other birds were all huddled at the far end. I quickly shut the door and put the padlock in the ring.

By the time I caught up with Sonya, she had dropped the stick and was examining the crinkled stripes of a croton; I escorted her, without another word, back to the house.

Jay strode in from the porch, his long white trousers flapping; he had a pair of black cycle clips in his hand. A tall boy grown taller. He pushed back a drift of hair. 'What's happened?'

Sonya's wayward body tightened as she braced herself; that once-delicate face puckered by rip lines half-pulled. A cloudiness in her expression suggested she knew there were no soft landings. 'Are those handcuffs for me?'

'I went to the lawyer with Uncle Elvin to sort out all the stuff about Pater.'

'What can those two do? You should never have brought those birds here. You know he can't stand them.' She had her fists bunched and her arms rigid like poles ready to shove into the ground.

Jay tensed up. 'What have you done now?'

'He'll never come back with those birds and the racket they make. You really shouldn't have tormented him, son.'

'Me?'

'I had to let them out. I didn't know what else to do.'

'You let the birds out?'

'You can't be happy in a cage. We all know that.'

'It's okay,' I tried to calm him. 'The birds stayed inside. I closed the door.'

'You were with her? You let this fucking nutcase near the birds?'

'No, I just saw your mother when I arrived.'

'Saw what?'

'She got upset.'

'I think I might be getting upset.' He turned on his mother, contorting his face into a cruder, crueller shape than I had yet seen. 'It's *your* fucking fault. *You* chased him away. Didn't Uncle Elvin tell you? My father's gone because of you. Not the bloody budgies. He's left you for another woman. Do you understand? Another bloody woman. Because he could not stand it anymore. Your gallivanting, your boozing, your heartlessness. He could not stand it. And neither can I.' His face sank gaunt and tight with the tribulations of a misplaced adolescence, forced growth, a sharpened tongue, a future of faults.

A sense of foreboding is hard for a young boy to separate from terror, but I felt everything was going wrong and there was nothing I could do to stop the crash.

6

At Casa Lihiniya, Jay unleashed a daily barrage of verbal rockets at his mother; in our house my mother chastised my father for his moral disarmament, his gambling and his politics, with a sniper's precision. His shield was a newspaper; Sonya's was incomprehension. The low heat that had kept small squabbles simmering in the corners of each house rose; tempers reached boiling point.

The book I had picked up at Mr Ismail's on family and property proved to be of no help. I flicked over the pages until a paragraph on the Iroquois caught my eye: Iroquois boys could be brothers even though they might not have the same biological parents. This chimed with my feelings regarding friendship and kinship, but it also suggested that fathers and mothers were interchangeable and that disturbed me. Could what had happened to Jay's parents also happen to mine, if they were all so connected? Could my father also up and leave? My indomitable mother lose her grip?

On Sunday night, at the end of the first week in September, my parents had their biggest row. Howls of protest: 'How, Clarence, how?' My mother was desperate for a safe home in a country she feared had begun to slide into anarchy. My father's response was to accuse her of paranoia instead of reassuring her: 'Always complaining, you are. There is no reign of terror, no?'

The next day I fled to Jay's house. Casa Lihiniya was no longer the place of wonder it had once been, but it still offered me respite. It was not, after all, my parents who were fighting there, and my presence usually had a bizarrely benign effect: I did not need to say or do anything. In that extravagant atmosphere, my silence drew the venom out like a sponge.

I found Jay's mother shaking with confusion. 'What are you talking about, son? You are the one who made him feel so useless. A son who never lifted a finger to help him, making cage after cage to taunt him. Sin, *aney*.'

Jay had shrugged off the role of son and donned the cloak of her intimidator. His voice, like his language, had coarsened with the strains of rancour that I had thought only adults knew how to nurture.

'Lock up this bloody drunk bitch, Kairo. Lock her up before I knock her blathering head off.'

'Help this boy of mine, please Kairo,' Sonya pleaded. 'I don't know what has happened to him. Wanting to lock everyone up. Putting cages everywhere, knocking people's heads off.' She always knew who I was, whatever else swam in and out of her consciousness throughout those harsh and damaging days. 'All I said was that he won't come back unless we get rid of those birds.'

I said nothing.

'Let's go. Vamoose.' Jay stormed out.

'He used to have such a soothing face. So round and kind. My God, I could watch that sweet child sleep for hours. Forget the dips and lows, you know. But now look at him – kicking and kicking like someone else is stuck inside and can't wait to get out.' Her eyes amplified her own sense of distress. She stared at me as though everything in her life had been diverted from its true purpose, including me. I wanted to hold her distraught hands in mine and reassure her as only a boy like her son could, but I did not.

I left her counting faults on her trembling fingers and followed Jay, worried that more anger than love filled his veins and wondering whether he, too, would spin out of kilter soon.

At the milk bar I hoped to curb his wrath, to remind him of the warning in the Book of Proverbs.

'You shouldn't swear so much at her. It's not right. She's your mother.'

'I can swear at her, and do what I like, precisely *because* she is my mother. She brought me into the world, so she must face the consequences. If I can't shout at my mother, who the fuck can I shout at? You?'

I had no answer. Jay was wrong, but he was challenging me; challenging me to take responsibility for my life. It made me feel hollow and empty and bewildered. Pretending seemed so right to do sometimes – imagining what is not there and bringing it to some kind of life – and yet so wrong to do now. Both houses had become a cage where we each found our only safe ground diminishing daily.

'When I'm on my own I sometimes feel so lost,' I confessed.

For a moment, Jay seemed disorientated. Perhaps I should not have divulged my fears, not when things were going so wrong for him, but I was trying to find a lifeline for us both. I wanted the two of us to face things together.

'Is it okay to go on like this?' I asked, not at all sure what I hoped he would say.

'Like what?'

'Dunno. Is it better not to pretend? Better to face things?'

'Are you talking about my mother again?'

'No.' My toes curled in. Everything shrank. 'Just us. All of us.'

☼

Even though Sonya feigned deafness, I could see her melt every time Jay shouted at her; she became smaller, stripped down layer by layer. Her reduced face still had a screen glow, but she no longer illuminated the room; her mouth had cut loose from the pull of her eyes. The curve straightened, the radiance subdued. I could not understand how Jay did not see what was happening to her, the anguish he caused day after day.

I tried to comfort her once, after a mauling he had given her over the empty larder. 'Auntie, he doesn't mean it.'

'I know, my dear. It's not me he's angry with. How could he be, really? It's himself. He feels guilty about his father. As you grow, you just soak in the guilt. That's what happens. It's the emptiness in himself, not in the larder, that's the problem. I know it well. The feeling is not nice.'

'Guilty for what?'

'His father is a man who wants everything. If he can't have it all, he'd rather have nothing. Jay needs a better example.'

'Uncle Elvin?'

She tilted her head, bereft of the once-playful, spray-held curls, the hive now remade as a more conventional bun badly done. Her lips bare. 'You are a good boy, like a son to me, but you see Jay is part of me. We are the same body, no? He's a part of me that is hurting badly, like a crushed arm. I have to bear it. The pain. Whatever is wrong, I will not cut it off. You can't.' Her breath emptied. 'When a husband and wife don't get on, they can cut loose. But a child and his mother have to amputate more than their hearts if they need to separate.'

☀

Sonya troubled me. Jay troubled me. My inability to solve the problems of my life, despite the remedies I'd read, troubled me. Freewheeling alone down Guildford Crescent, I spotted Channa climbing out of a grey Opel Rekord and taking the hand of a man in a pale suit. As they headed towards the entrance to the Lionel Wendt Theatre, Channa saw me.

'Hey, Kairo. This is my dad.'

I rolled up to them and stopped. Slipping off the saddle onto the middle bar, I waited for Channa's father to speak.

Ronny inclined his narrow Brylcreemed head. 'I've heard a lot about you, young man.'

I didn't know what to say. I never held my father's hand like that. I didn't go arm-in-arm with Jay the way other boys did with their friends. A man walks alone, hands free.

'Going to get tickets for the new show.' Channa jerked his thumb at a poster on the theatre wall.

Shaku, my father's friend, had star billing, his name painted in large black, crackly letters over the silhouette of a horse. 'That's my dad's friend. His new play,' I said.

'At a time like this, daring – but also perhaps somewhat foolhardy.' I detected a touch of scorn in Ronny's thick voice.

'He says London is the best place for plays.'

Ronny's free hand flew to his throat. 'London? You like London?'

'I'd like to see Hyde Park. Channa's so lucky.'

'So, Channa has been talking, has he?' The glance at his son was sharp, but swiftly sheathed. 'Well, perhaps one day you'll go there. Maybe your mother will take you.'

After they went inside the theatre, I wondered why he mentioned my mother and not my father. Mr Cha-cha-cha.

☀

The following week, September's Binara moon rose sluggishly, weighted by the hopes of new evangelists. The government, in an effort to appease their growing demands and win the support of the Buddhist vote bank, promised new licencing regulations and more holidays. My father was appalled: 'The real ferment is in the poor bloody youth outside the Colombo precinct whose heroes wear beards and berets,' he muttered. 'Not in the shaven heads of monks.' For me the important result was that soon school would be shut even more often. Strikes plus holidays guaranteed at least a day off every week. One more day to spend loafing. Ferment for me was entirely domestic. My mother noticed.

'Kairo, you must learn to rise above, not run away.'

'But you don't. You just shout.'

'An argument is sometimes unavoidable when you want different things.'

'I heard you both.'

She stiffened. 'But we will never run from each other, your father and me, *putha*. You know that, no?'

I wanted to believe her but at that point I didn't know how anyone could know anything for sure. Maybe neither of them had anyone else to run to. Their parents had died before I was born; there were no other seedlings. We were a modern nuclear family – maybe the smallest one in the country.

At Casa Lihiniya, Jay suggested we make a lookout seat for the breadfruit tree that overlooked Bertie's back garden; he seemed calmer as we set to work on the patio where his father used to smoke. In the four months I had known him, Jay had grown longer and lankier. Now under a bell jar of koel calls and mynah squawks, gathering his tools, he was as big as any man in the world. Elvin peered in from the archway. He waited until Jay had finished the frame before stepping closer.

'You know, Jay, your mother is not at all well. She needs help.' One of his hands paddled the air aimlessly.

'So, what's new? She's always been a case.'

'She needs to go away for a few weeks. I've found a place where she can recuperate.'

Jay checked the measurement of the wood he had cut. 'Only a few weeks? Why not a few years? Why not forever?'

'I am serious, Jay. I am taking her to America.'

'America?' He tossed aside the ruler. 'Are you taking me too?'

'Maybe later, but she needs professional help and my friends in Washington are arranging consultations.' Elvin's flailing hand returned to his chest which he patted nervously.

Jay remained silent; my throat was dry, but I spoke. 'She'll be all alone there.'

'I'll be staying close by until she's ready to come back. They say it could take a couple of months. She'll be in a clinic while I attend to some business matters.' Elvin reached out and placed his hand on Jay's arm. 'You see, even though they were never exactly happy together, it has been a huge shock. It is not easy for a beautiful diva to come to terms with the idea of another woman. Or, indeed, another man. But your father has his reasons too: Eros is blind. Jealousy unchannelled is always a problem. Perhaps one day Marty will be able to talk to you, man to man.'

'That's never going to happen.'

'You are his dear future. He will do what he can. He is providing for you, Jay. He has made all the arrangements.

There will be a divorce, once your mother is ready to deal with it. It is quite a thing in an old-fashioned town like this, but she has me. I will always be there for her. Your father understands. So, for now, you'll have to hold the fort on your own. I'm sure you are entirely capable, but I've asked Mrs Peiris to keep an eye.' The speech had been difficult for him; he turned to me and tried to end on a more upbeat note. 'And you, young man, you'll make sure he doesn't get up to too much mischief, won't you?'

'Will Mrs Peiris stay here?'

'Sonya wouldn't like that. It's all rather complicated. Not for you boys to worry about now. Iris will be here.' As a sweetener, he added, 'And Jay, can you take the cars out once in a while to give them a run?'

Jay pretended not to care. 'What for? They're not horses.'

'Those engines need running; the wheels need a spin. Just keep it under fifty.'

'Fifty miles per hour?' I asked in disbelief.

'He likes a bit of a race, our Jay. But don't egg him on, boy. As for the horses, they'll be looked after by Major Carson. He's been grieving since he lost his poor Tamerlane in the polo.' He paused over another recalcitrant nut that needed to be cracked. 'I'd avoid Sulaiman though, if he turns up. Fellow has developed a grudge after that business with the son's eye.'

Elvin waited but neither of us said anything more. After a while, he lit a cigarette and retreated inside the house.

We continued building the tree-seat: cutting wood, dove-tailing joints, passing each other chisels and files, our thoughts buried in sawdust. I tried to look into the future but saw no hint of the intersections to come.

Eventually I broke the silence. 'She'll get better soon.'

'Going to America won't fix it.' Jay traced a knot in the piece of wood with his finger and coaxed a hidden matur-ity into his narrow throat. 'You can cover it up, but it will always be there: failure. Longer than anything you use to hide it.'

True: I could not erase the guilt I felt for not ever meeting my father's expectations. My sense of inadequacy flared when I could least resist it, stemming from the time when my father had handed me a cricket bat and I had held it the wrong way unthinkingly. 'The blade has to face the ball, no?' My father had snorted, baffled by my incompe-tence. Nothing could mask the failure. Not then, not now.

I watched Jay carve an intricate pattern around the knot with his whittling knife, expressing with his hands more than he ever could with words.

Since the trip to the estate I had been trying to under-stand how Jay saw other people: Gerry, Niromi, his mother. How could he switch his feelings so swiftly? Was it a strategy of survival, or of alienation – another word I puzzled over. Might Jay turn away from me too? I wanted to know if he reacted the way he did because of what had happened to his family, or to him, growing up. And was there something I should do to protect myself?

I was not with Jay the day Sonya swept all her make-up into her red leather box bag and set off for America. I wanted to be there, afraid it might be the last time I would see her, but my mother insisted I finish my homework and I was not going to argue with her; I had learnt from Jay what not to do with parents. Even Sonya had pleaded once: 'You must understand, a mother may have faults but we have an impossible job trying to keep a sieve afloat. Listen to yours, Kairo. Don't do everything Jay does. He's still learning and he has his father's faults to deal with. Marty is a very jealous man. He gets jealous even of my lipstick when he sees me put it on. And jealousy wrecks everything.' I had coaxed her to play the harp again to ease her mind while Jay was out but her fingers had grown sluggish, the notes unkind. I sensed then that she would not find the right ones again until many things had changed in her life and mine and all that had unspooled was wound again tighter and firmer.

By the time I got to Casa Lihiniya that day, Sonya and Jay had already left for the airport. I could only hope that there had been a reconciliation between them as he helped her into the car, or maybe even at the airport where, in films, people pin their hopes to metal railings and kiss and wave and forgive, but I knew the scene was unlikely. Even at that unfledged, uncertain age, I knew reconciliation required recognition. You needed to see the one you had to say sorry to; it didn't work if all you saw were reflections in a mirror, or the flaws of the past.

I waited for Jay to call but no signal of any kind came that night.

When we met up the next day, I asked him if he was all right.

Jay stroked the long curve of his slender neck and let a hint of clemency wrinkle his face. 'So scared she looked. She kept searching her handbag like she'd lost something.'

'America will help her.'

His expression altered and he gave me the same withering look he'd given his mother every time she'd spoken to him since the first signs of corrosion appeared. 'Are you a doctor now?'

☼

In the days that followed, with neither of his parents around, Jay became both the master and the child of Casa Lihiniya; the house adjusted itself around him like a shell. I envied the freedom he had to grow, not knowing then the limits within which we must each find equanimity.

His interests shifted from the birds to the fish, the trees, the plots, in quick succession; then the cars. He seemed to be always one step ahead of me. Every time I caught up, he'd spring ahead or dive to the side with a quick grin. I did my best to keep the tanks clean, the fish fed, the birds supplied with seeds and fruit, whether he noticed or not.

The biggest problem I had was with Sinbad, who seemed to suffer the most from Jay's unpredictable bouts of neglect. If the parrot had not seen Jay, and talked to him or been talked to by him, it would creep into Sunbeam's old birdcage and sharpen its beak on the wires.

Some days, left alone at Casa Lihiniya, I was surprised to discover that I longed to go home.

☀

Although my mother had shed the most conventional aspects of her colonial-era upbringing, she was not a bohemian in the world of broadcasting; she marked Jackie Kennedy, and ordered her tailor to cut her slacks accordingly. Usually she gathered her thoughts silently at breakfast, before taking charge of the coordination of the morning pre-office routines once my father appeared, string vest awry, rubbing the faint memory of trumpeting from the bridge of his nose. But this sun-filled morning she was on the edge of her chair, on doubled-up seat-cushions, with her face close to the table, whispering into a steaming teacup.

'What are you doing, Ma?'

She put the cup down and quickly spread some cold margarine on her toast.

'Practising. I have an announcement to make.'

My heart dropped down to a new low. More tuition? Another lasso to dodge? 'What?'

'Malini can't do it next week, so Lazlo asked me to give it a go.'

'A go?'

'Programme announcements. He says I have the perfect voice. If I pass the audition, I could be on the All Asia

Service.' She tightened her shoulders, drawing them in. 'Your father won't like it. So, let's not tell him, okay?'

It could hardly be kept a secret, if her voice was going to be on the airwaves. My father would have to switch off even shortwave to keep her out of earshot. But instead of deriding her, I said, 'Let's hear you, Ma.'

She began to intone the sort of sentences people keep in the background as broadcast burble.

'Sounds just like the radio. You could do even the news dead easy.'

A coil in her eased; she flopped back and added a spoonful of pineapple jam to the toast. 'Now that would really upset him. For all his talk, he gets so discombobulated when things change.'

I was relieved and proud of her – of her sanity and her career, her pink rayon blouse and beige slacks. I did not say anything more to her, but I let her catch my hand and hold it briefly as I brushed past.

I didn't mention her plans to Jay, not wishing him to compare her to Sonya – someone who lived in a limelight, who needed special protection the way glossy photographs did, or Hollywood movie reels. But I could sense, even if not quite understand, that what they both sought was independence – their own form of independence. My mother needed it to feel secure and safe; Sonya to feel free from the sadness of unfathomable loss.

☼

That evening I was selecting which of my collection of *Mad* mags to trade for something seriously steamy, when I heard my father's actor friend Shaku boom out: 'Hail, Clarence, "Why looks your grace so heavily today?" Trouble afoot?'

Shaku always had two or three buttons of his candy-stripe shirt undone showing his broad, coppery chest like Charlton Heston in *Ben-Hur*. Things extraterrestrial fascinated him and he could recite Brecht as well as Shakespeare at the drop of a button.

I peeped from the landing and saw him swagger in, cap cocked, arms open, and do an exaggerated bow. 'Hiding at home from the tumult, art thou?' His deep, resonant voice always mesmerised me.

'Not hiding, working. Monica is out tonight and it is a good chance to get the form sorted for tomorrow.'

'Never say die, eh? Good man. So, what's the old girl up to?'

'New job at the radio. They've apparently asked her to do announcing now. Next thing I know, she'll be in my bloody ear every time I turn the wireless on.'

She must have called and told him she had passed the test; I was disappointed not to have been the first to know.

'So, she'll need some voice training then? Tell her to come to me.'

'Training?' My father sounded a little wary. 'No, she'll be fine. She can put it on fine. Come, sit, sit.'

'Will she do the news? High time someone started announcing real news on air. Place is buzzing – MPs ready to cross the floor at the glimpse of a toffee wrapper – but the radio might as well be in the House of Usher.'

A chair scraped the floor; I wiggled closer to the banister.

'Can't see her exchanging *Pot Luck* on a Tuesday evening for a reading from *Das Kapital*. You have to understand, Radio Ceylon is broadcasting from the site of the original Jawatte lunatic asylum. Same damn place. There is more than a residual effect.' My father undercut the dubious joke with a sharp snort. 'Have a drink?'

He called Siripala and asked for the bottle of arrack and two glasses. Ice and ginger ale, he added, not that Siripala needed to be told.

'How's the play?'

'Over, *men*.'

'So soon?'

'You didn't come?'

'Sorry, Shaku. Too much right now on my mind.'

'We might put it on again next year. Lorca is not exactly the bundle of fun people want right now.'

My father's face seemed to lose the joviality he kept for show. 'Ah, yes. The people.'

For him, 'the people' were a mass of misled victims who needed to be saved from tyranny; for Shaku, they were an audience who mostly needed to be entertained. Their common ground was not unlike mine and Jay's: an area of bonded hope and unbounded freedom, perhaps best left unexamined at its core.

'What about the new theatre project? Your People's Palladium?'

'Helluva how-do-you-do, that was. That bugger Tootsie put a spoke in it. You know the chap, don't you?' He raked his fingers through his thick, curly hair.

'A real-life Sooty Banda. What's the joker done now?'

'Hospitality and tourism is the thing, he says. That's the future for this country. Hotels and sin bins, not amateur dramatics.'

'Does he really expect people from other countries will be tempted to come here?'

'No, *men*.' Shaku waggled a hand indicating continuity more than the stated contradiction. He put on the voice of an arch inveigler: 'From England, Holland, Portugal, all those old imperialist countries, they'll come rushing – in their bathing costumes instead of their gunboats. This time we will be the ones to plunder them. Stolen enough, no? Now let them come and pay through the nose for sun-stroke and malaria.'

'Don't be ridiculous.'

The conversation paused as Siripala handed out the drinks. Glasses clinked. Ice cracked. Shaku resumed.

Face pressed against the uprights like a jailbird, I basked in the baritone flow.

'Seriously, Clarence, fellows like Tootsie not only have plans, they have contingency plans. Plan A, B, C. One for this government, one for the next, and one for anything in-between. If by some miracle the government survives, he'll spin socialism into a cup of tea – and if it falls, he'll make Colombo the capitalist beacon of the East.'

My father sank deeper into his chair at the prospect. 'The prime minister is too distracted by foreign issues, so her Press Bill is bound to fail, no? We have no left left.' He stopped, momentarily stumped by unexpected repetition in his line, jolting me out of a reverie.

'That's no bad thing, no? Who wants a press gag?'

'I disagree. On this newspaper issue, I have to say, I am with madam PM all the way. Lenin made the same point – to let the bourgeoisie run the press is to aid the enemy. You cannot have one family controlling all our newspapers.'

'But if the government tries to take over the press the agitation will be huge. People prefer a family driven by profit to a bunch of politicians after power.'

'You really think so?' My father rattled the ice cubes in his glass. Hearing the doubt in his voice, I realised I wanted my father to be right, always right. Not to lose the high ground. Neither man said anything for a while. Then, as another light dimmed in the house, my father asked, 'Does it not bother you, Shaku, this business about language?'

'Why? On stage we are always speaking somebody else's words.'

'What about the slogans? Things being whipped up.'

'You mean like Tootsie's nonsense?'

'Out on the streets. The crowds braying. If you are Tamil, or Muslim...'

'You know, Clarence, maybe it is time to put on *Mother Courage* and say to hell with the bloody handcart. Permit me to adapt a line, my friend, to our dark days.' Shaku pulled at the front of his shirt, opening it some more, before declaiming: 'O unhappy land, where be our true heroes?'

☀

In war, a city would be choked with sandbags, roads blocked by oil drums and barriers, gun bunkers and security posts. In a state of emergency, there would be curfews and clampdowns. Jay's balcony, under siege, had sheets pinned from the roof to the railings, all the fish tanks were covered with asbestos boards. I crept in from the outside stairs and found Jay fitting a bolt to his bedroom door.

'The trouble is women. They go mad when they come here. What is it with this fucking house?' He banged the door shut and secured it.

Niromi sprang into my mind, but I acted bemused. 'Who?'

'Mrs P. She wants to fumigate the whole place. One lunatic is pumping smoke into Pater's room and she's got two other assholes spraying DDT outside the kitchen. They'll be up here any minute.'

'Shelltox. We do that.' I often sprayed it from a pump-can pretending I was wielding a flamethrower, whooshing out an oily mist over the back garden battling the axis powers of cockroaches and mosquitoes.

'You don't have fish tanks to worry about. Birds. It could kill them all.'

'So, tell her. Maybe she doesn't understand.'

'She can't hear reason whatever you shout at her. Can't she see that fish eat larvae? My system keeps everything in balance. I've shown you, no?'

Hammering started on the other side of the door, followed by a plea. 'Open up, Jay. Have to purify your room, no?'

'Not with DDT, you don't.'

'No, *aney*, special incense. Have to clean the place of all these bad things, *putha*. Someone put a *hooni-pooni*, no? Now must do the reverse.'

A lifetime of childhood battles puckered below Jay's lip. 'Stupid woman doesn't know what she's talking about.'

He didn't let Mrs Peiris in and eventually she retreated to supervise the appeasement of the demons prowling around the garden.

'She's only trying to help, isn't she?'

'Uncle Elvin is the one she's after. Obsessed. Convinced my mother is going to destroy her chances. Haven't you seen how she juts her front every time his name is mentioned? Now she wants to put a charm in the house, first to neutralise my mother a million miles away, then to trap him. That's what.'

'Isn't she married?'

'The husband is a drunk. Stuck in Bandarawela. She's always preening herself for a knight to come galloping to her rescue. She's even got the horse saddled for him. Only Uncle Elvin doesn't see that.'

Jay sounded like a grown-up again, sketching out the shape of a whole life in a phrase, pinpointing the links that bound one person to another, their frailties; sticking pins mercilessly. This was a different Jay from the one who tick-led sloth bears and coddled parrots. This was a Jay accus-tomed to the fluttering of clipped wings, the cracks of a weakened heart. A boy who was becoming a man I didn't want to understand.

The days and the weeks merged; the moon lost its glow and its phases began to collapse into each other. Lancelot, the lamplighter, cycled increasingly shakily with his long teeter-ing pole to flick the switches of the streetlights; electricity began to fluctuate in houses small and large. I returned in my mind to the magic of Elvin's estate; the night hours sprawled out under the trees talking in that strange, still atmosphere where our words seemed the only human sounds for miles around. Would anywhere ever be like that again? I imagined our slumbering town turning into a metropolis with modern subways and futuristic flyovers, traffic lights at every street corner. Miss Universe and Mr Atlas both on the same stage at the planetarium, in the middle of the racecourse, and no one realising that this was once a playground for a pair of kids – sometimes a trio, potentially a foursome – who had nothing better to do from morning till night than make up stories of gangsters and rustlers, braves and warriors, and hope that their lives would prosper like the celluloid stories of a panoramic screen.

From time to time, my mother would implore me to study more.

'While your school is in such chaos, you must see your tuition master as your educator. Make sure you do the homework for him.'

'Why do we need a school at all then, Ma? Should be closed down completely if it is so useless that it takes thirty hours a week to do what he does in forty-five minutes.'

'What thirty hours?'

'Six hours a day, five days a week. Isn't that the new plan for schools? I saw in Thaththa's newspaper.'

'Nothing wrong with his maths,' my father chortled from the dining table. I wondered if the Iroquois were wrong. Perhaps a special bond that linked a son to a single father did exist, hidden deep in the general mess of tribal life and mixed chromosomes.

'The tuition master says you make mistakes all the time with the easiest of things, Kairo. You are not trying to fool him, are you son?'

'Can't concentrate, Ma. In this house, how to concentrate?'

More approving noises percolated from my father's throat.

'Well, you better do it anyhow.' My mother gave him a scornful look before leaving on her round of errands.

He came over and inspected the Sinhala textbook I had been pretending to read.

'Any good, son?' he asked.

'Makes me ill.' I made a face. 'Smell the paper.'

'Never mind the paper, what about the story? Can you follow?'

'So boring. They should put a detective or outlaw in it. Who wants to read about bullock carts and pumpkins?'

He screwed up his eyes to track the plump, curvy script. 'Can't even follow a newspaper in the mother tongue. Wish I could at least do that. It's not enough to have a dream any more, it has to be dreamt in the right language. Maybe they are right, son; English may not be it. We should try doing this together. Isn't that how you learnt to ride a bike?'

'But you never rode a bike.'

'I know. but I was there, wasn't I?'

'Thaththa, this stuff is really boring.'

Unlike my father, I had no reservations about the language I used; its private uses were more important to me than the shared use at home, or with Jay. I wanted it to keep secrets, provide a lifeline for my thoughts, a page that opens a door into another world whenever I wanted to escape.

Halfway through my daily ritual with pen and paper, a horn beeped from outside the gate. Jay called out my name.

I found him bright-eyed and beaming in the driving seat of a poppy-red VW Beetle, his arm hanging out of the wound-down window.

'Come on,' he drawled. 'Get in.'

'What are you doing in that?'

'Giving Uncle Elvin's beasts a run. Come on.' He gunned the engine, scattering the crows that had gathered pecking at the potholes on the road. 'Time for another lesson, pardner. I've seen just the place for it.' He did a triple beep, reverting to his old self. 'Every boy should learn to drive. How else can you be the captain of your destiny?'

'Sure.' I had feared the chance might never come. I jumped in and stuck my thumb up. 'Chocks away.'

The engine whirred, more an aeroplane than a car. We taxied down past the last house.

'Almost brought the jeep. You are big enough, but the gears are tough for a rookie.' He stopped the car. 'Right, let's give it a go then.' We exchanged places.

'What do I do if another car comes?'

'Nobody comes this way. The road just finishes nowhere.' Half a mile down the slope the savannah — a scrubland of grass — and the swamp oozing from the canal mingled.

'What about gangsters?' Siripala's stories of bootleggers who collected *kasippu* from the illegal stills by the canal and did devil dances on the graves of their victims swarmed in my head.

'No one can catch us,' Jay grinned. 'We could fly in this, if we had to.'

He made me go over the foot routines and do the gear changes again and soon we were rolling down past a donkey field with me at the controls.

'If you practise, soon we can take two cars out and do a chase like in the movies.'

'I like this Beetle,' I patted the dash and let my hand dance above the gear stick.

'She loves you, yeah, yeah, *machang*, but keep both hands on the wheel.' Jay reached over and steadied it.

At the end of the road, Jay took over and showed me the first of his repertoire of stunts: a swift three-point turn. Then he got me to time him doing nought-to-sixty back up the road, with his watch up against the speedometer, keen to match the test-drive stats from *Autocar*. We were out by five seconds. 'It's the gradient,' Jay muttered. 'We need to find a flatter road.' He did an emergency stop, nearly snapping my neck. 'Always be prepared,' he warned. Then he made me drive again, for hours it seemed, my heart racing as much as the VW engine. Then he announced: 'Time to try a big road.'

I gripped the wheel. 'What about the traffic?'

'Don't worry. You'll be fine.'

We headed back past our house and onto Fife Road. I had to skirt a bicycle first, then a godamba-roti handcart; on the main road, a bus and a tricky yellow-top taxi that couldn't decide between going left or right. By the time we made it back to Elvin's garages, the sky had turned dark. Exhausted, I closed my eyes.

Jay climbed out and delved into the toolboxes on the workshop table, hunting for a timing gauge. He turned on the radio. The tipsy crooner reminded me of Sonya wafting through her airy house in those carefree early days, even though it might have been my own mother who had programmed the show.

'Have you heard from your mother?' I asked Jay.

'One postcard.'

'From Washington?'

'Her handwriting is like a little girl's. She says she's all cut up that Harpo Marx has died – like it matters fuck all.'

'Has your uncle said how she's doing?'

'He wrote too. Says America is more complicated than he expected. I guess he means the treatment. Says he may be back for a few days before Christmas, but she won't.'

'He'll leave her there?'

'For a week, then he'll go back to America.'

'With you?' I joked, daring to voice the unthinkable.

'Would you mind?'

'What about your father? If she isn't here and you are alone, won't he come back?'

'Luckily there are legal and financial reasons that make it difficult. He has to stay abroad, thank God. Don't know what I'd do if he showed up now.'

'You prefer to be alone?'

A neon glow blinked near the gate, pricking the shrouds of a lasiandra bush.

'A firefly is never alone because when he looks up all the stars sparkle with him,' Jay said solemnly. I believed him, but I wanted my life to be more than a brief dance of sparks.

When I got home, I hung around the garage examining our old car with a fresh interest. Siripala had dropped my mother and my father at their separate functions earlier and brought the Anglia home to await their next instructions. The procedure on these occasions was for one or the other to call and ask for a pick-up when they were ready. Some nights, like this one, my father was dropped back home by his friend Abey who'd shout out a 'Cheerio' even before he had climbed out of the car. Now my father's arracky breath wafted through the concrete air-bricks of the garage wall as he fumbled for its support, cursing the shoe-flowers in his way and carrying on an argument in his head.

'Siripala,' he swung for the wall as Abey drove off. '*Kohedtha?*'

'Sir?'

'Where? Where is madam?'

'Madam not back yet.'

My father harrumphed, reeling into the house.

I heard him bellow down the telephone. 'I'm in, yes, I am bloody in,' as if he had broken into a fortress. 'Count me in.'

Then he clumped up the stairs and Siripala retreated to his quarters to smoke in the dark. A gecko chuck-chucked and the bullfrogs across the road began to croak. Soon the chorus was joined by flamboyant snores from the master bedroom.

I slipped into the driver's seat of the Anglia. I did the checklist that Jay had taught me: adjust the mirror, test the pedals, find neutral pumping the clutch. I ran my hands around the steering wheel trying to find the balance between a light touch and confident control and urged the car to silently roll down the slope and run like a trickle of silver towards the adventures that would make me a man.

I was determined to become a real driver, independent and free, an equal partner, sooner than Jay would expect.

☀

The next Sunday, Jay drove us over to Independence Square in the VW. I took the wheel and did a few fast laps circling the hall. Then Jay wanted to do the road tests again: quarter-mile top speed, nought-to-sixty. He had brought a piece of chalk to mark the starting point on the surface of the road and a stopwatch for precision.

'If we can break the twenty-second barrier, we'll be ready to put the Austin Healey through its paces. It'll do it in half the time.' Jay grinned. 'Imagine that.'

'Won't your uncle mind?'

'The race horse is the one for the workout, much more than the cart horse.'

'But he said not to go over fifty.'

'You didn't complain the other day. Anyway, he's not here.'

We swapped places. I opened the tiny triangular window and directed the airflow onto my chest, wriggling to keep my bare skin from sticking to the vinyl seat. I didn't complain because I wanted to go as fast as he did, faster.

We did three runs but couldn't reach sixty in under twenty-three seconds.

'I need to tune the engine again. Listen. Doesn't sound right, does it? You have to get the idle just right.'

'Is it the fuel pipe like on that Landmaster on the estate?'

'It's the carb. Have to strip it and clean it out, but for now just an adjustment with the fuel mixture might do the trick. I showed you the screw, didn't I?'

A black Ford Prefect came around the bend of the sports ground. Mrs Peiris was driving, head held high, eyes firmly on the road ahead. The car wobbled as she used the tail of her sari to swat something on the dashboard, not noticing us.

'A real menace,' Jay nodded at her car as it picked up speed. 'You can't tell what people are up to. Be careful of who you trust.'

'Mrs Peiris?'

'Adults. The whole lot.'

'I can look after myself.' The words sounded hollow in my soft mouth, but I had to be brave.

Jay turned the mixture screw right down and asked me to start the engine again. He pulled the throttle cable to race the engine and made another adjustment. I returned to his side.

'When you move up into the next form in school, you need to watch out. Some of the boys in college do nothing but fiddle with their things. Some teachers are even worse. Dixie especially. He's a pederast.'

'I'll be fine,' I said, although I did not know what he meant.

'The trouble is fellows just give in. Bugger flexes his fat doo-dah and everyone folds up.'

'I won't.'

'Good. Don't ever stand near him. Even if he asks you to come right up to his desk. Watch out for his hands. He'll get you to put a string down your trousers and leer like a prick.'

'Don't worry. I'm never the favourite in class.'

'People like us never are.'

I hesitated. 'Like us?'

'You can see beyond, Kairo, can't you? See better things.' Jay's eyes drew back, the pupils shrinking. 'What do you wish for, most of all?'

'Dunno.' I could not put it into words. Sometimes, at night, a massive weight would pull me into a dark pit; I wished then for a hand to reach out and save me. I knew every detail of that hand: the long supple fingers, ring-marked, with smiling folds around each knuckle; a smooth palm soothing an interrupted life line; a slender powerful wrist that would winch me back from the brink. Please God. I tried: 'Maybe I wish I could know what's going to happen. What I will be.'

'I wish I could make something both beautiful and unbreakable,' Jay said. 'When I was seven, my mother gave me a fabulous glass gondola. I could hold it in the palm of my hand. It had amazing coloured drops floating in the glass. She'd brought it back from Venice as a souvenir. She seemed so happy then. I used to stare at it for hours wondering how they made it so smooth and how they got the colours so bright. But then one day, she barged in and grabbed it off my table. She said she couldn't bear it in the house anymore and threw it out of the window. Smashed into a hundred pieces.'

'She really threw it out?'

'Why she suddenly hated it, I don't know. My father was the one who didn't like it.'

In that moment, watching him, I saw how our imaginations hovered at separate levels, a palimpsest of clouds that seemed to merge when seen from below but which floated at different altitudes: the cumulus, the altostratus, the cirrus. I knew them all. The shapes, the names, even if not the word to describe their interaction any more than our own. Jay's usually buoyant face had faint creases; some aspect of its structure – the bones – had shifted and cast shadows on the surface of the skin.

'I need to go see Niromi now.' Jay closed the engine cover and got back in the driving seat. 'We'll try the timing again another time.'

'The girl?'

Jay noticed the awkwardness in my voice. 'Yeah. You know, Niromi. I'll drop you off at the top of Jawatte Road.' I squeezed my eyes tight to stop anything escaping.

❈

At home, I snuck upstairs and sank into a Western for old times' sake: purple sage, tumbleweed, cottonwood. Easy riders.

At a quarter to four, my mother's colleague, Dilini, arrived to pick her up for bridge.

'Come in for two minutes, have a cool drink. I've got to finish this incident report. You won't believe what happened.'

'Why? What happened?' Dilini, a tall woman, rarely stood straight; her tone was always inquiring, her posture tipped forward by her unnecessary heels and the impeded height of men she said she was doomed to meet.

I crawled to my listening post on the landing.

'You know, that fellow with his silly chilli bomb at the reception desk?'

'Why was he dressed up like a gladiator? What was that all about?'

'God knows. All only cardboard armour, but he went berserk. They say he's from Angoda. Maybe looking for another mental asylum. But the thing is, what the hell was Edmund thinking? He put his ghastly arm around me? Can you believe it? What kind of excuse…'

'Oh, I can well believe that. Once they've been on air, they think they can get away with anything. They all imagine they are bigger bongos than they are.'

'Fatheads. Not real men.'

Dilini snorted in agreement.

I wanted to be a man like no other man. Tall and lean; I wanted my mother, and my father, to be proud of me.

After my mother left with her friend, I returned to the ranch in Wyoming until the heavy throb of a pickup truck drew me onto the balcony. Three men got out of the vehicle: two empty-handed, one with a briefcase.

They fanned out across the road; the mongrel that licked its paws outside the house next door slunk away. It could have been high noon in a different time zone. The one with the briefcase stood in the middle of the road and surveyed the patch of wild trees. 'You see what I mean, *machang*? Put the apartment block diagonal and you can really have the windows facing Adam's Peak.' He pulled up one of the strands of barbed wire and ducked in. The other two checked the road and followed him in.

I reckoned I should alert Jay. I slipped downstairs and telephoned his house. Iris answered: 'Baba gone, not even finished the omelette…' She put the phone down, not completing her complaint.

I tried Channa. 'Can you come? Something sinister is going on.'

'Okay. I'll be over soon as I can.'

Channa would not admit it, but I was sure he was doing maths prep for his tutor. The sort of thing a swot would do on a free afternoon between tennis and swimming, or that kind of laudable activity.

I resumed watch. An hour later, Channa turned up.

'Sorry, *men*. Had to say hello to this lady my parents had invited for tea – Mrs Walton. She had a lot of info about England.' He nudged the gate with his front wheel. 'So, where's the gang?'

'They've gone,' I said, flatly. 'You missed the whole shebang.'

'What did they do?'

'A bunch of desperadoes came in a massive jeep and combed through that whole jungle. Definitely planning to build something big, but Jay is completely wrong. They are building apartment blocks, not casinos.'

'A jeep like Jay's uncle's?'

'You've been in it?' I knew I should not mind, we were all in it together.

'Guess what?' Channa changed the subject. 'My father says someone's started a new secret joint in Wellawatta. The Giramal Club. With go-go dancers!'

'What are they?'

'Girls who dance without any clothes.'

'In Wellawatta?'

'In the buff.' Channa fiddled with the end of his shirt. 'Mrs Walton's husband works for the British Council. She said that when they were in Cuba before the revolution, it had been chock-a-block with "colourful places" like that – casinos. Then Fidel Castro came and chased them all to Las Vegas.'

I had an image of dancing girls of every colour running naked down the street and leaping into ships steaming out of a harbour, and a big man in a beard shaking his fist at them from the shore.

'My father says gambling is not a problem for real social-ists.' I said. 'Let's check it out, just you and me.'

'I'll get some more info.'

※

But Channa told Jay first and Jay immediately planned a mission. He came over the next evening in Elvin's stately grey Humber with Channa already in the front seat.

'Come on,' Jay jerked a thumb. 'Operation Wadiya.'

I got in the back, noting how Channa avoided my eye.

We drove up to Galle Road and past the ramshackle teashops and hopper hawkers. I counted three cars with dud lights. Even if Colombo turned into a Las Vegas one day, I couldn't imagine the dingy dens with their rows of brown bottles and stacks of betel leaves giving way to glitzy hotels and sparkling gem shops. Could there be neon lights, limousines, billboards and burger joints here? Would everyone wear blue jeans and shake their hips and grow wings? The possibility pleased me less than I expected.

Jay flicked an indicator and turned into one of the lanes dribbling down to the sea. He drove with the indifference of a big shot, elbow on sill, chewing a pellet of paper. The villa at the end of the lane, tipping towards the sea, had a few cars parked outside. Jay stopped several houses away, dimming the lights but keeping the engine running.

'That's it. The one at the end,' Channa whispered, taking the role of number one scout. 'If we go any closer, it might look suspicious.'

'Drive past slowly,' I said, wanting to show I was braver, wanting Jay to recognise how close my heart was to his own, despite everything. We were the ones who had been on a trail together, shot snipe, caught fish, pipe-dreamed on a raft. The future was ours, nobody else's. 'The road goes around the corner and then up the other lane.'

'Okay.' Jay spat the paper pellet out. 'Take a good look.'

As we passed the house, I whispered, 'Curtains closed.'

'Nothing to see,' Channa added. 'Top secret.'

On the corner, I recognised the rust bucket parked by the telegraph pole.

'Not nothing. That's our Anglia. My father must be inside.'

'You sure?'

'They must do betting there.'

'Slot machines, not racing. That's what Mrs Walton said they had in the clubs in Havana. It's the fast way to gamble.'

'You said they have naked girls in there. That can't be true, can it, Jay?'

'They are doing a test run,' Channa knitted an amalgamation of half-heard adult arguments into an explanation that slowly eased the tension in his face. 'If they make pots of money at this Giramal Club, they'll open more. In Dehiwela, Havelock Town, Colpetty. After the elections, my dad says, if Mrs B loses, it'll be buffet for all. Gambling is the thing. They'll make it the fashion.'

I tried to imagine my father's reaction. He'd be out every night, placing his own bets. Maybe my mother would accompany him. They used to go to places together, she'd once reminisced, in the days when she used to do her nails in bright colours and wear earrings that dangled. The Giramal might become like the famous Italian supper club where jacketed waiters lit candles for dinner and couples ate lasagne with olives. Maybe my father would no longer have to hide behind a hopeless sneer. I wanted his life to become better, and my mother's. I wanted them both to be happy, as they surely must have been once – like at the time of their wedding photo when they had their hands locked together. Two slim young people in a black and white world with no inkling of the days ahead or the impression they would make. It did not cross my mind that Channa might be wrong and that the Giramal was not the kind of club that we had

imagined, nor indeed that the election might spell a rad-
ically different future for my father; that the smiles in the
photo and their marital grip concealed panic as much as
love's innocent bloom.

When Jay dropped me back home, he gave me a grown-
up wink. 'Find out what's going on from your dad.'

'How?'

'Have a chat, he's bound to let something slip about this
new club.'

I figured Jay was beginning to forget what it was like to
have a father. Maybe, like the way we dream of the future,
we also dream up the past, smoothing all the edges for the
sake of our present longings.

Down the road, the Selvarajahs' dogs started barking.
That set another lot off farther down, and soon a rippling
circle of yapping and barking drowned out the crackling
radio at the back of the house.

☀

In the weeks that followed, Channa avoided us. At first, in
short, strained phone calls he would make excuses citing
chores, or relatives and family friends, until eventually he
confided, 'My dad won't let me out on the roads.'

'Grounded?'

'Not my fault. It's getting dangerous.'

'Those fellows in the Wolseley?'

'He's trying to get us all to England by Christmas.'

'My father says everything will be different in the
New Year.'

I had asked my father about the rising chants from loud-speakers mounted on vans calling for rallies, protest marches, strikes; the warnings of impending dictatorship and the demands for early elections. He had dithered between truthfulness and reassurance, both of which he must have wanted to offer me – his only son. He explained how the opposition was angry at the prospect of being muzzled, the government was angry at being stymied on every proposal, the left was angry at its growing impotence, the clergy were angry at being ridiculed or forgotten. 'We're heading for a helluva showdown but it may be what we need to make us ponder our fate.'

Without Channa around, I became Jay's sole focus. He launched himself into a programme of mentoring overdrive.

I never learnt so much, so fast, so excitingly, ever before in my life or since. Jay seemed to want to take the whole mechanical world apart and show me how every tiny bit of it worked by itself and in connection with everything else. One day it would be an air pump for the aquarium, another day a radio, or the carburettor of a car engine. We were in a world of our own: goldfish bustled, mynahs chattered, orioles sang. The rasp of malice sharpening its claws on the other side of town did not breach the calm of Jay's house or Elvin's rambling grounds. I did not care what was happening anywhere except what was happening between Jay and me.

'Practise, practise, practise,' was his mantra. My life became a testing ground for something bigger and more important to come. Every day he would get me to drive, teaching me to understand a vehicle as a live animal. Always the red Beetle for lessons so that I recognised all its quirks. No doom could threaten our future.

'Jay really needs a friend like you, sweetie,' his mother had told me holding my hand in her brittle fingers. 'A friend for life. Don't ever leave him, will you?'

I was determined not to.

On the last Sunday of November, Jay said he wanted to see how well I could handle a bigger car.

'The Bentley?'

He laughed, sounding years older, having unconsciously imbibed his uncle's spirit while pottering in his garages. He put on Elvin's pukka accent. 'Not that one, old man. We'll take out the trusty warhorse. How would you like that?'

The first time I had seen Jay drive flashed across my mind – coming back from the fabled estate – and how impressed I had been and how much I wanted to be like Jay and take the wheel of the jeep with a champion's assurance.

'I'm ready for it.'

'We'll go to the beach – a special beach.' Jay's cheeks bunched up as he made a sucking sound: 'We'll take Niromi with us. Okay?'

'Sure.' We had some rapport after the business with the violin at Mrs De Souza's house. I had kept my mouth shut as she wanted me to, so we must be quits. The monkey in my ear urged me to reveal her girly plans, but at that point in a boy's life a girl just complicated everything, whatever the greater design. I didn't know why she had changed the way she looked at me; maybe Jay had reassured her in some way – and she had succumbed as people seemed to do.

In the afternoon sun, Elvin's house glowed pink. Jay got me to bring the jeep out of the garage. The warhorse was the heaviest thing I had ever handled; my hands, my feet, my whole body strained with the weight of it.

'Ease up,' Jay said.

'Can't.'

'It has an engine, you know. Wheels. It'll roll. You only have to guide it.'

By the time we got to Niromi's house on Vajira Road, I felt more in control. I waited in the jeep while Jay popped inside to fetch her.

Coming out, she led the way, a pale shirt knotted at the waist, tripping up to the jeep with a cheerful, 'Hi.'

No secret signals, no indication that she had ever had a cross word to say – or a good one. I figured I too should pretend we had no history: play it cool, acknowledge her manfully. She climbed in the back where I had once sat and Jay jumped into the passenger seat next to me. I checked the rear-view mirror. She'd put something smeary around her eyes and on her lips.

She grinned. 'So, Kairo, you can drive?'

'Yeah.'

'He's a great driver,' Jay said.

'I've driven a tractor.' Niromi leant back.

'A two-wheeler?' Was nothing inviolate anymore?

'Don't be silly. A real one.'

'No way,' Jay said.

'It's true. In Batty. A Massey Ferguson on Uncle Vernon's farm.' She laughed, 'My daddy used to let me steer our car when I was like six.'

That shut us up.

Jay's special beach was far down the coast, past Mount Lavinia, Ratmalana, Moratuwa; it didn't seem to matter to him, and soon it did not matter to me either. The road hardly had any other vehicles on it. Our lives floated free, all constraints melted. I believed we could do anything we wanted for no reason except a desire to do so. Now, installed as driver, I was no longer a little boy. For the moment, for me, this was no longer a country of confusion, simply a road where a boy could be in control and nothing need ever go wrong.

After an hour, the road crossed a railway line; the sea loomed closer.

'Slow down,' Jay leant forwards. 'Look for a turn-off opposite a Madonna shrine-like thing.'

Niromi spotted it first. A pale, moony figure draped in a blue cape with a cross in her hand. Marigold garlands and lotus flowers circled her bare feet as though she had reverted to an older religion while standing by the roadside.

'Go straight to the end,' Jay instructed.

The red dirt surface of the lane, dipping in and out of craters, rippled with the tide marks of hard rain and small forgotten floods.

'Should I shift to four-wheel drive?'

'Go ahead.'

I yanked the second, shorter gear stick and the jeep juddered as all the wheels engaged.

The terrain turned sandier; ranawara and lantana scrambled for a sharper, salt-seeded light while coconut trees swayed, rangier, their tops mashed up by the winds that came sweeping in from the ocean. The sky curved with an emery edge. I couldn't understand why Jay wanted to come all this way when within half an hour night would fall and there would be nothing to see but gnats reeling in the beam of the headlamps.

'At the bottom, take a left and then drive right onto the beach. That's my favourite spot for a swim.'

'You didn't say anything about a sea-bath,' Niromi protested. 'I didn't bring my swimsuit.'

'Who needs swimsuits?'

Maybe that was why. So we could undress in the dark and all go in the sea without our clothes.

I changed gear again and wove the jeep between the blue-chipped palm trees, popping sea grapes, onto the beach and stopped on the dry, powdery sand with the engine panting and the surf foaming in front of us.

'Now what?' My heart had never felt so close to the bone and I did not know why.

'First, we walk,' Jay said. 'Up to those rocks. Have to climb to the top, then you'll see.'

This time Jay led the way; Niromi and I followed. Me, unsure if I should hold her hand. Not for her sake, but for mine. The soft, relentless sand, the deceptive sea, the serrated light combing the water and the violent strands of the sinking sun rupturing the sky both excited me and frightened me as I became aware that I might be on the verge of too much yearning.

At the rocks, Jay slipped into tracker mode and gestured for us to climb up quietly over the dry, brown, rubbery sea kelp and whitening barnacles. Niromi clambered ahead; I placed my hands and feet where she had put hers, matching her every move.

At the top of the ridge, Jay chose a flat rock where we could perch, cross-legged, next to each other. Niromi's bare knee touched mine, scalding me. The new faint hairs on my leg strayed and lifted, whetted by the sea breeze; my skin tightened. Jeans would have been safer than shorts; I wished I had a pair and tight straps to hold things in.

Below us, the beach was narrow and steep. The surf rolled softly against it, cushioned and hushed for something momentous and unavailable anywhere else along the coast.

'It's nice but what are we here for?' Niromi asked.

She had tied her hair into a bunch at the back with an elastic band which left her neck naked. The colour had seeped away from it into her shoulders except for a black mole an inch below the hairline which she may never have seen but I had.

'Wait,' Jay put a finger to his lips. 'Watch the sky above the water. That's where it'll begin.'

At first, I assumed the storm of dark dots that swirled and swerved across the gloaming sky, a dark, prickly genie of massive proportions shifting its shape from moment to moment, was a phantasmagorical rain cloud, or even a tornado. It banked and flipped and doubled itself and rushed across the water right before us, sweeping across the cove and folding into the line of short-form palm trees while a low wall of sound, of crunching and chirping, began to grow over the vibrations from the swaying coconut lyres. Then another cloud of tiny birds, and another, appeared in the sky. They danced and swirled, like the first, before swooping down into the trees. With each wave, the sound grew louder: a crescendo as the scarlet light in the sky dwindled. Jay whistled with the birds, as if he might be raising their song a note higher, as they raised his, and all the while new clouds of birds descended to merge with those in the trees. Cloud after zooming, twisting, dancing cloud.

'There must be thousands.' Niromi's hand strayed and found mine. She gripped it hard, stronger and more charged than I had thought possible for a girl. The clouds of birds coalesced and the patterns dispersed momentarily before others took their place. I noticed she no longer had a ring on her finger; her nails were pink with identical white tips. Her wrist had a bone so round I wanted to cover it with my lips.

Jay spoke in a rapture of his own: 'Tens of thousands. Barn swallows. They've flown across oceans and continents to be here. Just to be here tonight. Look. Look how they fly.'

I watched him: the outline of his face, the ridge of his brow, the wide-open eyes, the slope of his nose and slightly turned out lips, the dip of his chin. Then hers, which seemed to match his in every curve and flourish. Could they both be the other half of mine?

The last traces of the sun blackened and early stars began to speckle the receding dome. The birds fell silent. Huddled in their lines of thirty or forty on each frond of the hundreds of branches, muffling the strings, they became the silent puffs that helped the earth to turn. From our vantage point I saw how they were only one measure of the millions of birds that aerated the earth, wings beating, singing, churning clouds and wondered how in among those millions a grey parrot, or an Atlantic puffin, or an eagle will find a mate they would stay with for the rest of their lives.

We walked back to the jeep in the glow of silvery sealight, skirting the froth of low waves, each lost in mysterious flights to secret places, my uncertainty sharpened by an unfamiliar slippery desire.

'That was worth it, no?' Jay pulled out a knapsack from the back of the jeep. 'To witness that?'

'I've never seen anything like it.' Niromi's breath sounded heavier than his. 'Felt they were coming like that just for you. How did you find this place, Jay?'

'Instinct, I guess. I was staying with my uncle at a beach house farther along and I just found it.' Jay drew his initial in the sand with his foot. 'One day you're just playing in the sand, and then suddenly everything looks so different.'

'How long have they been coming like that?'

'Congregating? Hundreds of years maybe. Like those bats, no, Kairo? You remember those bats we wanted to follow? We should still do it, you know. Find out what the hell they are up to.'

I did not say anything. Things that had seemed almost crystalline a moment ago were no longer clear. The barn swallows in their cloud formations now confused me. The bats in their unresolved straight lines confused me. Jay confused me, and Niromi confused me. The suggestion of swimming naked in the sea with her worried me; driving all the way home in the night worried me. I had not done either before. Skinny-dipping in the pond on Elvin's estate was not the same. Could I undress in front of Niromi? What does one do with a girl? Jay had not given me any coaching.

'What about the sea?' I asked.

'You wanna go in?'

'How?' I saw her chest rising and falling, fish gulping, and felt a stirring; a rush inside clouding everything, singing and clapping. My hand burned. 'Will you do the driving, going back?'

'It's a good feeling. A quick dip, then just follow your homing instinct.'

'I haven't done it at night. Isn't it scary?' Not just the driving, but the night currents, the deep sea. The girl and boy thing.

'If you are not ready, you are not ready.' He pulled out a small flat bottle from the knapsack. 'I need a drink first.'

'What's that? Gin?' Niromi asked.

'Schnapps. Gal Oya Schnapps. Want some? Dutch courage before you jump in the water?' He laughed.

They each had a swig.

I reached out for mine.

'No, not for you.'

'Why not?'

'You're too young.'

'I am not.' I snatched the bottle and took a big swig as Jay had done. The alcohol ignited in my throat and made me retch. In one searing second, I hated Jay for making me grow up this way.

'No, please don't,' Jay pleaded. 'No more.'

The heat in my chest and stomach gave me no courage, only a dull metallic welding of bones to make me sink. A sense of uncaring. I took another gulp before letting go of the bottle.

The three of us waited in a silence that grew thicker and pricklier. Nobody touched the bottle again. I understood something had happened, or was about to happen, that should not ever happen. Maybe Jay had to kiss her before she took her clothes off. Maybe if I took another sip, I could too. I wanted to. If Jay could, I could too. We were the same. All for one, one for all. I was not a little boy. Not anymore. I could see him roll his tongue in his mouth, running it over his teeth in preparation.

Then Jay grabbed the bottle and hurled it into the sea.

The waves had stopped. After the splash, the silence became intolerable.

'I better drive back, no?' Niromi said and started to climb into the driving seat.

'No.' Jay unclasped her hand from the steering wheel.

She stiffened for a moment before relinquishing her place. Jay took control without another word. He started the engine and raced it higher and higher until it seemed it might break into a million tiny pieces.

I curled into the back seat swallowing air. Fighting the urge to drown. Niromi settled in the front; her eyes caught a beam of stray light off the water. She released her hair and shook it. Then she turned to me and I saw she was as seared as I was by the carelessness of the night.

'Are you all right?' she asked in a tone that my mother might have used. Squirming in the dark, I hated the tears I could feel so unfairly welling up. I hated the sun. I hated the moon. I hated what had happened.

Over the next few days and nights I found it hard to keep Niromi out of my thoughts. Every time I tried to make up with Jay in my mind, she would eclipse him and leave me in a kind of limbo that resolved nothing.

In my pictorial guide to the story of America, I had been fascinated to discover that Pocahontas was the one who had kept the peace between the Powhatans and the English in Virginia. She had even gone to England and met Elizabeth I. No king to speak of overshadowed the story; she and the Queen were the ones that mattered. I kept thinking about that.

By the time the December holidays started, things were jumbled up for everyone. My father shot out of the house early one morning, even though it was not a working day for him.

'Have to catch a fellow. Call Quickshaws for a taxi if you need to go out,' he yelled.

Before my mother could unleash a word, the car had lurched out with Siripala at the wheel, the routine gone haywire.

She banged the door to her room shut. I had a bad feeling about the day.

I set off for the milk bar under a sky swollen with low, dark clouds, but as I approached I noticed the flags and awning had disappeared. The counter folded up, shuttered.

Not so long ago the milk bar had been our central mooring, the safe harbour where we could not only meet, but where we could leave messages, catch up with the news, anchor and replenish. A neutral place for the three of us – with Mahela watching over us. Now he too was gone. It seemed everyone above a certain age was in danger of disappearing, and the threshold was dropping.

I stole round the back and peered through the air vents hoping to see the ice boxes and stacks of cups waiting for the milkshake maestro. I did not want things to change so much so unexpectedly. A temporary stop would be all right. A pause to catch your breath, refill a water bottle, but then let things return to those first golden days when even the green caterpillars glowed. I wanted to begin again. With no bad things ever having to happen.

A crow landed on the roof of the kiosk and started to caw. I threw a pebble at it, but it only flapped back a few paces, as if it recognised me from the time Jay shot its friend and now it had plans. I wheeled my bike down the trail to the spot from where we had viewed the planetarium taking shape and found some comfort in seeing that the building work had not finished yet, concrete rings still jutted out of mounds of earth; bare ribs of buildings.

I rode over to the other side of the racecourse. The grandstand car park was open. Right in the corner, by the old members' notice board, Elvin's Austin Healey stood parked. I started towards it, but then saw Jay was not alone in the car. He was with Niromi. She raised her head from his shoulder and a moment later the two shapes fused into one. The blister in my head finally burst.

Everything sank to a blur. Everything. First her: the day I saw her by Independence Hall; the day I bumped into her outside the radio station; the time at Mrs De Souza's house when I knocked over the vase; the drive down to the beach; and the hot slosh of Gal Oya firewater, which I had hoped would prepare me for the worst. Then him.

☀

Maybe we had to be rivals. Maybe he knew that from the beginning. I began to see Jay's world might have only ever been make-believe – a playland of phoney con-spiracies and plots, stupid chicken farms and ridiculous gambling dens.

I blazed a circle of anger and hurt to Casa Lihiniya and let myself in through the side door. The cook woman, Iris, was nowhere to be seen. Slipping in under the arch into the garden, I headed straight for the aviary.

'Hail-lo, hail-lo.' Sinbad rolled an eye.

I slid the door open. Jay didn't bother to lock it after his mother left. 'Vamoose, Sinbad. He doesn't care. You can go free.'

I turned on the budgies that had gathered at the far end. 'Go, go, you dumb mutts.'

'Hail-lo, hail-lo,' Sinbad mocked. 'Va-moose.'

I pulled at the wire mesh. The cage was my cage. Not Niromi's. Not even Channa's. I made it with Jay. How could he abandon me so easily? What was the point of attention and affection if they could be switched so easily? Then I panicked that I was turning into Sonya and that I'd be trapped forever like her.

I fled – cycled hard, brushing aside the hateful ever-dormant tears, wanting them to drain away and leave me in perpetual drought.

At the temple close to home, I stopped. The curve of the huge, white dagoba dome rising out of the ground filled the sky. Although this was where a young man had been killed in a riot fifty years earlier, its apparent vast emptiness and impassivity obliterated history. It could swallow more than my anxieties. I yearned to simply stop thinking, to stop the jostling, stop the random fear and even the longing that mystified me. I wanted to cease to be so that I would stop being lonely and yet I did not want to ever die.

☀

On Sunday, the 13th of December 1964, nearly six months after we had first met, Jay came racing down our road in the Beetle and sounded the horn outside our house. In the ten days or so since the drive to the beach we had not spoken to each other, but Jay acted as if nothing had altered.

'Come on. Final driving lesson. You did fine with the jeep. Tomorrow, you can take this one out on your own.' He played a dampened tune on the horn.

'Stop horning.' I found it hard to breathe, to swallow. 'I've got algebra to finish, or my mother will throw a fit.'

'So? They all throw fits. You should have seen the fit Iris went into when I blaggarded her about the birds.'

Nervously I fingered the chrome trim of the sill. 'What happened?'

'Damn fool woman left the cage door wide open. They could have all gone to Timbuktu. I gave her hell.'

'Who escaped? Sinbad?'

'Just the two blue budgies. Sinbad kept the others in, although all he says now is *va-moose*.'

'Yeah.' Sinbad was a smart bird but I wished he would shut up.

'How's about a quick spin? Go for a Chocolac?'

'Milk bar is closed.'

'How come?'

'It's boarded up. Empty. Nobody there.'

Jay squashed his round face into a clumsy attempt to display disdain. 'I've gone off shakes anyway.'

'Mahela's gone.'

'Maybe selling peanuts is more lucrative.' Jay paused as a prior sense of responsibility pricked him. 'Unless those thugs in the Wolseley came back and did something.' He revved the engine, dismissing the thought. 'Tomorrow then. No excuses, okay?'

A second later, the Beetle whirred away, drawing down the trees and the bushes of the gardens along the road in its wake. My anger seeped away but I was left uneasy.

☼

Towards the end of the day, a green Hillman parked right up against the front wall. My father's friend, Abey, clambered out from the passenger side because he hadn't left enough room to open his door, and then stood in the middle of the road and stared at his car as if he couldn't understand how it had arrived there.

'So, where were you today, comrade?' My father greeted him from the front steps. 'You didn't come to the meeting.'

'Sorry, *men*.' Abey stretched his neck from side to side, freeing it but losing air. 'I've been composing my resignation letter. Not easy, I tell you. Helluva thing.'

Abey could usually be counted on to put his friends into a good mood – a dose of liver salts in a cotton suit – but this time barely a bubble broke the tightly tailored gloom that encased him.

'We haven't even hammered out the constitution for this new party and you are already resigning?' My father rarely masked his disapproval of political wavering.

'Not from our Giramal People's Party. Have to resign from the job, no?'

'Why?'

'My name has been put on the list as a refusenik – you know, for still using English in my memos. What next? Into the clink if you say "how do you do"? All my years of service have been in English. Wasn't even this country's independence negotiated in English? All to no avail. So, now I have written my letter of resignation. A damn good one too, in sound English prose that regrettably will not be appreciated by the minister of tomfoolery.'

From my eyrie at the end of the balcony, I could see both men at the front door. My father's hair looked thinner viewed from above, his shoulders not as broad as before, his feet splayed out in peeling brown sandals. He nudged aside the brick doorstop and ushered his friend in. 'We are all dinosaurs, Abey. All these years of dreaming, dreaming in the wrong bloody language. How did it come to seem so natural to us? Is it because of reading? Did reading books only in English blind us? I never thought I was missing anything reading Dickens, Shelley, Auden. Even Tolstoy and Marx seemed perfected in translation. But when I look at that boy of mine, I can see how it shapes everything you see.'

Curious to know more about the dangers of reading, and its remedies, I slipped indoors too and took up position at my regular spot upstairs.

Abey, burdened by the practicalities of early retirement, grasped for the consolations of the aggrieved. 'Trouble is all our leaders are now led by the nose; they can smell the power of the language issue to agitate the masses.'

'The point, surely, is to awaken them. A world language is to be seized, not abandoned.' My father sniffed. 'So, you've really resigned?'

'You should consider your position too, Clarence. These proficiency tests are not going to be scrapped. Maybe they'll delay full implementation for the technical officers like doctors, but for the likes of us – no reprieve.'

'How to quit? Need the salary, no? My son, after all...'

'You better negotiate something before they kick you out.'

'But why would they do that? I'm not the class enemy. I'm not even Tamil like Shaku.'

'Between you, me and the lamppost, let me tell you, I think that Amirthalingam might be right. If humiliation of the Tamils is the aim, one day the youth really will rise. Next thing, they'll all be calling for a separate state, not just the extremists. Wouldn't you? Then we'll be in helluva bloody mess.'

'Sit, *men*, sit, will you. You are making me nervous fidgeting so much. Have a drink before that too is banned by the righteous right. And bloody left too. But, no, Abey, I can't see any appetite for such extremist action, separate state or any kind of Shangri La – theocratic or bureaucratic. Everybody gets humiliated, no, hurt even? But that doesn't make us all run amok. Maybe confused, but not berserk. It's all talk. Hot air and fervour. How can anyone understand anything when the language we use has become so warped? Even the word "communal" is now so corrupted.'

Siripala brought their drinks, ready poured and cleverly cut, clinking chunkily in Johnny Walker freebie glasses. Abey took his with a breezy mix of English and Sinhala. 'Ah, Siripala. Thank you. *Kohomadha?*' He parked his drink with reverence before continuing. 'You underestimate the pulling power of wrath and fury. You should know better from all those books you read. Frustration, rage – it's like a locomotive stoked up. But I agree, Clarence, I agree. Right now we do need a new left party, we do – the old parties are corrupted. And I am impressed with the new Giramal Party – a progressive alternative – but with the general election now set for March we have no time to prepare. For me, the tipping point was when the leader of the house spoke. You have to respect the man, no, whether or not you agree with his policies? Ours is not a sensitive tribe, but when he made that speech in parliament, it moved me.'

My father placed his hands on the back of one of the dining chairs and leant on it; nothing short of an earthquake would move him. But Abey's remarks about the Giramal being a political party and not a gambling club changed everything for me. All Jay's theories, and Channa's, lay exposed as absurd mafia fantasies. I listened on even though I wanted no more revelations.

'You don't believe that nonsense about "unadulterated totalitarianism", do you? Press control does not lead to liquidating critics nor, as that venerable whatsit claims, "putting the people to eternal sleep".'

'It's a slippery slope. That's all I'm saying.'

'Nothing to slip. I've always maintained, the press barons are the same as robber barons.'

I could vouch for that, although I had always assumed my father was describing a romantic combination of adventure heroes.

'Clarence, for me that phrase of his, "Whither are we transiting?" hits the nail on the head whichever way you look. That's the thing, no? We are not here just to gorge ourselves, or feather our nest, are we?'

'Is that what they are all doing?' My father's voice dropped, flame extinguished, heat off. He presented his empty cupped hands to his friend. 'Have we not a more noble purpose?'

※

'Today is the day,' Jay said when he came to collect me in the Beetle the next afternoon. 'The day you go solo.'

Jay slid over and I slipped into the driving seat. Jay's face had hardened in places – around the jaw and above his cheekbones. Uneven patches. The beginnings of a beard? I wondered if he'd started to shave.

'Solo? Where?'

'We'll go to Elvin's first and I'll take the Buick – the convertible. Then we do a race.'

'Already?'

Jay's face tightened. 'We don't have much time left.'

'Why?'

He hesitated. 'I've found the perfect place. Havelock golf course. It's deserted. Abandoned. Not a soul there.

There's a fantastic fairway. Nearly half a mile on the flat. We can do whatever the fuck we like.'

I turned on the ignition. Maybe I'd learn to swear without flinching too. 'It's closed because the Royal Colombo has finally opened up its membership, my father says.'

'Bet Wilbur's got his eye on the land.'

I eased the car into gear. As you get older do your mistakes become deeper? Can you not help but see plots in accidents, confuse love and desire?

'I heard they are going to build a church there.'

'I told Channa I'll give him a ride in the Buick. He's desperate to get out of the house. Sez he can sneak out if we can pick him up at the roundabout.'

'And Niromi?'

'She's been already.' He slapped the dashboard. 'So, let's go.'

He didn't try to guide but let me prove I had regained confidence after the way the drive to the coast had ended. I did not own up and tell Jay I'd been out in our Anglia alone already – practising. I don't know why I kept it secret. I was ready. A gear change was only shifting a stick; growing up was recalibrating your life. I could feel it happening from my toes to my fingertips. I took the main road to the big house and picked up speed. Jay said nothing, but his cheeks were full and proud.

On Elvin's drive, the huge blue convertible was already out, top folded down, polished and gleaming.

'If you are driving that, maybe I should race you in the Austin Healey?' The picture of Jay in it with Niromi flashed briefly, smarting.

Jay laughed lightly. 'Next time. We have to keep the best for next time, no? Anyway, we'll have to go in that one together first.'

Jay let himself out and sauntered over to the convertible with the calm confidence of a boy who knew the best was yet to come. The complications receded.

Jay climbed into the blue car, swinging his long legs over the curved door without opening it and started the massive American engine. The car gave a shiver, preparing to fly. I pressed the accelerator with my bare toe in response and the Beetle whirred noisily. I was in full control, more than I had ever been before. I ran my fingers down the two halves of the hard plastic steering wheel – from twelve to six – to make a circle. Jay cocked a thumb and the blue car eased out, the large whitewall tyres crunching the gravel of the drive. I followed it out of the gate and we set off in convoy, each alone and yet inseparably together.

Channa was lurking by the bakery near the roundabout. Jay stopped. The bold tail lights glowed. Seeing Channa get in the car, I felt another of those twinges that tighten the knots around the heart. But Jay had trusted me with a car of my own. That counted for more, surely? And soon he would let me drive the Austin Healey, too. Jay gave a blast from his horn and shot ahead in a swirl of flamboyance that belonged in a cinema. I chased after him. Pressed the accelerator pedal halfway and latched on right behind. The road was a blur on each side.

We flew past the closed-up milk bar, the radio station, Independence Square, leaving behind the crow circles and the flame trees. The convertible swung into the entrance of the disused golf course. I followed in my Beetle and came to a stop, fender to fender. Channa got out and opened the gates. We drove in, one after the other, churning road rubble, right up to the dilapidated clapboard clubhouse. In the rolling emptiness of the fairways I felt uneasy. Not because of driving alone, or trying to keep up with Jay. Just uneasy, seeing the burnt edges of the evening sky, the light beginning to go.

Jay called out from his car: 'Drive around and get a feel for the grass under your wheels. I'll figure out a cool circuit for a race, okay?'

His words brought back our first trials downhill on bikes, cycling on the racecourse from Mahela's milk bar. Sunbeam. I stared at the clubhouse trying to recall what my father had said about the golfers who had frequented it. The white paint was peeling and two of the windows had broken panes.

Jay sounded his horn – a brash clarion blast. 'Okay?'

I tried to catch his eye but Channa in the passenger seat of the Buick was in the way. Why had Jay brought him? Why did he always let someone come between us?

I beeped the horn and took off. The Beetle had no trouble on grass and the undulations below the first tee made it seem to soar. At one point, the engine revved as if the wheels were spinning in the air. Accelerator flattened right down to the floor, the needle hit fifty. I crossed to the other fairway.

The convertible with Jay and Channa in it rushed the forsaken green and swerved between two disintegrating bunkers two hundred yards away while I drove back up to the clubhouse.

The crows in the trees nearby started up.

The convertible raced back. Jay stopped it right next to the Beetle. He had one hand on the gearstick and his other arm hanging out, leaving the wheel hands-free.

'How?'

'Cool.' The Beetle was on form. My next target was sixty and in fewer seconds than Jay had ever managed in our test drives. I knew I could do it.

'You see the mango tree down there? That's the marker. First one to get down there, circle the tree, do a slalom between the bunkers and make it back here, wins. Channa, you be the judge. You draw the finishing line and stand by it.'

Channa made a face as he climbed out of the car.

'You'll need a flag.' I could see Channa had been hoping Jay would give him a go at the wheel.

'I brought one.' Channa pulled a yellow school pennant out of his pocket. 'I'll go find a stick for it.'

While he was gone, Jay turned his car to face the mango tree down at the dog-leg. I did the same with mine. The clouds, low and red, were beginning to pile up.

'Hey, you know what I'd like to do with this space?' he asked from his car.

'Make a race track?'

Jay blinked and brushed a strand of hair out of his eyes. 'Make a safari park. Build Noah's ark out here. We should do that you know, bring pairs of all sorts of animals here. Have elephants and bears and leopards and deer roaming around.'

'No birds?'

'Yeah, birds also. Herons and parrots and peacocks. Swallows. All of them here.' The soft collar of his pale cotton shirt lay flat and damp on the thin round bone below his neck. 'Make this place really special.'

Channa came back with three flagsticks. 'I found these at the back. You guys ready?'

'Sure.' All those weeks of cycling, fishing, shooting, driving, practising, was to get me ready for this moment when I could show Jay just who I was.

Channa stuck two of the flagsticks in the ground five yards apart. 'First one to get through that wins.' Wide enough for one car, but not two abreast. There could only be one winner.

'So, let the best man win.' Despite the difficulties of the last few weeks, Jay's face still had glimpses of the buoyancy that I had seen when he first wheeled into the church car park on his bike. A kind of glee that kept fighting to burst out.

I had only a slim chance of winning, but that did not matter. Jay was treating me as an equal already and that counted for more. I should never have doubted him.

'Yours is a V-8,' I said. 'A Buick Skylark is a lot faster.'

'On grass, it's not just speed. Yours is designed for adversity, you know. Rommel used Volkswagens in the desert.'

Above the noise of the engines, I heard the high screams of parakeets winging between the shreds of the late light in the trees. From the corner of my eye, I caught a spark in the sky: an early star.

Channa took up his position and raised the yellow flag. 'Ready?' I stuck my thumb up. Jay did the same. Channa started his countdown: three, two, one. Go. The flagged dropped and I let go of the clutch. The car jerked, almost stalled but then took off. Jay flew ahead. I fastened on to his tail, racing to forty, fifty, fifty-five, sixty. The mango tree loomed up, Jay took the turn close, brake lights winking in alarm. I went wider, not daring to go as tight as he did. Then I saw Jay's convertible slide on the long grass, wheels spinning. For a delicious moment I hoped I might get in front, but the Buick Skylark shot ahead with Jay whooping and waving a fist in the air. Channa, at the finishing line, started jumping up and down jabbing the air with his flag. I urged the car faster: hit sixty-five, or at least sixty-three, but by then Jay was through the finishing line. I slowed down, bringing the car in, rolling to the pits of our own Grand Prix track in the lost acres of an unpoliced town.

Grasping the key to turn the engine off seemed beyond me, and yet the exhilaration in my veins suggested anything was possible.

Jay got out of the Buick and came over. He leant in and put his hand on my shoulder. He squeezed it briefly. 'Great stuff. Silver medallist, huh?'

Was there a touch of disappointment in his voice? Maybe he had hoped his protégé would win. The speedometer, I wanted to blurt out, you should have seen it – the needle quivering – but I played it cool instead.

'So, what now?'

His face softened. 'You choose, Kairo. Another race, or we could try chicken? Test your nerve.'

'Like in that movie?' He couldn't mean destroy the cars. Elvin's beautiful cars.

'No, man. Go at each other. A real showdown.'

'I know the score.' I had read about brinkmanship. Daredevil driving. The Bay of Pigs. Keeping control, not letting go.

'Okay. I'll drive down to the tree again. We face each other. Then I'll flash my headlights. On the third flash, we charge. First to swerve is chicken. Stay in line as long as you can, but don't fuckin' crash into me.' He smiled, cracking the small acres of wild sunlit honey.

'Sure.' If he was up for it, so was I. Who needs the movies?

'I wanna come,' Channa, ever hopeful, pleaded.

'Okay. Hop in,' Jay said.

There was a moment then when I could have stopped the crazy game. It would have only taken one small word: *no*, *stop*, *wait*. One of those slow words that Jay hated to use. But they barely fluttered in my throat as the big blue car rumbled away, the chrome fins sharpened and shining in the heavy yellow sun. I watched it go down the fairway and circle the tree.

When it came to a stop, the large brazen headlights flashed. From that moment on, everything that happened on that rough patch of land has been in permanent slow motion. The fastest car in the slowest motion. I counted the seconds, the ebb and flow of my confused feelings folded in to form a still moment of grace. I was only a boy but I felt the two of us were bound together by a desire to be more than our uncertain selves. My fears evaporated.

The lights flashed a second time. A couple of crows swooped into the tree by the Buick.

I fumbled for the switches: turning on the windscreen wipers before finding the control for the headlamps. A few seconds late, I returned the flash. I kept my foot down on the clutch, racing the engine, talking myself through the actions I needed to do, and shifted into gear. I was ready to be the boy I wanted to be: strong, brave, clear. Ready to prove myself to my mother, my father, Niromi. The convertible seemed to shrug as the engine raced. The third flash of the headlights. I released the clutch as I flashed back and slipped into a dream. I did everything without having to think. All my fears, my hopes, drained away. I did the gear changes as Jay had taught me to, by instinct. My hands were steady. The engine pitched high, pumping. The speedometer needle climbed up, tick by tick. Staring through the windscreen, I put Jay in my sights. We were heading straight for each other. The gap between us in every sense shortening by the second. Ten, nine, eight, seven… hurtling.

And then, as if on a signal, the crows rose out of the bordering trees, flapping their black capes, cawing crazily, chasing a clumsy coucal out onto the fairway. It lurched into the path of the convertible, flat tan wings on a fat black body. Jay swerved right to avoid it and I swerved in the same direction, following his actions, mirroring him, trying to keep my nerve. Jay pulled in some more – hard, too hard, much too hard. The car slewed into a skid, out of control. I manoeuvred out of the way and braked. The blue convertible charged on, vaulted up the front of a bunker, rose in the air as if in a whirlwind. Channa was thrown out of the car as it spun, but Jay stayed stuck to the driver's seat, girdled, as it landed upside down, smashing the windscreen and crushing the steering wheel into his chest.

I couldn't move, I didn't even open the door. I kept the engine running, thinking I should not have risen to his challenge: if I had not wanted the thrill, if I had been more the kid I should have been, he wouldn't have been in that car going the way he was, at that speed. We would not have been playing games we should not have been playing.

A bunch of people on a bus on the main road who had seen the blue car rising in the air quickly swarmed across to surround it. Messages were taken to nearby houses, an ambulance called. Mrs Peiris arrived and took charge of my car. The convertible was a write-off. Channa's father came for him, and my mother for me. She took me home, stunned and silent as I was.

There were no recriminations from her that I can remember. She put me to bed and I slept as if I never wanted to wake again. When I did, late the next afternoon, rain clouds had obscured the sun; the world seemed irrevocably altered.

I found my mother in the kitchen. My father next to her, a newspaper crumpled in his hand, shoulders drooping.

'I have to see Jay,' I said. 'Where did they take him?'

My mother reached out and held me with both her hands. 'I'm sorry, son.'

'What?'

'Jay is dead.'

'He can't be.'

'He died before the ambulance reached the hospital.'

I couldn't breathe; something was wrong with the air.

'His Uncle Elvin is here, sorting things out.'

'He came from America? Already?' It was impossible: all lies. Grown-up, adult lies. Jay had warned me: do not trust them. Fucking adults.

'Didn't he tell you, son? His uncle was coming to take him to a high school over there after Christmas. It was all arranged.'

Words would not do. I could not find any then.

'Elvin arrived on the flight this morning,' my father added in a voice of solace tinged with a measure of unexpected respect. 'He called us straightaway.'

I held back my tears but when my mother said, 'Oh, my sweet darling,' I buried my face in her arms and cried. The sap drained out of me. I wept for the life I had lost. Mine as much as his.

IV

FIREFLIES

7

December is a cruel month, my father would complain in his later years deploring the commercialisation of religion as a double fault. I, too, have made it a habit to avoid festive gatherings and try to get away from the tinsel, Chinese crackers and false good cheer whenever I can. This year, I have rented a secluded estate bungalow on the slopes overlooking the south coast far from any church. No temple nearby either. No mosque. There will be no carols. No pirith chants. No call of the muezzin.

Instead, the garden, fringed with low-country tea bushes, is filled with birdsong. The air teeming with invisible cogs and wheels: turning, squeaking, rubbing, creaking. The mechanism of nature's great timepiece. I can't but wonder, even now, what Jay would make of this abundance. The woodpeckers, the sunbirds, the fly-catchers with their long tail feathers. My notebook is full of sightings; whenever my pen touches the paper the intervening years vanish. A kingfisher dips into the water of the lily pond.

The lawn is curved and the garden sunlit. The care-taker reminds me of Gerry, the way he rises on his toes to listen to a distant hoot – a signal – holding an ekel broom in his hand.

'You look after the whole place on your own?' I ask him.

'*Mama vitharai.*' I am the only one. He sweeps a few fallen leaves and proudly adds, 'I planted the flowers and started the spice garden. Before that only three coconut trees and the rest a hopeless jungle. No good for anyone. Now we have even a resident malkoha.'

All the way along my drive down the coast to the house, I searched for Jay's cove. I call it Jay's cove, but after that single visit of ours it became as much mine as his. Or Niromi's. Several times I thought I had found the turn-off but the beachfront at the end never looked right – everywhere the shoreline crammed with new hastily built guest houses for budget tourists, and flimsy wooden shacks. Between them blackened fishing nets strung out to dry. Fences. Makeshift walls. Even if any of those side roads had led to the beach that had so enraptured us, the birds would not have been there. I could see no trees for sheltering. No roosting places. There was no room for them. No room for a lot of things from that time.

'Is there a place by the sea nearby where lots of small birds come when the sun goes down? Thousands of birds. I saw it once as a boy – a special beach – but I can't remember exactly where.'

'I know. I can take you, sir.' The caretaker cranes his neck, lifted by the prospect of the chance to guide. 'Not far. You cross the main road and then about ten minutes only to walk.'

'Small birds filling the whole sky?'

'Yes, yes. From the sea they come. Evening time.'

I feel immensely relieved.

I picture Jay as he was that evening, as the red sun softened and clouds of barn swallows appeared, flying in across the blue water and into the trees as if swirling in the refrain of a celestial choir; tiny birds that filled the gilt sky and dropped like small jewels to bead every string of the hundreds of green harps that lined his sanctuary, calling and calling and Jay singing back to them, his face broad and glowing in the last ruffled rays of the sun.

☀

I don't now remember much from the days and weeks that followed his death. I wanted the world to stop. For nothing more to ever happen. For the cage of guilt, and pretence, to melt. Channa soon left with his parents for England. I was not allowed to see him again, or he was not allowed to see me. Because he had been in the car with Jay, he was questioned by the police and blamed more than me by people like Mrs Peiris. He never said anything to defend himself. I also said nothing. I did not blurt out: 'Not Channa's fault. We were the ones racing, not him.' I could not say: 'All for one, one for all.' We were each on our own. We had been growing further apart each day instead of closer. Each with a story of his own to tell. Stories of hope and freedom, the benevolence of nature – even human nature – faultless friendship, love, genderless love. Or perhaps the reversal of all that.

Elvin quickly smoothed over the procedures, ensuring a swift verdict of misadventure and arranging a rapid funeral; even securing the brief appearance of Marty tugging clumsily at his tie. At the graveyard, I stayed in the shadows watching them. Iris began a low wail, gathering the tidal force of pent-up grief. I saw Sulaiman shuffle away from her with Gerry – his bad eye sewn shut. Our wrongs unrighted.

Elvin came over and put his arm around me. 'It was not your fault, Kairo, nor a fault in the world. Jay would be the first to say it.'

I tried to find something to say in return but couldn't. I wanted to tell him, 'Jay taught me to drive' – as though that might make a difference.

During the funeral, Niromi had kept her head lowered. I noticed her hair was oiled and tamed. At the end, when filing out, she accosted me. The skin around her mouth, her nose, was coarsened; her eyes rubbed hard. 'Why did you all do it? Why did you let him do it?' Fresh small streams of tears, and perspiration, trickled down her swollen cheeks and into the folds around her neck.

I wished I could put things right. Fix the mess of our shrunken young lives.

'Will I see you again?' I asked, unaware of the circularity that bends time and shapes survival.

Inexplicably she yielded then, softened. She clasped my hand and squeezed it as she had done that time on the beach.

A few days later, Elvin flew back to Sonya in her clinic in Washington. She didn't want to come back home and Elvin never carried out his business plans. When land reform came, years later, his estate was one of the first to be nationalised. Sulaiman lost his job but by then Gerry had become a pop singer. He ended up as a vocalist in a resort band in Phuket, escaping the fate of many of his rural peers when the troubles came.

I never visited Elvin's mansion again, or Casa Lihiniya with its garden and rooftop, the balcony, the fish, the birds, the vale of my blossoming; that whole magical world of discovery shifted out of reach and into a place of permanent impossibilities.

☀

The lily pond at the bottom of the garden is choked with duckweed. Spindly waterbirds step gingerly from pad to pad, pecking with their long bills at insects skating on the water. The pond is decorative rather than agricultural, there is a concrete path that goes up to it and a curved wooden footbridge over the narrower end. It is not a shortcut but another ornamental feature of the garden. I have walked across it several times since I arrived and watched the tadpoles nipping the brown, murky water. I can't tell whether it is the water or the bridge that attracts me, or the possibility of being between one place and another, waiting for a signal.

At five fifteen, the caretaker knocks on my door. He has buttoned up his shirt.

'Ready, sir?'

'Let's go.'

He takes me past a dell filled with scarlet heliconia and candy-coloured gandapana. 'You see, sir, these flowers need light. I had to cut down some of the old trees to allow new things to grow.'

'We used to play with those gandapana seeds.' I pick a few clusters and squeeze the berries apart, remembering.

'Gandapana is the big challenge. Have to keep in check, otherwise it'll take over the whole place. Lot of nectar for insects but a real pest if you just let it be. You see, sir, we want it all to look plentiful but to keep it tip-top is hard work. You have to be on the job every day. There's a lot that has to be done. Not everyone in this country understands that.'

'Are you talking about the future? The political future?' For some time, my concerns have been more mundane.

'The future feeds on the past, no? And the past comes from what you do today. Can see that in any garden.'

Above us a flight of parakeets shoots past, heading inland, ignoring the mangoes on the trees he has nurtured. I search the branches to see if a green-billed coucal might be hiding: a species now endangered.

On the lane leading to the main road a bunch of kids are playing cricket with a soft ball. One hits the ball with his bat and a small boy runs after it. In the jingle of child-ish make-believe I remember again how one thing leads to another and see how much we need to embellish even the smallest life with light more wondrous than we are given. The kids cheer. They are barefoot and could be of any denomination – as we might have been – but they have local heroes. Real ones.

At the main road, I study the rifts and fissures in the tar-mac that has softened through the day. I'd like to understand how that happens: the process by which heat and time disrupts the material world; why surfaces shift, things buckle, break, burn. Why in this world we live with waste and negligence. War. Serial damage. Is it needed to melt us into one?

My father once asked, 'How does it compare: the things you have done and the things you have left undone?' The question was aimed at himself, but I think I should ask it of myself too.

I notice a lull in the birdsong. Over the years, I have come to believe that for a new song to be heard, the old one has to end.

A three-wheeler beeps and putters past, the driver smiling in a yellow shirt, his red tuk-tuk packed with Christmassy shopping bags and young children who wave excitedly. It scoots around the bend and disappears in a puff of oily smoke.

Approaching the beach, we seem to be in no man's land. The coconut palms are gangly, tousled. The patch of grass leading to the beach is dry. The wind has dropped. The sea is calm. The sand has a rose tinge to it.

I have seen the sun go down into the sea many times and yet there is nothing familiar about the colour of the sky or the glow in the clouds today.

'Where are they, the birds?'

'I don't know, sir,' my guide says, puzzled. 'This is the place but no sign, no?'

I'd noticed the bats in Colombo no longer fly in straight lines; their flight paths, too, are in disarray.

'Are we too early?'

'The time is right. Something must have happened somewhere to disrupt things.'

We wait. There is nothing else to do. The light slowly seeps away undesired.

'Getting dark, sir. Go back?'

We retrace our steps in silence. I think back and reckon Jay must also have been waiting for the right moment.

When we reach the garden, the caretaker climbs to the upper terrace to lock the other gates. I take the path to the edge of the pond. The frogs have not started their night chorus yet. The duckweed is motionless. I am not sure where to go next in search of the barn swallows, that lost time. The bird sanctuary near Yala, or the game reserve itself? Then, I see a firefly, a bluish-green flicker above the lantana bushes higher up, on safer ground, illuminating a path from one point of darkness to another, beckoning.

ACKNOWLEDGEMENTS

My thanks to sharp-eyed agents, editors, birders, guides, especially Curtis Gillespie, Bill Hamilton, Alexandra Pringle, Faiza Khan, Katherine Ailes, Lauren Whybrow. And Helen, as always, for her forensic lens and steady hand. Also the teams at Bloomsbury, The New Press and A M Heath.

I am grateful to have had some special breathing places for this book: Ateneo de Manila; Armitage Hill; the Banff Centre in the lands of Treaty 7 territory where the past, present and future generations of Stoney Nakoda, Blackfoot, and Tsuut'ina Nations are acknowledged and honoured; haciendas and gardens of friends, and absent friends. Thanks also to the British Library, the Department of National Archives in Colombo – unsuspecting memories, unexpected bookshelves and other sources. Guiding lights: Shanthi and Tanisa.

Fiction being what it is, I have taken liberties with the timing of Education Reform Acts, some elections, public events and the flight paths of bats, birds and winged friends.

A NOTE ON THE AUTHOR

Born in Sri Lanka, Romesh Gunesekera is the award-winning author of five novels and three short story collections. His debut novel *Reef* was shortlisted for both the Booker Prize for Fiction and the Guardian Fiction Prize; *The Sandglass*, his second novel, was awarded the inaugural BBC Asia Award; his most recent short story collection, *Noontide Toll*, was shortlisted for the 2015 Gordon Burn Prize. Gunesekera has been awarded the Premio Mondello Five Continents in Italy, a National Honour for his writing in Sri Lanka and is an elected Fellow of the Royal Society of Literature. He lives in London.

A NOTE ON THE TYPE

The text of this book is set in Perpetua. This typeface is an adaptation of a style of letter that had been popularised for monumental work in stone by Eric Gill. Large scale drawings by Gill were given to Charles Malin, a Parisian punch-cutter, and his hand-cut punches were the basis for the font issued by Monotype. First used in a private translation called 'The Passion of Perpetua and Felicity', the italic was originally called Felicity.